TISH

WORLD CLASSICS IN LARGE PRINT

American Authors Series

The aim of World Classics in Large Print is to make the most enduring and popular works of literature available in comfortable softcover editions printed in clear, easy-to-read large type.

TISH

Mary Roberts Rinehart

Illustrations by May Wilson Preston

SANBORNVILLE, NEW HAMPSHIRE

East Baton Rouge Parish Library
Baton Rouge, Louisiana

First published in 1916
Typeset in 16 point Adobe Caslon type

ISBN 978-1-59688-127-3
This Large Print edition of
Tish by Mary Roberts Rinehart
published in September 2009
by
The Large Print Book Company
Post Office Box 970
Sanbornville, New Hampshire 03872-0970

TISH

Tish was already on the ice. "The outside edge, by George!" said Charlie Sands. "The old sport!"
[see page 233]

MIND OVER MOTOR

How Tish Broke the Law and Some Records

I

So many unkind things have been said of the affair at Morris Valley that I think it best to publish a straightforward account of everything. The ill nature of the cartoon, for instance, which showed Tish in a pair of khaki trousers on her back under a racing-car was quite uncalled for. Tish did not wear the khaki trousers; she merely took them along in case of emergency. Nor was it true that Tish took Aggie along as a mechanician and brutally pushed her off the car because she was not pumping enough oil. The fact was that Aggie sneezed on a curve and fell out of the car, and would no doubt have been killed had she not been thrown into a pile of sand.

It was in early September that Eliza Bailey, my cousin, decided to go to London, ostensibly for a rest, but really to get some cretonne at Liberty's. Eliza wrote me at Lake Penzance asking me to go to Morris Valley and look after Bettina.

I must confess that I was eager to do it. We three were very comfortable at Mat Cottage, "Mat" being the name Charlie Sands, Tish's nephew, had given it, being the initials of "Middle-Aged Trio." Not that I regard the late forties as middle-aged. But Tish, of course, is fifty. Charlie Sands, who is on a newspaper, calls us either the "M.A.T." or the "B.A.'s," for "Beloved Aunts," although Aggie and I are not related to him.

Bettina's mother's note:—

> Not that she will allow you to do it, or because she isn't entirely able to take care of herself; but because the people here are a talky lot. Bettina will probably look after you. She has come from college with a feeling that I am old and decrepit and must be cared for. She maddens me with pillows and cups of tea and woolen shawls. She thinks Morris Valley selfish and idle, and is disappointed in the church, preferring her Presbyterianism pure. She is desirous now of learning how to cook. If you decide to come I'll be grateful if you can keep her out of the kitchen.
>
> Devotedly, Eliza.
>
> P.S. If you can keep Bettina from getting married while I'm away I'll be very glad. She believes a woman should marry and rear a large family!
>
> E.

We were sitting on the porch of the cottage at Lake Penzance when I received the letter, and I read it aloud. "Humph!" said Tish, putting down the stocking she was knitting and looking over her spectacles at me—"Likes her Presbyterianism pure and believes in a large family! How old is she? Forty?"

"Eighteen or twenty," I replied, looking at the letter. "I'm not anxious to go. She'll probably find me frivolous."

Tish put on her spectacles and took the letter. "I think it's your duty, Lizzie," she said when she'd read it through. "But that young woman needs handling. We'd better all go. We can motor over in half a day."

That was how it happened that Bettina Bailey, sitting on Eliza Bailey's front piazza, decked out in chintz cushions,—the piazza, of course,—saw a dusty machine come up the drive and stop with a flourish at the steps. And from it alight, not one chaperon, but three.

After her first gasp Bettina was game. She was a pretty girl in a white dress and bore no traces in her face of any stern religious proclivities.

"I didn't know—" she said, staring from one to the other of us. "Mother said—that is—won't you go right upstairs and have some tea and lie down?" She had hardly taken her eyes from Tish, who had lifted the engine hood and was poking at the carbureter with a hairpin.

"No, thanks," said Tish briskly. "I'll just go around to the garage and oil up while I'm dirty. I've got a short circuit somewhere. Aggie, you and Lizzie get the trunk off."

Bettina stood by while we unbuckled and lifted down our traveling trunk. She did not speak a word, beyond asking if we wouldn't wait until the gardener came. On Tish's saying she had no time to wait, because she wanted to put kerosene in the cylinders before the engine cooled, Bettina lapsed into silence and stood by watching us.

Bettina took us upstairs. She had put Drummond's "Natural Law in the Spiritual World" on my table and a couch was ready with pillows and a knitted slumber robe. Very gently she helped us out of our veils and dusters and closed the windows for fear of drafts.

"Dear mother is so reckless of drafts," she remarked. "Are you sure you won't have tea?"

"We had some blackberry cordial with us," Aggie said, "and we all had a little on the way. We had to change a tire and it made us thirsty."

"Change a tire!"

Aggie had taken off her bonnet and was pinning on the small lace cap she wears, away from home, to hide where her hair is growing thin. In her cap Aggie is a sweet-faced woman of almost fifty, rather ethereal. She pinned on her cap and pulled her crimps down over her forehead.

"Yes," she observed. "A bridge went down with us and one of the nails spoiled a new tire. I told Miss Carberry the bridge was unsafe, but she thought, by taking it very fast—"

Bettina went over to Aggie and clutched her arm. "Do you mean to say," she quavered, "that you three women went through a bridge—"

"It was a small bridge," I put in, to relieve her mind; "and only a foot or two of water below. If only the man had not been so disagreeable—"

"Oh," she said, relieved, "you had a man with you!"

"We never take a man with us," Aggie said with dignity. "This one was fishing under the bridge and he was most ungentlemanly. Quite refused to help, and tried to get the license number so he could sue us."

"Sue you!"

"He claimed his arm was broken, but I distinctly saw him move it." Aggie, having adjusted her cap, was looking at it in the mirror. "But dear Tish thinks of everything. She had taken off the license plates."

Bettina had gone really pale. She seemed at a loss, and impatient at herself for being so. "You—you won't have tea?" she asked.

"No, thank you."

"Would you—perhaps you would prefer whiskey and soda."

Aggie turned on her a reproachful eye. "My dear girl," she said, "with the exception of a little home-made wine used medicinally we drink nothing. I am the secretary of the Woman's Prohibition Party."

Bettina left us shortly after that to arrange for putting up Letitia and Aggie. She gave them her mother's room, and whatever impulse she may have had to put the Presbyterian Psalter by the bed, she restrained it. By midnight Drummond's "Natural Law" had disappeared from my table and a novel had taken its place. But Bettina had not lost her air of bewilderment.

That first evening was very quiet. A young man in white flannels called, and he and Letitia spent a delightful evening on the porch talking spark-plugs and carbureters. Bettina sat in a corner and looked at the moon. Spoken to, she replied in monosyllables in a carefully sweet tone. The young man's name was Jasper McCutcheon.

It developed that Jasper owned an old racing-car which he kept in the Bailey garage, and he and Tish went out to look it over. They very politely asked us all to go along, but Bettina refusing, Aggie and I sat with her and looked at the moon.

Aggie in her capacity as chaperon, or as one of an association of chaperons, used the opportunity to examine Bettina on the subject of Jasper.

"He seems a nice boy," she remarked. Aggie's idea of a nice boy is one who in summer wears fresh flannels outside, in winter less conspicuously. "Does he live near?"

"Next door," sweetly but coolly.

"He is very good-looking."

"Ears spoil him—too large."

"Does he come around—er—often?"

"Only two or three times a day. On Sunday, of course, we see more of him."

Aggie looked at me in the moonlight. Clearly the young man from the next door needed watching. It was well we had come.

"I suppose you like the same things?" she suggested. "Similar tastes and—er—all that?"

Bettina stretched her arms over her head and yawned.

"Not so you could notice it," she said coolly. "I can't thick of anything we agree on. He is an Episcopalian; I'm a Presbyterian. He approves of suffrage for women; I do not. He is a Republican; I'm a Progressive. He disapproves of large families; I approve of them, if people can afford them."

Aggie sat straight up. "I hope you don't discuss that!" she exclaimed.

Bettina smiled. "How nice to find that you are really just nice elderly ladies after all!" she said. "Of course we discuss it. Is it anything to be ashamed of?"

"When I was a girl," I said tartly, "we married first and discussed those things afterward."

"Of course you did, Aunt Lizzie," she said, smiling alluringly. She was the prettiest girl I think I have ever seen, and that night she was beautiful. "And you raised enormous families who religiously walked to church in their bare feet to save their shoes!"

"I did nothing of the sort," I snapped.

"It seems to me," Aggie put in gently, "that you

make very little of love." Aggie was once engaged to be married to a young man named Wiggins, a roofer by trade, who was killed in the act of inspecting a tin gutter, on a rainy day. He slipped and fell over, breaking his neck as a result.

Bettina smiled at Aggie. "Not at all," she said. "The day of blind love is gone, that's all—gone like the day of the chaperon."

Neither of us cared to pursue this, and Tish at that moment appearing with Jasper, Aggie and I made a move toward bed. But Jasper not going, and none of us caring to leave him alone with Bettina, we sat down again.

We sat until one o'clock.

At the end of that time Jasper rose, and saying something about its being almost bedtime strolled off next door. Aggie was sound asleep in her chair and Tish was dozing. As for Bettina, she had said hardly a word after eleven o'clock.

Aggie and Tish, as I have said, were occupying the same room. I went to sleep the moment I got into bed, and must have slept three or four hours when I was awakened by a shot. A moment later a dozen or more shots were fired in rapid succession and I sat bolt upright in bed. Across the street some one was raising a window, and a man called "What's the matter?" twice.

There was no response and no further sound. Shaking in every limb, I found the light switch and looked at the time. It was four o'clock in the morning and quite dark.

Some one was moving in the hall outside and whimpering. I opened the door hurriedly and Aggie half fell into the room.

"Tish is murdered, Lizzie!" she said, and collapsed on the floor in a heap.

"Nonsense!"

"She's not in her room or in the house, and I heard shots!"

Well, Aggie was right. Tish was not in her room. There was a sort of horrible stillness everywhere as we stood there clutching at each other and listening.

"She's heard burglars downstairs and has gone down after them, and this is what has happened! Oh, Tish! brave Tish!" Aggie cried hysterically.

And at that Bettina came in with her hair over her shoulders and asked us if we had heard anything. When we told her about Tish, she insisted on going downstairs, and with Aggie carrying her first-aid box and I carrying the blackberry cordial, we went down.

The lower floor was quiet and empty. The man across the street had put down his window and gone back to bed, and everything was still. Bettina in her dressing-gown went out on the porch and turned on the light. Tish was not there, nor was there a body lying on the lawn.

"It was back of the house by the garage," Bettina said. "If only Jasper—"

And at that moment Jasper came into the circle of light. He had a Norfolk coat on over his pajamas and a pair of slippers, and he was running, calling over his shoulder to some one behind as he ran.

"Watch the drive!" he yelled. "I saw him duck round the corner."

We could hear other footsteps now and somebody panting near us. Aggie was sitting huddled in a porch chair, crying, and Bettina, in the hall, was trying to get down from the wall a Moorish knife that Eliza Bailey had picked up somewhere.

"John!" we heard Jasper calling. "John! Quick! I've got him!"

He was just at the corner of the porch. My heart stopped and then rushed on a thousand a minute. Then:—

"Take your hands off me!" said Tish's voice.

The next moment Tish came majestically into the circle of light and mounted the steps. Jasper, with his mouth open, stood below looking up, and a hired man in what looked like a bed quilt was behind in the shadow.

Tish was completely dressed in her motoring clothes, even to her goggles. She looked neither to the right nor left, but stalked across the porch into the house and up the stairway. None of us moved until we heard the door of her room slam above.

"Poor old dear!" said Bettina. "She's been walking in her sleep!"

"But the shots!" gasped Aggie. "Some one was shooting at her!"

Conscious now of his costume, Jasper had edged close to the veranda and stood in its shadow.

"Walking in her sleep, of course!" he said heartily. "The trip to-day was too much for her. But think of her getting into that burglar-proof garage with her eyes shut—or do sleep-walkers have their eyes shut?—and actually cranking up my racer!"

Aggie looked at me and I looked at Aggie.

"Of course," Jasper went on, "there being no muffler on it, the racket wakened her as well as the neighborhood. And then the way we chased her!"

"Poor old dear!" said Bettina again. "I'm going in to make her some tea."

"I think," said Jasper, "that I need a bit of tea too. If you will put out the porch lights I'll come up and have some."

But Aggie and I said nothing. We knew Tish never walked in her sleep. She had meant to try out Jasper's racing-car at dawn, forgetting that racers have no mufflers, and she had been, as one may say, hoist with her own petard—although I do not know what a petard is and have never been able to find out.

We drank our tea, but Tish refused to have any or to reply to our knocks, preserving a sulky silence. Also she had locked Aggie out and I was compelled to let her sleep in my room.

I was almost asleep when Aggie spoke:—

"Did you think there was anything queer about the way that Jasper boy said good-night to Bettina?" she asked drowsily.

"I didn't hear him say good-night."

"That was it. He didn't. I think"—she yawned—"I think he kissed her."

II

Tish was down early to breakfast that morning and her manner forbade any mention of the night before. Aggie, however, noticed that she ate her cereal with her left hand and used her right arm only when absolutely necessary. Once before Tish had almost broken an arm cranking a car and had been driven to arnica compresses for a week; but this time we dared not suggest anything.

Shortly after breakfast she came down to the porch

where Aggie and I were knitting.

"I've hurt my arm, Lizzie," she said. "I wish you'd come out and crank the car."

"You'd better stay at home with an arm like that," I replied stiffly.

"Very well, I'll crank it myself."

"Where are you going?"

"To the drug store for arnica."

Bettina was not there, so I turned on Tish sharply. "I'll go, of course," I said; "but I'll not go without speaking my mind, Letitia Carberry. By and large, I've stood by you for twenty-five years, and now in the weakness of your age I'm not going to leave you. But I warn you, Tish, if you touch that racing-car again, I'll send for Charlie Sands."

"I haven't any intention of touching it again," said Tish, meekly enough. "But I wish I could buy a second-hand racer cheap."

"What for?" Aggie demanded.

Tish looked at her with scorn. "To hold flowers on the dining-table," she snapped.

It being necessary, of course, to leave a chaperon with Bettina, because of the Jasper person's habit of coming over at any hour of the day, we left Aggie with instructions to watch them both.

Tish and I drove to the drug store together, and from there to a garage for gasoline. I have never learned to say "gas" for gasoline. It seems to me as absurd as if I were to say "but" for butter. Considering that Aggie was quite sulky at being left, it is absurd for her to assume an air of virtue over what followed that day. Aggie was only like a lot of people—good because she was not tempted; for it was at the garage that we met

Mr. Ellis.

We had stopped the engine and Tish was quarreling with the man about the price of gasoline when I saw him—a nice-looking young man in a black-and-white checked suit and a Panama hat. He came over and stood looking at Tish's machine.

"Nice lines to that car," he said. "Built for speed, isn't she? What do you get out of her?"

Tish heard him and turned. "Get out of her?" she said. "Bills mostly."

"Well, that's the way with most of them," he remarked, looking steadily at Tish. "A machine's a rich man's toy. The only way to own one is to have it endowed like a university. But I meant speed. What can you make?"

"Never had a chance to find out," Tish said grimly. "Between nervous women in the machine and constables outside I have the twelve-miles-an-hour habit. I'm going to exchange the speedometer for a vacuum bottle."

He smiled. "I don't think you're fair to yourself. Mostly—if you'll forgive me—I can tell a woman's driving as far off as I can see the machine; but you are a very fine driver. The way you brought that car in here impressed me considerably."

"She need not pretend she crawls along the road," I said with some sarcasm. "The bills she complains of are mostly fines for speeding."

"No!" said the young man, delighted. "Good! I'm glad to hear it. So are mine!"

After that we got along famously. He had his car there—a low gray thing that looked like an armored cruiser.

"I'd like you ladies to try her," he said. "She can move,

but she is as gentle as a lamb. A lady friend of mine once threaded a needle as an experiment while going sixty-five miles an hour."

"In this car?"

"In this car."

Looking back, I do not recall just how the thing started. I believe Tish expressed a desire to see the car go, and Mr. Ellis said he couldn't let her out on the roads, but that the race-track at the fair-ground was open and if we cared to drive down there in Tish's car he would show us her paces, as he called it.

From that to going to the race-track, and from that to Tish's getting in beside him on the mechanician's seat and going round once or twice, was natural. I refused; I didn't like the look of the thing.

Tish came back with a cinder in her eye and full of enthusiasm. "It was magnificent, Lizzie," she said. "The only word for it is sublime. You see nothing. There is just the rush of the wind and the roar of the engine and a wonderful feeling of flying. Here! See if you can find this cinder."

"Won't you try it, Miss—er—Lizzie?"

"No, thanks," I replied. "I can get all the roar and rush of wind I want in front of an electric fan, and no danger."

He stood by, looking out over the oval track while I took three cinders from Tish's eye.

"Great track!" he said. "It's a horse-track, of course, but it's in bully shape—the county fair is held there and these fellows make a big feature of their horse-races. I came up here to persuade them to hold an automobile meet, but they've got cold feet an the proposition."

"What was the proposition?" asked Tish.

"Well," he said, "it was something like this. I've been turning the trick all over the country and it works like a charm. The town's ahead in money and business, for an automobile race always brings a big crowd; the track owners make the gate money and the racing-cars get the prizes. Everybody's ahead. It's a clean sport too."

"I don't approve of racing for money," Tish said decidedly.

But Mr. Ellis shrugged his shoulders. "It's really hardly racing for money," he explained. "The prizes cover the expenses of the racing-cars, which are heavy naturally. The cars alone cost a young fortune."

"I see," said Tish. "I hadn't thought of it in that light. Well, why didn't Morris Valley jump at the chance?"

He hesitated a moment before he answered. "It was my fault really," he said. "They were willing enough to have the races, but it was a matter of money. I made them a proposition to duplicate whatever prize money they offered, and in return I was to have half the gate receipts and the betting privileges."

Tish quite stiffened. "Clean sport!" she said sarcastically. "With betting privileges!"

"You don't quite understand, dear lady," he explained. "Even in the cleanest sport we cannot prevent a man's having an opinion and backing it with his own money. What I intended to do was to regulate it. Regulate it."

Tish was quite mollified. "Well, of course," she said, "I suppose since it must be, it is better—er,—regulated. But why haven't you succeeded?"

"An unfortunate thing happened just as I had the deal about to close," he replied, and drew a long breath. "The town had raised twenty-five hundred. I was to duplicate the amount. But just at that time a—a young brother of mine in the West got into difficulties, and I—but why go into family matters? It would have been easy enough for me to pay my part of the purse out of my share of the gate money; but the committee demands cash on the table. I haven't got it."

Tish stood up in her car and looked out over the track.

"Twenty-five hundred dollars is a lot of money, young man."

"Not so much when you realize that the gate money will probably amount to twelve thousand."

Tish turned and surveyed the grandstand.

"That thing doesn't seat twelve hundred."

"Two thousand people in the grandstand—that's four thousand dollars. Four thousand standing inside the ropes at a dollar each, four thousand more. And say eight hundred machines parked in the oval there at five dollars a car, four thousand more. That's twelve thousand for the gate money alone. Then there are the concessions to sell peanuts, toy balloons, lemonade and palm-leaf fans, the lunch-stands, merry-go-round and moving-picture permits. It's a bonanza! Fourteen thousand anyhow."

"Half of fourteen thousand is seven," said Tish dreamily. "Seven thousand less twenty-five hundred is thirty-five hundred dollars profit."

"Forty-five hundred, dear lady," corrected Mr. Ellis, watching her. "Forty-five hundred dollars profit to be made in two weeks, and nothing to do to get it but sit still and watch it coming!"

I can read Tish like a book and I saw what was in her mind. "Letitia Carberry!" I said sternly. "You take my warning and keep clear of this foolishness. If money comes as easy as that it ain't honest."

"Why not?" demanded Mr. Ellis. "We give them their money's worth, don't we? They'd pay two dollars for a theater seat without half the thrills—no chances of seeing a car turn turtle or break its steering-knuckle and dash into the side-lines. Two dollars' worth? It's twenty!"

But Tish had had a moment to consider, and the turning-turtle business settled it. She shook her head. "I'm not interested, Mr. Ellis," she said coldly. "I couldn't sleep at night if I thought I'd been the cause of anything turning turtle or dashing into the side-lines."

"Dear lady!" he said, shocked; "I had no idea of asking you to help me out of my difficulties. Anyhow, while matters are at a standstill probably some shrewd money-maker here will come forward before long and make a nice profit on a small investment."

As we drove away from the fair grounds Tish was very silent; but just as we reached the Bailey place, with Bettina and young Jasper McCutcheon batting a ball about on the tennis court, Tish turned to me.

"You needn't look like that, Lizzie," she said. "I'm not even thinking of backing an automobile race—although I don't see why I shouldn't, so far as that goes. But it's curious, isn't it, that I've got twenty-five hundred dollars from Cousin Angeline's estate not even earning four per cent?"

I got out grimly and jerked at my bonnet-strings.

"You put it in a mortgage, Tish," I advised her with severity in every tone. "It may not be so fast as an automobile race or so likely to turn turtle or break its steering-knuckle, but it's safe."

"Huh!" said Tish, reaching for the gear lever. "And

about as exciting as a cold pork chop."

"And furthermore," I interjected, "if you go into this thing now that your eyes are open, I'll send for Charlie Sands!"

"You and Charlie Sands," said Tish viciously, jamming at her gears, "ought to go and live in an old ladies' home away from this cruel world."

Aggie was sitting under a sunshade in the broiling sun at the tennis court. She said she had not left Bettina and Jasper for a moment, and that they had evidently quarreled, although she did not know when, having listened to every word they said. For the last half-hour, she said, they had not spoken at all.

"Young people in love are very foolish," she said, rising stiffly. "They should be happy in the present. Who knows what the future may hold?"

I knew she was thinking of Mr. Wiggins and the icy roof, so I patted her shoulder and sent her up to put cold cloths on her head for fear of sunstroke. Then I sat down in the broiling sun and chaperoned Bettina until luncheon.

III

Jasper took dinner with us that night. He came across the lawn, freshly shaved and in clean white flannels, just as dinner was announced, and said he had seen a chocolate cake cooling on the kitchen porch and that it was a sort of unwritten social law that when the Baileys happened to have a chocolate cake at dinner they had him also.

There seemed to be nothing to object to in this. Evidently he was right, for we found his place laid at the table. The meal was quite cheerful, although Jasper ate the way some people play the piano, by touch, with his eyes on Bettina. And he gave no evidence at dessert of a fondness for chocolate cake sufficient to justify a standing invitation.

After dinner we went out on the veranda, and under cover of showing me a sunset Jasper took me round the corner of the house. Once there, he entirely forgot the sunset.

"Miss Lizzie," he began at once, "what have I done to you to have you treat me like this?"

"I?" I asked, amazed.

"All three of you. Did—did Bettina's mother warn you against me?"

"The girl has to be chaperoned."

"But not jailed, Miss Lizzie, not jailed! Do you know that I haven't had a word with Bettina alone since you came?"

"Why should you want to say anything we cannot hear?"

"Miss Lizzie," he said desperately, "do you want to hear me propose to her? For I've reached the point where if I don't propose to Bettina soon, I'll—I'll propose to somebody. You'd better be warned in time. It might be you or Miss Aggie."

I weakened at that. The Lord never saw fit to send me a man I could care enough about to marry, or one who cared enough about me, but I couldn't look at the boy's face and not be sorry for him.

"What do you want me to do?" I asked.

"Come for a walk with us," he begged. "Then sprain your ankle or get tired, I don't care which. Tell us to go on and come back for you later. Do you see? You can sit down by the road somewhere."

"I won't lie," I said firmly. "If I really get tired I'll say so. If I don't—"

"You will." He was gleeful. "We'll walk until you do! You see it's like this, Miss Lizzie. Bettina was all for me, in spite of our differing on religion and politics and—"

"I know all about your differences," I put in hastily.

"Until a new chap came to town—a fellow named Ellis. Runs a sporty car and has every girl in the town lashed to the mast. He's a novelty and I'm not. So far I have kept him away from Bettina, but at any time they may meet, and it will be one-two-three with me."

I am not defending my conduct; I am only explaining. Eliza Bailey herself would have done what I did under the circumstances. I went for a walk with Bettina and Jasper shortly after my talk with Jasper, leaving Tish with the evening paper and Aggie inhaling a cubeb cigarette, her hay fever having threatened a return. And what is more, I tired within three blocks of the house, where I saw a grassy bank beside the road.

Bettina wished to stay with me, but I said, in obedience to Jasper's eyes, that I liked to sit alone and listen to the crickets, and for them to go on. The last I saw of them Jasper had drawn Bettina's arm through his and was walking beside her with his head bent, talking. I sat for perhaps fifteen minutes and was growing uneasy about dew and my rheumatism when I heard footsteps and, looking up, I saw Aggie coming toward me. She was not surprised to see me and addressed me coldly.

"I thought as much!" she said. "I expected better of you, Lizzie. That boy asked me and I refused. I dare say he asked Tish also. For you, who pride yourself on your strength of mind—"

"I was tired," I said. "I was to sprain my ankle," she observed sarcastically. "I just thought as I was sitting there alone—"

"Where's Tish?"

"A young man named Ellis came and took her out for a ride," said Aggie. "He couldn't take us both, as the car holds only two."

I got up and stared at Aggie in the twilight. "You come straight home with me, Aggie Pilkington," I said sternly.

"But what about Bettina and Jasper?"

"Let 'em alone," I said; "they're safe enough. What we need to keep an eye on is Letitia Carberry and her Cousin Angeline's legacy."

But I was too late. Tish and Mr. Ellis whirled up to the door at half-past eight and Tish did not even notice that Bettina was absent. She took off her veil and said something about Mr. Ellis's having heard a grinding in the differential of her car that afternoon and that he suspected a chip of steel in the gears. They went out together to the garage, leaving Aggie and me staring at each other. Mr. Ellis was carrying a box of tools.

Jasper and Bettina returned shortly after, and even in the dusk I knew things had gone badly for him. He sat on the steps, looking out across the dark lawn, and spoke in monosyllables. Bettina, however, was very gay.

It was evident that Bettina had decided not to take her Presbyterianism into the Episcopal fold. And although I am a Presbyterian myself I felt sorry.

Tish and Mr. Ellis came round to the porch about ten o'clock and he was presented to Bettina. From that moment there was no question in my mind as to how affairs were going, or in Jasper's either. He refused to move and sat doggedly on the steps, but he took little part in the conversation.

Mr. Ellis was a good talker, especially about himself.

"You'll be glad to know," he said to me, "that I've got this race matter fixed up finally. In two weeks from now we'll have a little excitement here."

I looked toward Tish, but she said nothing.

"Excitement is where I live," said Mr. Ellis. "If I don't find any waiting I make it."

"If you are looking for excitement, we'll have to find you some," Jasper said pointedly.

Mr. Ellis only laughed. "Don't put yourself out, dear boy," he said. "I have enough for present necessities. If you think an automobile race is an easy thing to manage, try it. Every man who drives a racing-car has a *coloratura* soprano beaten to death for temperament. Then every racing-car has quirky spells; there's the local committee to propitiate; the track to look after; and if that isn't enough, there's the promotion itself, the advertising. That's my stunt—the advertising."

"It's a wonderful business, isn't it?" asked Bettina. "To take a mile or so of dirt track and turn it into a sort of stage, with drama every minute and sometimes tragedy!"

"Wait a moment," said Mr. Ellis; "I want to put that down. I'll use it somewhere in the advertising." He wrote by the light of a match, while we all sat rather stunned by both his personality and his alertness. "Everything's grist that comes to my mill. I suppose you all remember when I completed the speedway at Indianapolis and had the Governor of Indiana lay a gold brick at the entrance? Great stunt that! But the best part of that story never reached the public."

Bettina was leaning forward, all ears and thrills. "What was that?" she asked.

"I had the gold brick stolen that night—did it myself and carried the brick away in my pocket—only gold-plated, you know. Cost eight or nine dollars, all told, and brought a million dollars in advertising. But the papers were sore about some passes and wouldn't use the story. Too bad we can't use the brick here. Still have it kicking about somewhere."

It was then, I think, that Jasper yawned loudly, apologized, said good-night and lounged away across the lawn. Bettina hardly knew he was going. She was bending forward, her chin in her palms, listening to Mr. Ellis tell about a driver in a motor race breaking his wrist cranking a car, and how he—Ellis—had jumped into the car and driven it to victory. Even Aggie was enthralled. It seemed as if, in the last hour, the great world of stress and keen wits and endeavor and mad speed had sat down on our door-step.

As Tish said when we were going up to bed, why shouldn't Mr. Ellis brag? He had something to brag about.

IV

Although I felt quite sure that Tish had put up the prize money for Mr. Ellis, I could not be certain. And Tish's attitude at that time did not invite inquiry. She took long rides daily with the Ellis man in his gray car, and I have reason to believe that their objective point was always the same—the race-track.

Mr. Ellis was the busiest man in Morris Valley. In

the daytime he was superintending putting the track in condition, writing what he called "promotion stuff," securing entries and forming the center of excited groups at the drug store and one or other of the two public garages. In the evenings he was generally to be found at Bettina's feet.

Jasper did not come over any more. He sauntered past, evening after evening, very much white-flanneled and carrying a tennis racket. And once or twice he took out his old racing-car, and later shot by the house with a flutter of veils and a motor coat beside him.

Aggie was exceedingly sorry for him, and even went the length of having the cook bake a chocolate cake and put it on the window sill to cool. It had, however, no perceptible effect, except to draw from Mr. Ellis, who had been round at the garage looking at Jasper's old racer, a remark that he was exceedingly fond of cake, and if he were urged—

That was, I believe, a week before the race. The big city papers had taken it up, according to Mr. Ellis, and entries were pouring in.

"That's the trouble on a small track," he said—"we can't crowd 'em. A dozen cars will be about the limit. Even with using the cattle pens for repair pits we can't look after more than a dozen. Did I tell you Heckert had entered his Bonor?"

"No!" we exclaimed. As far as Aggie and I were concerned, the Bonor might have been a new sort of dog.

"Yes, and Johnson his Sampler. It's going to be some race—eh, what!"

Jasper sauntered over that evening, possibly a late result of the cake, after all. He greeted us affably, as if his defection of the past week had been merely incidental, and sat down on the steps.

"I've been thinking, Ellis," he said, "that I'd like to enter my car."

"What!" said Ellis. "Not that—"

"My racer. I'm not much for speed, but there's a sort of feeling in the town that the locality ought to be represented. As I'm the only owner of a speed car—"

"Speed car!" said Ellis, and chuckled. "My dear boy, we've got Heckert with his ninety-horse-power Bonor!"

"Never heard of him." Jasper lighted a cigarette. "Anyhow, what's that to me? I don't like to race. I've got less speed mania than any owner of a race car you ever met. But the honor of the town seems to demand a sacrifice, and I'm it."

"You can try out for it anyhow," said Ellis. "I don't think you'll make it; but, if you qualify, all right. But don't let any other town people, from a sense of mistaken local pride, enter a street roller or a traction engine."

Jasper colored, but kept his temper.

Aggie, however, spoke up indignantly. "Mr. McCutcheon's car was a very fine racer when it was built."

"*De mortuis nil nisi bonum*," remarked Mr. Ellis, and getting up said good-night.

Jasper sat on the steps and watched him disappear. Then he turned to Tish.

"Miss Letitia," he said, "do you think you are wise to drive that racer of his the way you have been doing?"

Aggie gave a little gasp and promptly sneezed, as she does when she is excited.

"I?" said Tish.

"You!" he smiled. "Not that I don't admire your courage. I do. But the other day, now, when you lost a tire and went into the ditch—"

"Tish!" from Aggie.

"—you were fortunate. But when a racer turns over the results are not pleasant."

"As a matter of fact," said Tish coldly, "it was a wheat-field, not a ditch."

Jasper got up and threw away his cigarette. "Well, our departing friend is not the only one who can quote Latin," he said. "*Verbum sap.*, Miss Tish. Good-night, everybody. Good-night, Bettina."

Bettina's good-night was very cool. As I went up to bed that night, I thought Jasper's chances poor indeed. As for Tish, I endeavored to speak a few word of remonstrance to her, but she opened her Bible and began to read the lesson for the day and I was obliged to beat a retreat.

It was that night that Aggie and I, having decided the situation was beyond us, wrote a letter to Charlie Sands asking him to come up. Just as I was sealing it Bettina knocked and came in. She closed the door behind her and stood looking at us both.

"Where is Miss Tish?" she asked.

"Reading her Bible," I said tartly. "When Tish is up to some mischief, she generally reads an extra chapter or two as atonement."

"Is she—is she always like this?"

"The trouble is," explained Aggie gently, "Miss Letitia is an enthusiast. Whatever she does, she does with all her heart."

"I feel so responsible," said Bettina. "I try to look after her, but what can I do?"

"There is only one thing to do," I assured her—"let her alone. If she wants to fly, let her fly; if she wants to race, let her race—and trust in Providence."

"I'm afraid Providence has its hands full!" said Bettina, and went to bed.

For the remainder of that week nothing was talked of in Morris Valley but the approaching race. Some of Eliza Bailey's friends gave fancy-work parties for us, which Aggie and I attended. Tish refused, being now openly at the race-track most of the day. Morris Valley was much excited. Should it wear motor clothes, or should it follow the example of the English Derby and the French races and wear its afternoon reception dress with white kid gloves? Or—it being warm—wouldn't lingerie clothes and sunshades be most suitable?

Some of the gossip I retailed to Jasper, oil-streaked and greasy, in the Baileys' garage where he was working over his car.

"Tell 'em to wear mourning," he said pessimistically. "There's always a fatality or two. If there wasn't a fair chance of it nothing would make 'em sit for hours watching dusty streaks going by."

The race was scheduled for Wednesday. On Sunday night the cars began to come in. On Monday Tish took us all, including Bettina, to the track. There were half a dozen tents in the oval, one of them marked with a huge red cross.

"Hospital tent," said Tish calmly. We even, on permission from Mr. Ellis, went round the track. At one spot Tish stopped the car and got out.

"Nail," she said briefly. "It's been a horse-racing track for years, and we've gathered a bushel of horse-shoe nails."

Aggie and I said nothing, but we looked at each other. Tish had said "we." Evidently Cousin Angeline's legacy was not going into a mortgage.

The fair-grounds were almost ready. Peanut and lunch stands had sprung up everywhere. The oval, save by the tents and the repair pits, was marked off into parking-spaces numbered on tall banners. Groups of dirty men in overalls, carrying machine wrenches, small boys with buckets of water, onlookers round the tents and track-rollers made the place look busy and interesting. Some of the excitement, I confess, got into my blood. Tish, on the contrary, was calm and businesslike. We were sorry we had sent for Charlie Sands. She no longer went out in Mr. Ellis's car, and that evening she went back to the kitchen and made a boiled salad dressing.

We were all deceived.

Charlie Sands came the next morning. He was on the veranda reading a paper when we got down to breakfast. Tish's face was a study.

"Who sent for you?" she demanded.

"Sent for me! Why, who would send for me? I'm here to write up the race. I thought, if you haven't been out to the track, we'd go out this morning."

"We've been out," said Tish shortly, and we went in to breakfast. Once or twice during the meal I caught her eye on me and on Aggie and she was short with us both. While she was upstairs I had a word with Charlie Sands.

"Well," he said, "what is it this time? Is she racing?"

"Worse than that," I replied. "I think she's backing the thing!"

"No!"

"With her cousin Angeline's legacy." With that I told him about our meeting Mr. Ellis and the whole story. He listened without a word.

"So that's the situation," I finished. "He has her hypnotized, Charlie. What's more, I shouldn't be surprised to see her enter the race under an assumed name."

Charlie Sands looked at the racing list in the Morris Valley Sun.

"Good cars all of them," he said. "She's not here among the drivers, unless she's—Who are these drivers anyhow? I never heard of any of them."

"It's a small race," I suggested. "I dare say the big men—"

"Perhaps." He put away his paper and got up. "I'll just wander round the town for an hour or two, Aunt Lizzie," he said. "I believe there's a nigger in this woodpile and I'm a right nifty little nigger-chaser."

When he came back about noon, however, he looked puzzled. I drew him aside.

"It seems on the level," he said. "It's so darned open it makes me suspicious. But she's back of it all right. I got her bank on the long-distance 'phone."

We spent that afternoon at the track, with the different cars doing what I think they called "trying out heats." It appeared that a car, to qualify, must do a certain distance in a certain time. It grew monotonous after a while. All but one entry qualified and Jasper just made it. The best showing was made by the Bonor car, according to Charlie Sands.

Jasper came to our machine when it was over, smiling without any particular good cheer.

"I've made it and that's all," he said. "I've got about

as much chance as a watermelon at a colored picnic. I'm being slaughtered to make a Roman holiday."

"If you feel that way why do you do it?" demanded Bettina coldly. "If you go in expecting to slaughtered—"

He was leaning on the side of the car and looked up at her with eyes that made my heart ache, they were so wretched.

"What does it matter?" he said. "I'll probably trail in at the last, sound in wind and limb. If I don't, what does it matter?"

He turned and left us at that, and I looked at Bettina. She had her lips shut tight and was blinking hard. I wished that Jasper had looked back.

V

Charlie Sands announced at dinner that he intended to spend the night at the track.

Tish put down her fork and looked at him. "Why?" she demanded.

"I'm going to help the boy next door watch his car," he said calmly. "Nothing against your friend Mr. Ellis, Aunt Tish, but some enemy of true sport might take a notion in the night to slip a dope pill into the mouth of friend Jasper's car and have her go to sleep on the track to-morrow."

We spent a quiet evening. Mr. Ellis was busy, of course, and so was Jasper. The boy came to the house to get Charlie Sands and, I suppose, for a word with Bettina, for when he saw us all on the porch he looked, as you may say, thwarted.

When Charlie Sands had gone up for his pajamas and dressing-gown, Jasper stood looking up at us.

"Oh, Association of Chaperons!" he said, "is it permitted that my lady walk to the gate with me—alone?"

"I am not your lady," flashed Bettina.

"You've nothing to say about that," he said recklessly. "I've selected you; you can't help it. I haven't claimed that you have selected me."

"Anyhow, I don't wish to go to the gate," said Bettina.

He went rather white at that, and Charlie Sands coming down at that moment with a pair of red-and-white pajamas under his arm and a toothbrush sticking out of his breast pocket, romance, as Jasper said later in referring to it, "was buried in Sands."

Jasper went up to Bettina and held out his hand. "You'll wish me luck, won't you?"

"Of course." She took his hand. "But I think you're a bit of a coward, Jasper!"

He eyed her. "Coward!" he said. "I'm the bravest man you know. I'm doing a thing I'm scared to death to do!"

* * * * *

The race was to begin at two o'clock in the afternoon. There were small races to be run first, but the real event was due at three.

From early in the morning a procession of cars from out of town poured in past Eliza Bailey's front porch, and by noon her cretonne cushions were thick with dust. And not only automobiles came, but hay-wagons, side-bar buggies, delivery carts—anything and everything that could transport the crowd.

At noon Mr. Ellis telephoned Tish that the grand-stand was sold out and that almost all the parking-places that had been reserved were taken. Charlie Sands came home to luncheon with a curious smile on his face.

"How are you betting, Aunt Tish?" he asked.

"Betting!"

"Yes. Has Ellis let you in on the betting?"

"I don't know what you are talking about," Tish said sourly. "Mr. Ellis controls the betting so that it may be done in an orderly manner. I am sure I have nothing to do with it."

"I'd like to bet a little, Charlie," Aggie put in with an eye on Tish. "I'd put all I win on the collection plate on Sunday."

"Very well." Charlie Sands took out his notebook. "On what car and how much?"

"Ten dollars on the Fein. It made the best time at the trial heats."

"I wouldn't if I were you," said Charlie Sands. "Suppose we put it on our young friend next door."

Bettina rather sniffed. "On Jasper!" she exclaimed.

"On Jasper," said Charlie Sands gravely.

Tish, who had hardly heard us, looked up from her plate.

"Bettina is betting," she snapped. "Putting it on the collection plate doesn't help any." But with that she caught Charlie Sands' eye and he winked at her. Tish colored. "Gambling is one thing, clean sport is another," she said hotly.

I believe, however, that whatever Charlie Sands may have suspected, he really knew nothing until the race had started. By that time it was too late to prevent it, and the only way he could think of to avoid getting Tish involved in a scandal was to let it go on.

We went to the track in Tish's car and parked in the oval. Not near the grandstand, however. Tish had picked out for herself a curve at one end of the track which Mr. Ellis had said was the worst bit on the course. "He says," said Tish, as we put the top down and got out the vacuum bottle—oh, yes, Mr. Ellis had sent Tish one as a present—"that if there are any smashups they'll occur here."

Aggie is not a bloodthirsty woman ordinarily, but her face quite lit up.

"Not really!" she said.

"They'll probably turn turtle," said Tish. "There is never a race without a fatality or two. No racer can get any life insurance. Mr. Ellis says four men were killed at the last race he promoted."

"Then I think Mr. Ellis is a murderer," Bettina cried. We all looked at her. She was limp and white and was leaning back among the cushions with her eyes shut. "Why didn't you tell Jasper about this curve?" she demanded of Tish.

But at that moment a pistol shot rang out and the races were on.

The Fein won two of the three small races. Jasper was entered only for the big race. In the interval before the race was on, Jasper went round the track slowly, looking for Bettina. When he saw us he waved, but did not stop. He was number thirteen.

I shall not describe the race. After the first round or two, what with dust in my eyes and my neck aching from turning my head so rapidly, I just sat back and let them spin in front of me.

It was after a dozen laps or so, with number thirteen doing as well as any of them, that Tish was arrested.

Charlie Sands came up beside the car with a gentleman named Atkins, who turned out to be a county detective. Charlie Sands was looking stern and severe, but the detective was rather apologetic.

"This is Miss Carberry," said Charlie Sands. "Aunt Tish, this gentleman wishes to speak to you."

"Come around after the race," Tish observed calmly.

"Miss Carberry," said the detective gently, "I believe you are back of this race, aren't you?"

"What if I am?" demanded Tish.

Charlie Sands put a hand on the detective's arm. "It's like this, Aunt Tish," he said; "you are accused of practicing a short-change game, that's all. This race is sewed up. You employ those racing-cars with drivers at an average of fifty dollars a week. They are hardly worth it, Aunt Tish. I could have got you a better string for twenty-five."

Tish opened her mouth and shut it again without speaking.

"You also control the betting privileges. As you own all the racers you have probably known for a couple of weeks who will win the race. Having made the Fein favorite, you can bet on a Brand or a Bonor, or whatever one you chance to like, and win out. Only I take it rather hard of you, Aunt Tish, not to have let the family in. I'm hard up as the dickens."

"Charlie Sands!" said Tish impressively. "If you are joking—"

"Joking! Did you ever know a county detective to arrest a prominent woman at a race-track as a little jest between friends? There's no joke, Aunt Tish. You've financed a phony race. The permit is taken in your name—L.L. Carberry. Whatever car wins, you and Ellis take the prize money, half the gate receipts, and what you have made out of the betting—"

Tish rose in the machine and held out both her hands to Mr. Atkins.

"Officer, perform your duty," she said solemnly. "Ignorance is no defense and I know it. Where are the handcuffs?"

"We'll not bother about them, Miss Carberry", he said. "If you like I'll get into the car and you can tell me all about it while we watch the race. Which car is to win?"

"I may have been a fool, Mr. County Detective," she said coldly; "but I'm not a knave. I have not bet a dollar on the race."

We were very silent for a time. The detective seemed to enjoy the race very much and ate peanuts out of his pocket. He even bought a red-and-black pennant, with "Morris Valley Races" on it, and fastened it to the car. Charlie Sands, however, sat with his arms folded, stiff and severe.

Once Tish bent forward and touched his arm.

"You—you don't think it will get in the papers, do you?" she quavered.

Charlie Sands looked at her with gloom. "I shall have to send it myself, Aunt Tish," he said; "it is my duty to my paper. Even my family pride, hurt to the quick and quivering as it is, must not interfere with my duty."

It was Bettina who suggested a way out—Bettina, who had sat back as pale as Tish and heard that her Mr. Ellis was, as Charlie Sands said later, as crooked as a pretzel.

"But Jasper was not—not subsidized," she said. "If

he wins, it's all right, isn't it?"

The county detective turned to her.

"Jasper?" he said.

"A young man who lives here." Bettina colored.

"He is—not to be suspected?"

"Certainly not," said Bettina haughtily; "he is above suspicion. Besides, he—he and Mr. Ellis are not friends."

Well, the county detective was no fool. He saw the situation that minute, and smiled when he offered Bettina a peanut. "Of course," he said cheerfully, "if the race is won by a Morris Valley man, and not by one of the Ellis cars, I don't suppose the district attorney would care to do anything about it. In fact," he said, smiling at Bettina, "I don't know that I'd put it up to the district attorney at all. A warning to Ellis would get him out of the State."

It was just at that moment that car number thirteen, coming round the curve, skidded into the field, threw out both Jasper McCutcheon and his mechanician, and after standing on two wheels for an appreciable moment of time, righted herself, panting, with her nose against a post.

Jasper sat up almost immediately and caught at his shoulder. The mechanician was stunned. He got up, took a step or two and fell down, weak with fright.

I do not recall very distinctly what happened next. We got out of the machine, I remember, and Bettina was cutting off Jasper's sweater with Charlie Sands' penknife, and crying as she did it. And Charlie Sands was trying to prevent Jasper from getting back into his car, while Jasper was protesting that he could win in two or more laps and that he could drive with one hand—he'd only broken his arm.

The crowd had gathered round us, thick. Suddenly they drew back, and in a sort of haze I saw Tish in Jasper's car, with Aggie, as white as death, holding to Tish's sleeve and begging her not to get in. The next moment Tish let in the clutch of the racer and Aggie took a sort of flying leap and landed beside her in the mechanician's seat.

Charlie Sands saw it when I did, but we were both too late. Tish was crossing the ditch into the track again, and the moment she struck level ground she put up the gasoline.

It was just then that Aggie fell out, landing, as I have said before, in a pile of sand. Tish said afterward that she never missed her. She had just discovered that this was not Jasper's old car, which she knew something about, but a new racer with the old hood and seat put on in order to fool Mr. Ellis. She didn't know a thing about it.

Well, you know the rest—how Tish, trying to find how the gears worked, side-swiped the Bonor car and threw it off the field and out of the race; how, with the grandstand going crazy, she skidded off the track into the field, turned completely round twice, and found herself on the track again facing the way she wanted to go; how, at the last lap, she threw a tire and, without cutting down her speed, bumped home the winner, with the end of her tongue nearly bitten off and her spine fairly driven up into her skull.

All this is well known now, as is also the fact that Mr. Ellis disappeared from the judges' stand after a word or two with Mr. Atkins, and was never seen at Morris Valley again.

Tish came out of the race ahead by half the gate money—six thousand dollars—by a thousand dollars from concessions, and a lame back that she kept all winter. Even deducting the twenty-five hundred she had put up, she was forty-five hundred dollars ahead, not counting the prize money. Charlie Sand brought the money from the track that night, after having paid off Mr. Ellis's racing-string and given Mr. Atkins a small present. He took over the prize money to Jasper and came back with it, Jasper maintaining that it belonged to Tish, and that he had only raced for the honor of Morris Valley. For some time the money went begging, but it settled itself naturally enough, Tish giving it to Jasper in the event of—but that came later.

On the following evening—Bettina, in the pursuit of learning to cook, having baked a chocolate cake— we saw Jasper, with his arm in a sling, crossing the side lawn.

Jasper stopped at the foot of the steps. "I see a

chocolate cake cooling on the kitchen porch," he said. "Did you order it, Miss Lizzie?"

I shook my head.

"Miss Tish? Miss Aggie?"

"I ordered it," said Bettina defiantly—"or rather I baked it."

"And you did that, knowing what it entailed? He was coming up the steps slowly and with care.

"What does it entail?" demanded Bettina.

"Me."

"Oh, that!" said Bettina. "I knew that."

Jasper threw his head back and laughed. Then:—

"Will the Associated Chaperons," he said, "turn their backs?"

"Not at all," I began stiffly. "If I—"

"She baked it herself!" said Jasper exultantly. "One—two. When I say three I shall kiss Bettina."

And I have every reason to believe he carried out his threat.

* * * * *

Eliza Bailey forwarded me this letter from London where Bettina had sent it to her:—

Dearest Mother: I hope you are coming home soon. I really think you should. Aunt Lizzie is here and she brought two friends, and, mother, I feel so responsible for them! Aunt Lizzie is sane enough, if somewhat cranky; but Miss Tish is almost more than I can manage—I never know what she is going to do next—and I am worn out with chaperoning her. And Miss Aggie, although she is very sweet, is always smoking cubeb cigarettes for hay fever, and it looks terrible! The neighbors do not know they are cubeb, and, anyhow, that's a habit, mother. And yesterday Miss Tish was arrested, and ran a motor race and won it, and to-day she is knitting a stocking and reciting the Twenty-third Psalm. Please, mother, I think you should come home.

Lovingly, BETTINA.

P.S. I think I shall marry Jasper after all. He says he likes the Presbyterian service.

I looked up from reading Eliza's letter. Tish was knitting quietly and planning to give the money back to the town in the shape of a library, and Aggie was holding a cubeb cigarette to her nose. Down on the tennis court Jasper and Bettina were idly batting a ball round.

"I'm glad the Ellis man did not get her," said Aggie. And then, after a sneeze, "How Jasper reminds me of Mr. Wiggins."

The library did not get the money after all. Tish sent it, as a wedding present, to Bettina.

LIKE A WOLF ON THE FOLD

I

Aggie has always been in the habit of observing the anniversary of Mr. Wiggins's death. Aggie has the anniversary habit, anyhow, and her life is a succession: of small feast-days, on which she wears mental crape or wedding garments—depending on the occasion. Tish and I always remember these occasions appropriately, sending flowers on the anniversaries of the passing away of Aggie's parents; grandparents; a niece who died in birth; her cousin, Sarah Webb, who married a missionary and was swallowed whole by a large snake,—except her shoes, which the reptile refused and of which Aggie possesses the right, given her by the stricken husband; and, of course, Mr. Wiggins.

For Mr. Wiggins Tish and I generally send the same things each year—Tish a wreath of autumn foliage and I a sheaf of wheat tied with a lavender ribbon. The program seldom varies. We drive to the cemetery in the afternoon and Aggie places the sheaf and the wreath on Mr. Wiggins's last resting-place, after first removing the lavender ribbon, of which she makes cap bows through the year and an occasional pin-cushion or fancy-work bag; then home to chicken and waffles, which had been Mr. Wiggins's favorite meal. In the evening Charlie Sands generally comes in and we play a rubber or two of bridge.

On the thirtieth anniversary of Mr. Wiggins's falling off a roof and breaking his neck, Tish was late in arriving, and I found Aggie sitting alone, dressed in black, with a tissue-paper bundle in her lap. I put my sheaf on the table and untied my bonnet-strings.

"Where's Tish?" I asked.

"Not here yet."

Something in Aggie's tone made me look at her. She was eyeing the bundle in her lap.

"I got a paler shade of ribbon this time," I said, seeing she made no comment on the sheaf. "It's a better color for me if you're going to make my Christmas present out of it this year again. Where's Tish's wreath?"

"Here." Aggie pointed dispiritedly to the bundle in her lap and went on rocking.

"That! That's no wreath."

In reply Aggie lifted the tissue paper and shook out, with hands that trembled with indignation, a lace-and-linen centerpiece. She held it up before me and we eyed each other over it. Both of us understood.

"Tish is changed, Lizzie," Aggie said hollowly. "Ask her for bread these days and she gives you a Cluny-lace fandangle. On mother's anniversary she sent me a set of doilies; and when Charlie Sands was in the hospital with appendicitis she took him a pair of pillow shams. It's that Syrian!"

Both of us knew. We had seen Tish's apartment change from a sedate and spinsterly retreat to a riot of lace covers on the mantel, on the backs of chairs, on the stands, on the pillows—everywhere. We had watched her Marseilles bedspreads give way to hem-stitched covers, with bolsters to match. We had seen Tish go through a cold winter clad in a succession of sleazy silk kimonos instead of her flannel dressing-gown; terrible kimonos—green and yellow and red and pink, that looked like fruit salads and were just as heating.

"It's that dratted Syrian!" cried Aggie—and at that Tish came in. She stood inside the door and eyed us.

"What about him?" she demanded. "If I choose to take a poor starving Christian youth and assist him by buying from him what I need—what I need!—that's my affair, isn't it? Tufik was starving and I took him in."

"He took you in, all right!" Aggie sniffed. "A great, mustached, dirty, palavering foreigner, who's probably got a harem at home and no respect for women!"

Tish glanced at my sheaf and at the centerpiece. She was dressed as she always dressed on Mr. Wiggins's day—in black; but she had a new lace collar with a jabot, and we knew where she had got it. She saw our eyes on it and she had the grace to flush.

"Once for all," she snapped, "I intend to look after this unfortunate Syrian! If my friends object, I shall be deeply sorry; but, so far as I care, they may object until they are purple in the face and their tongues hang out. I've been sending my money to foreign missions long enough; I'm doing my missionary work at home now."

"He'll marry you!" This from Aggie.

Tish ignored her. "His father is an honored citizen of Beirut, of the nobility. The family is impoverished, being Christian, and grossly imposed on by the Turks. Tufik speaks French and English as well as Mohammedan. They offered him a high government position if he would desert the Christian faith; but he refused firmly. He came to this country for religious freedom; at any moment they may come after him and take him back."

A glint of hope came to me. I made a mental note to write to the mayor, or whatever they call him over there, and tell him where he could locate his wandering boy.

"He loves the God of America," said Tish.

"Money!" Aggie jeered.

"And he is so pathetic, so grateful! I told Hannah at noon to-day—that's what delayed me—to give him his lunch. He was starving; I thought we'd never fill him. And when it was over, he stooped in the sweetest way, while she was gathering up the empty dishes, and kissed her hand. It was touching!"

"Very!" I said dryly. "What did Hannah do?"

"She's a fool! She broke a cup on his head."

Mr. Wiggins's anniversary was not a success. Part of this was due to Tish, who talked of Tufik steadily—of his youth; of the wonderful bargains she secured from him; of his belief that this was the land of opportunity—Aggie sniffed; of his familiarity with the Bible and Biblical places; of the search the Turks were making for him. The atmosphere was not cleared by Aggie's taking the Cluny-lace centerpiece to the cemetery and placing it, with my sheaf, on Mr. Wiggins's grave.

As we got into Tish's machine to go back, Aggie was undeniably peevish. She caught cold, too, and was sneezing—as she always does when she is irritated or excited.

"Where to?" asked Tish from the driving-seat, looking straight ahead and pulling on her gloves. From where we sat we could still see the dot of white on the grass that was the centerpiece.

"Back to the house," Aggie snapped, "to have some chicken and waffles and Tufik for dinner!"

Tish drove home in cold silence. As well as we could tell from her back, she was not so much indignant as she was determined. Thus we do not believe that she willfully drove over every rut and thank-you-ma'am on the road, scattering us generously over the tonneau, and finally, when Aggie, who was the lighter, was tossed against the top and sprained her neck, eliciting a protest from us. She replied in an abstracted tone, which showed where her mind was.

"It would be rougher on a camel," she said absently. "Tufik was telling me the other day—"

Aggie had got her head straight by that time and was holding it with both hands to avoid jarring. She looked goaded and desperate; and, as she said afterward, the thing slipped out before she knew she was more than thinking it.

"Oh, damn Tufik!" she said.

Fortunately at that moment we blew out a tire and apparently Tish did not hear her. While I was jacking up the car and Tish was getting the key of the toolbox out of her stocking, Aggie sat sullenly in her place and watched us.

"I suppose," she gibed, "a camel never blows out a tire!"

"It might," Tish said grimly, "if it heard an oath from the lips of a middle-aged Sunday-school teacher!"

We ate Mr. Wiggins's anniversary dinner without any great hilarity. Aggie's neck was very stiff and she had turned in the collar of her dress and wrapped flannels wrung out of lamp oil round it. When she wished to address either Tish or myself she held her head rigid and turned her whole body in her chair; and when she felt a sneeze coming on she clutched wildly at her head with both hands as if she expected it to fly off.

Tufik was not mentioned, though twice Tish got as far as Tu— and then thought better of it; but her mind was on him and we knew it. She worked the conversation round to Bible history and triumphantly demanded whether we knew that Sodom and Gomorrah are towns to-day, and that a street-car line is contemplated to them from some place or other—it developed later that she meant Tyre and Sidon. Once she suggested that Aggie's sideboard needed new linens, but after a look at Aggie's rigid head she let it go at that.

No one was sorry when, with dinner almost over, and Aggie lifting her ice-cream spoon straight up in front of her and opening her mouth with a sort of lockjaw movement, the bell rang. We thought it was Charlie Sands. It was not. Aggie faced the doorway and I saw her eyes widen. Tish and I turned.

A boy stood in the doorway—a shrinking, timid, brown-eyed young Oriental, very dark of skin, very white of teeth, very black of hair—a slim youth of eighteen, possibly twenty, in a shabby blue suit, broken shoes, and a celluloid collar. Twisting between nervous brown fingers, not as clean as they might have been, was a tissue-paper package.

"My friends!" he said, and smiled.

Tish is an extraordinary woman. She did not say a word. She sat still and let the smile get in its work. Its first effect was on Aggie's neck, which she forgot. Tufik's timid eyes rested for a moment on Tish and brightened. Then like a benediction they turned to mine, and came to a stop on Aggie. He took a step farther into the room.

"My friend's friend are my friend," he said. "America is my friend—this so great God's country!"

Aggie put down her ice-cream spoon and closed her mouth, which had been open.

"Come in, Tufik," said Tish; "and I am sure Miss Pilkington would like you to sit down."

Tufik still stood with his eyes fixed on Aggie, twisting his package.

"My friend has said," he observed—he was quite calm and divinely trustful—"My friend has said that this is for Miss Pilk a sad day. My friend is my mother; I have but her and God. Unless—but perhaps I have two new friend also—no?"

"Of course we are your friends," said Aggie, feeling for the table-bell with her foot. "We are—aren't we, Lizzie?"

Tufik turned and looked at me wistfully. It came over me then what an awful thing it must be to be so far from home and knowing nobody, and having to wear trousers and celluloid collars instead of robes and turbans, and eat potatoes and fried things instead of olives and figs and dates, and to be in danger of being taken back and made into a Mohammedan and having to keep a harem.

"Certainly," I assented. "If you are good we will be your friends."

He flashed a boyish smile at me.

"I am good," he said calmly—"as the angels I am good. I have here a letter from a priest. I give it to you. Read!"

He got a very dirty envelope from his pocket and brought it round the table to me. "See!" he said. "The priest says: 'Of all my children Tufik lies next my heart.'"

He held the letter out to me; but it looked as if it had been copied from an Egyptian monument and was about as legible as an outbreak of measles.

"This," he said gently, pointing, "is the priest's blessing. I carry it ever. It brings me friends." He put the paper away and drew a long breath; then surveyed us all with shining eyes. "It has brought me you."

We were rather overwhelmed. Aggie's maid having responded to the bell, Aggie ordered ice cream for Tufik and a chair drawn to the table; but the chair Tufik refused with a little, smiling bow.

"It is not right that I sit," he said. "I stand in the presence of my three mothers. But first—I forget—my gift! For the sadness, Miss Pilk!"

He held out the tissue-paper package and Aggie opened it. Tufik's gift proved to be a small linen doily, with a Cluny-lace border!

We were gone from that moment—I know it now, looking back. Gone! We were lost the moment Tufik stood in the doorway, smiling and bowing. Tish saw us going; and with the calmness of the lost sat there nibbling cake and watching us through her spectacles—and raised not a hand.

Aggie looked at the doily and Tufik looked at her.

"That's—that's really very nice of you," said Aggie. "I thank you."

Tufik came over and stood beside her.

"I give with my heart," he said shyly. "I have had nobody—in all so large this country—nobody! And now—I have you!" Aggie saw—but too late. He bent over and touched his lips to her hands. "The Bible says: 'To him that overcometh I will give the morning star!' I have overcometh—ah, so much!—the sea; the cold, wet England; the Ellis Island; the hunger; the aching of one who has no love, no money! And now—I have the morning star!"

He looked at us all three at once—Charlie Sands said this was impossible, until he met Tufik. Aggie was fairly palpitant and Tish was smug, positively smug. As for me, I roused with a start to find myself sugaring my ice cream.

Charlie Sands was delayed that night. He came in about nine o'clock and found Tufik telling us about his home and his people and the shepherds on the hills about Damascus and the olive trees in sunlight. We half-expected Tufik to adopt Charlie Sands as a father; but he contented himself with a low Oriental salute, and shortly after he bowed himself away.

Charlie Sands stood looking after him and smiling to himself. "Pretty smooth boy, that!" he said.

"Smooth nothing!" Tish snapped, getting the bridge score. "He's a sad-hearted and lonely boy; and we are going to do the kindest thing—we are going to help him to help himself."

"Oh, he'll help himself all right!" observed Charlie Sands. "But, since his people are Christians, I wish you'd tell me how he knows so much about the inside of a harem!"

Seeing that comment annoyed us, he ceased, and we fell to our bridge game; but more than once his eye fell on Aggie's doily, and he muttered something about the Assyrian coming down like a wolf on the fold.

II

The problem of Tufik's future was a pressing one. Tish called a meeting of the three of us next morning, and we met at her house. We found her reading about Syria in the encyclopaedia, while spread round her on chairs and tables were numbers of silk kimonos, rolls of crocheted lace, shirt-waist patterns, and embroidered linens.

Hannah let us in. She looked surly and had a bandage round her head, a sure sign of trouble—Hannah always referring a pain in her temper to her ear or her head or her teeth. She clutched my arm in the hall and held me back.

"I'm going to poison him!" she said. "Miss Lizzie,

that little snake goes or I go!"

"I'm ashamed of you, Hannah!" I replied sternly. "If out of the breadth of her charity Miss Tish wishes to assist a fellow man—"

Hannah reeled back and freed my arm.

"My God!" she whispered. "You too!"

I am very fond of Hannah, who has lived with Tish for many years; but I had small patience with her that morning.

"I cannot see how it concerns you, anyhow, Hannah," I observed severely.

Hannah put her apron to her eyes and sniffled into it.

"Oh, you can't, can't you!" she wailed. "Don't I give him half his meals, with him soft-soapin' Miss Tish till she can't see for suds? Ain't I fallin' over him mornin', noon, and night, and the postman telling all over the block he's my steady company—that snip that's not eighteen yet? And don't I do the washin'? And will you look round the place and count the things I've got to do up every week? And don't he talk to me in that lingo of his, so I don't know whether he's askin' for a cup of coffee or insultin' me?"

I patted Hannah on the arm. After all, none of the exaltation of a good deed upheld Hannah as it sustained us.

"We are going to help him help himself, Hannah," I said kindly. "He hasn't found himself. Be gentle with him. Remember he comes from the land of the Bible."

"Humph!" said Hannah, who reads the newspapers. "So does the plague!"

The problem we had set ourselves we worked out

that morning. As Tish said, the boy ought to have light work, for the Syrians are not a laboring people.

"Their occupation is—er—mainly pastoral," she said, with the authority of the encyclopaedia. "Grazing their herds and gathering figs and olives. If we knew some one who needed a shepherd—"

Aggie opposed the shepherd idea, however. As she said, and with reason, the climate is too rigorous. "It's all well enough in Syria," she said, "where they have no cold weather; but he'd take his death of pneumonia here."

We put the shepherd idea reluctantly aside. My own notion of finding a camel for him to look after was negatived by Tish at once, and properly enough I realized.

"The only camels are in circuses," she said, "and our duty to the boy is moral as well as physical. Circuses are dens of immorality. Of course the Syrians are merchants, and we might get him work in a store. But then again—what chance has he of rising? Once a clerk, always a clerk." She looked round at the chairs and tables, littered with the contents of Tufik's pasteboard suitcase, which lay empty at her feet. "And there is nothing to canvassing from door to door. Look at these exquisite things!—and he cannot sell them. Nobody buys. He says he never gets inside a house door. If you had seen his face when I bought a kimono from him!"

At eleven o'clock, having found nothing in the "Help Wanted" column to fit Tufik's case, Tish called up Charlie Sands and offered Tufik as a reporter, provided he was given no nightwork. But Charlie Sands said it was impossible—that the editors and owners of the paper were always putting on their sons and relatives, and that when there was a vacancy the big advertisers got it. Tish insisted—she suggested that Tufik could run an Arabian column, like the German one, and bring in a lot of new subscribers. But Charlie Sands stood firm.

At noon Tufik came. We heard a skirmish at the door and Hannah talking between her teeth.

"She's out," she said.

"Well, I think she is not out," in Tufik's soft tones.

"You'll not get in."

"Ah, but my toes are in. See, my foot wishes to enter!" Then something soft, coaxing, infinitely wistful, in Arabian followed by a slap. The next moment Hannah, in tears, rushed back to the kitchen. There was no sound from the hallway. No smiling Tufik presented himself in the doorway.

Tish rose in the majesty of wrath. "I could strangle that woman!" she said, and we followed her into the hall.

Tufik was standing inside the door with his arms folded, staring ahead. He took no notice of us.

"Tufik!" Aggie cried, running to him. "Did she—did she dare—Tish, look at his cheek!"

"She is a bad woman!" Tufik said somberly. "I make my little prayer to see Miss Tish, my mother, and she—I kill her!"

We had a hard time apologizing to him for Hanna. Tish got a basin of cold water so he might bathe his face; and Aggie brought a tablespoonful of blackberry cordial, which is soothing. When the poor boy was calmer we met in Tish's bedroom and Tish was quite firm on one point—Hannah must leave!

Now, this I must say in my own defense—I was

sorry for Tufik; and it is quite true I bought him a suit and winter flannels and a pair of yellow shoes—he asked for yellow. He said he was homesick for a bit of sunshine, and our so somber garb made him heart-sad. But I would never have dismissed a cook like Hannah for him.

"I shall have to let her go," Tish said. "He is Oriental and passionate. He has said he will kill her—and he'll do it. They hold life very lightly."

"Humph!" I said. "Very well, Tish, that holding life lightly isn't a Christian trait. It's Mohammedan—every Mohammedan wants to die and go to his heaven, which is a sort of sublimated harem. The boy's probably a Christian by training, but he's a Mohammedan by blood."

Aggie thought my remark immoral and said so. And just then Hannah solved her own problem by stalking into the room with her things on and a suitcase in her hand.

"I'm leaving, Miss Tish!" she said with her eye-rims red. "God knows I never expected to be put out of this place by a dirty dago! You'll find your woolen stockings on the stretchers, and you've got an appointment with the dentist tomorrow morning at ten. And when that little blackguard has sucked you dry, and you want him killed to get rid of him, you'll find me at my sister's."

She picked up her suitcase and Tish flung open the door. "You're a hard-hearted woman, Hannah Mackintyre!" Tish snapped. "Your sister can't keep you. You'll have to work."

Hannah turned in the doorway and sneered at the three of us.

"Oh, no!" she said. "I'm going to hunt up three soft-headed old maids and learn to kiss their hands and tell 'em I have nobody but them and God!"

She slammed out at that, leaving us in a state of natural irritation. But our rage soon faded. Tufik was not in the parlor; and Tish, tiptoeing back, reported that he was in the kitchen and was mixing up something in a bowl.

"He's a dear boy!" she said. "He feels responsible for Hannah's leaving and he's getting luncheon! Hannah is a wicked and uncharitable woman!"

> "Man's inhumanity to man,
> Makes countless thousands mourn!"

quoted Aggie softly. From the kitchen came the rhythmic beating of a wooden spoon against the side of a bowl; a melancholy chant—quite archaic, as Tish said—kept time with the spoon, and later a smell of baking flour and the clatter of dishes told us that our meal was progressing.

"'The Syrians,'" read Tish out of her book, "'are a peaceful and pastoral people. They have not changed materially in nineteen centuries, and the traveler in their country finds still the life of Biblical times.' Something's burning!"

Shortly after, Tufik, beaming with happiness and Hannah clearly forgotten, summoned us to the dining-room. Tufik was not a cook. We realized that at once. He had made coffee in the Oriental way—strong enough to float an egg, very sweet and full of grounds; and after a bite of the cakes he had made, Tish remembered the dentist the next day and refused solid food on account of a bad tooth. The cakes were made of lard and flour, without any baking-powder or flavoring, and the tops were sprinkled thick with granulated sugar. Little circles of grease melted out of them on to the plate, and Tufik, wide-eyed with triumph, sweetly wistful over Tish's tooth, humble and joyous in one minute, stood by the cake plate and fed them to us!

I caught Aggie's agonized eye, but there was nothing else to do. Were we not his friends? And had he not made this delicacy for us? On her third cake, however, Aggie luckily turned blue round the mouth and had to go and lie down. This broke up the meal and probably saved my life, though my stomach has never been the same since. Tish says the cakes are probably all right in the Orient, where it is hot and the grease does not get a chance to solidify. She thinks that Tufik is probably a good cook in his own country. But Aggie says that a good many things in the Bible that she never understood are made plain to her if that is what they ate in Biblical times—some of the things they saw in visions, and all that. She dropped asleep on Tish's lounge and distinctly saw Tufik murdering Hannah by forcing one of his cakes down her throat.

The next month was one of real effort. We had planned to go to Panama, and had our passage engaged; but when we broke the news to Tufik he turned quite pale.

"You go—away?" he said wistfully.

"Only for a month," Tish hastened to apologize. "You see, we—we are all very tired, and the Panama Canal—"

"Canal? I know not a canal."

"It is for ships—"

"You go there in a ship?"

"Yes. A canal is a—"

"You go far—in a ship—and I—I stay here?"

"Only for a month," Aggie broke in. "We will leave you enough money to live on; and perhaps when we come back you will have found something to do—"

"For a month," he said brokenly. "I have no friends, no Miss Tish, no Miss Liz, no Miss Pilk. I die!"

He got up and walked to the window. It was Aggie who realized the awful truth. The poor lonely boy was weeping—and Charlie Sands may say what he likes! He was really crying—when he turned, there were large tears on his cheeks. What made it worse was that he was trying to smile.

"I wish you much happiness on the canal," he said. "I am wicked; but my sad heart—it ache that my friends leave me. I am sad! If only my seester—"

* * * * *

That was the first we had known of Tufik's sister, back in Beirut, wearing a veil over her face and making lace for the bazaars. We were to know more.

Well, between getting ready to go to Panama and trying to find something Tufik could do, we were very busy for the next month. Tufik grew reconciled to our going, but he was never cheerful about it; and finding that it pained him we never spoke about it in his presence.

He was with us a great deal. In the morning he would go to Tish, who would give him a list of her friends to see. Then Tish would telephone and make appointments for him, and he would start off hopefully, with his pasteboard suitcase. But he never sold anything—except a shirt-waist pattern to Mrs. Ostermaier, the minister's wife. We took day about giving him his carfare, but this was pauperizing and we knew it. Besides, he was very sensitive and insisted on putting down everything we gave him in a book, to be repaid later when he had made a success.

The allowance idea was mine and it worked well. We figured that, allowing for his washing,—which was not much, as he seemed to prefer the celluloid collar,— he could live in a sort of way on nine dollars a week. We subscribed equally to this; and to save his pride we mailed it to him weekly by check.

His failure to sell his things hurt him to the soul. More than once we caught tears in his eyes. And he was not well—he could not walk any distance at all and he coughed. At last Tish got Charlie Sands to take him to a lung specialist, a stupid person, who said it was a cigarette cough. This was absurd, as Tufik did not smoke.

At last the time came for the Panama trip. Tish called me up the day she packed and asked me to come over.

"I can't. I'm busy, Tish," I said.

She was quite disagreeable. "This is your burden as well as mine," she snapped. "Come over and talk to that wretched boy while I pack my trunk. He stands and watches everything I put in, and I haven't been able to pack a lot of things I need."

I went over that afternoon and found Tufik huddled on the top step of the stairs outside Tish's apartment, with his head in his hands.

"She has put me out!" he said, looking up at me with tragic eyes. "My mother has put me out! She does not love Tufik! No one loves Tufik! I am no good. I am a dirty dago!"

I was really shocked. I rang the bell and Tish let me

in. She had had no maid since Hannah's departure and was taking her meals out. She saw Tufik and stiffened.

"I thought I sent you away!" she said, glaring at him.

He looked at her pitifully.

"Where must I—go?" he asked, and coughed.

Tish sighed and flung the door wide open. "Bring him in," she said with resignation, "but for Heaven's sake lock him in a closet until I get my underwear packed. And if he weeps—slap him."

The poor boy was very repentant, and seeing that his cough worried us he fought it back bravely. I mixed the white of an egg with lemon juice and sugar, and gave it to him. He was pathetically grateful and kissed my hand. At five o'clock we sent him away firmly, having given him thirty-six dollars. He presented each of us with a roll of crocheted lace to take with us and turned in the doorway to wave a wistful final good-bye.

We met at Tish's that night so that we might all go together to the train. Charlie Sands had agreed to see us off and to keep an eye on Tufik during our absence. Aggie was in a palpitating travel ecstasy, clutching a patent seasick remedy and a map of the Canal Zone; Tish was seeing that the janitor shut off the gas and water in the apartment; and Charlie Sands was jumping on top of a steamer trunk to close it. The taxicab was at the door and we had just time to make the night train. The steamer sailed early the next morning.

"All ready!" cried Charlie Sands, getting the lid down finally. "All off for the Big Ditch!"

We all heard a noise in the hall—a sort of scuffling, with an occasional groan. Tish rushed over and threw open the door. On the top step, huddled and shivering, with streams of water running off his hair down over his celluloid collar, pouring out of his sleeves and cascading down the stairs from his trousers legs, was Tufik. The policeman on the beat was prodding at him with his foot, trying to make him get up. When he saw us the officer touched his hat.

"Evening, Miss Tish," he said, grinning. "This here boy of yours has been committing suicide. Just fished him out of the lake in the park!"

"Get up!" snapped Charlie Sands. "You infernal young idiot! Get up and stop sniveling!"

He stooped and took the poor boy by the collar. His brutality roused us all out of our stupor. Tish and I rushed forward and commanded him to stand back; and Aggie, with more presence of mind than we had given her credit for, brought a glass containing a tablespoonful of blackberry cordial into which she had poured ten drops of seasickness remedy. Tufik was white and groaning, but he revived enough to sit up and stare at us with his sad brown eyes.

"I wish to die!" he said brokenly. "Why you do not let me die? My friends go on the canal! I am alone! My heart is empty!"

Tish wished to roll him on a barrel, but we had no barrel; so, with Charlie Sands standing by with his watch in his hand, refusing to assist and making unkind remarks, we got him to Tish's room and laid out on her mackintosh on the bed. He did not want to live. We could hardly force him to drink the hot coffee Tish made for him. He kept muttering things about his loneliness and being only a dirty dago; and then he turned bitter and said hard things about this great America, where he could find no work and must be a burden on his three mothers, and could not bring his dear sister to be company for him. Aggie quite broke down and had to lie down on the sofa in the parlor and have a cracker and a cup of tea.

When Tish and I had succeeded in making Tufik promise to live, and had given him one of his own silk kimonos to put on until his clothing could be dried—Charlie Sands having disagreeably refused to lend his overcoat—and when we had given the officer five dollars not to arrest the boy for attempting suicide, we met in the parlor to talk things over.

Charlie Sands was sitting by the lamp in his overcoat. He had put our railway and steamer tickets on the table, and was holding his cigarette so that Aggie could inhale the fumes, she having hay fever and her cubebs being on their way to Panama.

"I suppose you know," he said nastily, "that your train has gone and that you cannot get the boat tomorrow?"

Tish was in an exalted mood—and she took off her things and flung them on a chair.

"What is Panama," she demanded, "to saving a life? Charlie, we must plan something for this boy. If you will take off your overcoat—"

"And see you put it on that little parasite? Not if I melt! Do you know how deep the lake is? Three feet!"

"One can drown in three feet of water," said Aggie sadly, "if one is very tired of life. People drown themselves in bathtubs."

Tish's furious retort to this was lost, Tufik choosing that moment to appear in the doorway. He wore a purple-and-gold kimono that had given Tish bronchitis early in the winter, and he had twisted a bath towel round the waist. He looked very young, very sad, very Oriental. He ignored Charlie Sands, but made at once for Tish and dropped on one knee beside her.

"Miss Tish!" he begged. "Forgive, Miss Tish! Tufik is wicked. He has the bad heart. He has spoil the going on the canal. No?"

"Get up!" said Tish. "Don't be a silly child. Go and take your shoes out of the oven. We are not going to Panama. When you are better, I am going to give you a good scolding."

Charlie Sands put the cigarette on a book under Aggie's nose and stood up.

"I guess I'll go," he said. "My nerves are not what they used to be and my disposition feels the change."

Tufik had risen and the two looked at each other. I could not quite make out Tufik's expression; had I not known his gentleness I would have thought his expression a mixture of triumph and disdain.

"'The Assyrian came down like a wolf on the fold, and his cohorts were gleaming in purple and gold!'" said Charlie Sands, and went out, slamming the door.

III

The next day was rainy and cold. Aggie sneezed all day and Tish had neuralgia. Being unable to go out for anything to eat and the exaltation of the night before having passed, she was in a bad humor. When I got there she was sitting in her room holding a hot-water bottle to her face, and staring bitterly at the plate containing a piece of burned toast and Tufik's specialty—a Syrian cake crusted with sugar.

"I wish he had drowned!" she said. "My stomach's gone, Lizzie! I ate one of those cakes for breakfast.

You've got to eat this one."

"I'll do nothing of the sort! This is your doing, Tish Carberry. If it hadn't been for you and your habit of picking up stray cats and dogs and Orientals and imposing them on your friends we'd be on the ocean to-day, on our way to a decent climate. The next time your duty to your brother man overwhelms you, you'd better lock yourself in your room and throw the key out the window."

Tish was not listening, however. Her eye and her mind both were on the cake.

"If you would eat it and then take some essence of pepsin—" she hazarded. But I looked her full it the eye and she had the grace to color. "He loves to make them," she said—"he positively beamed when he brought it. He has another kind he is making now—of pounded beans, or something like that. Listen!" I listened.

From back in the kitchen came a sound of hammering and Tufik's voice lifted in a low, plaintive chant. "He says that song is about the valleys of Lebanon," said Tish miserably. "Lizzie, if you'll eat half of it, I'll eat the rest."

My answer was to pick up the plate and carry it into the bathroom. Heroic measures were necessary: Tish was not her resolute self; and, indeed, through all the episode of Tufik, and the shocking denouement that followed, Tish was a spineless individual who swayed to and fro with every breeze.

She divined my purpose and followed me to the bathroom door.

"Leave some crumbs on the plate!" she whispered. "It will look more natural. Get rid of the toast too."

I turned and faced her, the empty plate in my

hands.

"Tish," I said sternly, "this is hypocrisy, which is just next door to lying. It's the first step downward. I have a feeling that this boy is demoralizing us! We shall have to get rid of him."

"As for instance?" she sarcastically asked.

"Send him back home," I said with firmness. "He doesn't belong here; he isn't accustomed to anything faster than a camel. He doesn't know how to work—none of them do. He comes from a country where they can eat food like this because digestion is one of their occupations."

I was right and Tish knew it. Even Tufik was satisfied when we put it up to him. He spread his hands in his Oriental way and shrugged his shoulders.

"If my mothers think best," he said softly. "In my own land Tufik is known—I sell in the bazaar the so fine lace my sister make. I drink wine, not water. My stomach—I cannot eat in this America. But—I have no money."

"We will furnish the money," Tish said gently. "But you must promise one thing, Tufik. You must not become a Mohammedan."

"Before that I die!" he said proudly.

"And—there is something else, Tufik,—something rather personal. But I want you to promise. You are only a boy; but when you are a man—" Tish stopped and looked to me for help.

"Miss Tish means this," I put in, "you are to have only one wife, Tufik. We are not sending you back to start a harem. We—we disapprove strongly of—er—anything like that."

"Tufik takes but one wife," he said. "Our people—we

have but one wife. My first child—it is called Tish; my next, Lizzie; and my next, Aggie Pilk. All for my so kind friends. And one I call Charlie Sands; and one shall be Hannah. So that Tufik never forget America."

Aggie was rather put out when we told her what we had done; but after eating one of the cakes made of pounded beans and sugar, under Tufik's triumphant eyes, she admitted that it was probably for the best. That evening, while Tufik took his shrunken and wrinkled clothing to be pressed by a little tailor in the neighborhood who did Tish's repairing, the three of us went back to the kitchen and tried to put it in order. It was frightful—flour and burned grease over everything, every pan dirty, dishes all over the place and a half-burned cigarette in the sugar bin. But—it touched us all deeply—he had found an old photograph of the three of us and had made a sort of shrine of the clock-shelf—the picture in front of the clock and in front of the picture a bunch of red geraniums.

While we were looking at the picture and Aggie was at the sink putting water in the glass that held the geraniums, Tufik having forgotten to do so, Tish's neighbor from the apartment below, an elderly bachelor, came up the service staircase and knocked at the door. Tish opened it.

"Humph!" said the gentleman from below. "Gone is he?"

"Is who gone?"

"Your thieving Syrian, madam!"

Tish stiffened.

"Perhaps," she said, "if you will explain—"

"Perhaps," snarled the visitor, "you will explain what you have done with my geraniums! Why don't you raise your own flowers?"

Tish was quite stunned and so was I. After all, it was Aggie who came to the rescue. She slammed the lid on to the teakettle and set it on the stove with a bang.

"If you mean," she said indignantly, "that you think we have any geraniums of yours—"

"Think! Didn't my cook see your thieving servant steal 'em off the box on the fire-escape?"

"Then, perhaps," Aggie suggested, "you will look through the apartment and see if they are here. You will please look everywhere!"

Tish and I gasped. It was not until the visitor had made the rounds of the apartment, and had taken an apologetic departure, that Tish and I understood. The teakettle was boiling and from its spout coming a spicy and familiar odor. Aggie took it off the stove and removed the lid. The geraniums, boiled to a pulp, were inside.

"Back to Syria that boy goes!" said Tish, viewing the floral remains. "He did it out of love and we must not chide him. But we have our own immortal souls to think of."

The next morning two things happened. We gave Tufik one hundred and twenty dollars to buy a ticket back to Syria and to keep him in funds on the way. And Tish got a note from Hannah:—

Dear Miss Tish: I here you still have the dago—or, as my sister's husband says, he still has you. I am redy to live up to my bargen if you are.
HANNAH.

P.S. I have lerned a new salud—very rich, but delissious.

H.

In spite of herself, Tish looked haunted. It was the salad, no doubt. She said nothing, but she looked round the untidy rooms, where everything that would hold it had a linen cover with a Cluny-lace edge—all of them soiled and wrinkled. She watched Tufik, chanting about the plains of Lebanon and shoving the carpet-sweeper with a bang against her best furniture; and, with Hannah's salad in mind, she sniffed a warning odor from the kitchen that told of more Syrian experiments with her digestion. Tish surrendered: that morning she wrote to Hannah that Tufik was going back to Syria, and to come and bring the salad recipe with her.

That was, I think, on a Monday. Tufik's steamer sailed on Thursday. On Tuesday Aggie and I went shopping; and in a spirit of repentance—for we felt we were not solving Tufik's question but getting rid of him—we bought him a complete new outfit. He almost disgraced us by kissing our hands in the store, and while we were buying him some ties he disappeared—to come back later with the rims of his eyes red from weeping. His gentle soul was touched with gratitude. Aggie had to tell him firmly that if he kissed any more hands he would get his ears boxed.

The clerks in the store were all interested, and two or three cash-boys followed us round and stood, open-mouthed, staring at us. Neither Aggie nor I knew anything about masculine attire, and Tufik's idea was a suit, with nothing underneath, a shirt-front and collar of celluloid, and a green necktie already tied and hooking on to his collar-button. He was dazed when we bought him a steamer trunk and a rug, and disappeared again, returning in a few moments with a small paper bag full of gumdrops. We were quite touched.

That, as I say, was on Tuesday. Tufik had been sleeping in Tish's guest-room since his desperate attempt at suicide, and we sent his things to Tish's apartment. That evening Tufik asked permission to spend the night with a friend in the restaurant business—a Damascan. Tish let him go against my advice.

"He'll eat a lot of that Syrian food," I objected, "and get sick and miss his boat, and we'll have the whole thing over again!"

But Tish was adamant. "It's his last night," she said, "and he has promised not to smoke any cigarettes and I've given him two pepsin tablets. This is the land of the free, Lizzie."

We were to meet Tufik at the station next morning and we arranged a lunch for him to eat on the train, Aggie bringing fried chicken and I sandwiches and cake. Tish's domestic arrangements being upset, she supplied fruit, figs and dates mostly, to make him think of home.

The train left early, and none of us felt very cheerful at having to be about. Aggie sat in the station and sneezed; Tish had a pain above her eye and sat by a heater. We had the luncheon in a large shoebox, wrapped in oiled paper to keep it moist.

He never appeared! The train was called, filled up, and left. People took to staring at us as we sat there. Aggie sneezed and Tish held her eye. And no Tufik! In a sort of helpless, breakfastless rage we called a taxicab and went to Tish's. No one said much. We were all thinking.

We were hungry; so we spread out the shoebox

lunch on one of the Cluny-lace covers and ate it, mostly in silence. The steamer trunk and the rug had gone. We let them go. They might go to Jerusalem, as far as we were concerned! After we had eaten,—about eleven o'clock, I think,—Tish got up and surveyed the apartment. Then, with a savage gleam in her eye, she whisked off all the fancy linens, the Cluny laces, the hemstitched bedspreads, and piled them in a heap on the floor. Aggie and I watched her in silence. She said nothing, but kicked the whole lot into the bottom of a cupboard. When she had slammed the door, she turned and faced us grimly.

"That roll of fiddle-de-dees has cost me about five hundred dollars," she said. "It's been worth it if it teaches me that I'm an old fool and that you are two others! If that boy shows his face here again, I'll hand him over to the police."

However, as it happened, she did nothing of the sort. At four o'clock that afternoon there was a timid ring at the doorbell and I answered it. Outside was Tufik, forlorn and drooping, and held up by main force by a tall, dark-skinned man with a heavy mustache.

"I bring your boy!" said the mustached person, smiling. "He has great trouble—sorrow; he faint with grief."

I took a good look at Tufik then. He was pale and shaky, and his new suit looked as if he had slept in it. His collar was bent and wilted, and the green necktie had been taken off and exchanged for a ragged black one.

"Miss Liz!" he said huskily. "I die; the heart is gone! My parent—"

He broke down again; and leaning against the door

jamb he buried his face in a handkerchief that I could not believe was one of the lot we had bought only yesterday. I hardly knew what to do. Tish had said she was through with the boy. I decided to close them out in the hallway until we had held a council; but Tufik's foot was on the sill, and the more I asked him to move it, the harder he wept.

The mustached person said it was quite true. Tufik's father had died of the plague; the letter had come early that morning. Beirut was full of the plague. He waved the letter at me; but I ordered him to burn it immediately—on account of germs. I brought him a shovel to burn it on; and when that was over Tufik had worked out his own salvation. He was at the door of Tish's room, pouring out to Aggie and Tish his grief, and offering the black necktie as proof.

We were just where we had started, but minus one hundred and twenty dollars; for, the black-mustached gentleman having gone after trying to sell Tish another silk kimono, I demanded Tufik's ticket—to be redeemed—and was met with two empty hands, outstretched.

"Oh, my friends,—my Miss Tish, my Miss Liz, my Miss Ag,—what must I say? I have not the ticket! I have been wikkid—but for my sister—only for my sister! She must not die—she so young, so little girl!"

"Tufik," said Tish sternly, "I want you to tell us everything this minute, and get it over."

"She ees so little!" he said wistfully. "And the body of my parent—could I let it lie and rot in the so hot sun? Ah, no; Miss Tish, Miss Liz, Miss Ag,—not so. To-day I take back my ticket, get the money, and send it to my sister. She will bury my parent, and then—she comes to this so great America, the land of my good friends!"

There was a moment's silence. Then Aggie sneezed!

IV

I shall pass over the next month, with its unpleasantnesses; over Charlie Sands's coming one evening with a black tie and, on the strength of having killed a dog with his machine, asking for money to bury it, and bring another one from Syria! I shall not more than mention Hannah, who kept Tish physically comfortable and well fed and mentally wretched, having a teakettle of boiling water always ready if Tufik came to the apartment; I shall say nothing of our success in getting him employment in the foreign department of a bank, and his ending up by washing its windows; or of the position Tish got him as elevator boy in her hospital, where he jammed the car in some way and held up four surgeons and three nurses and a patient on his way to the operating-room—until the patient changed his mind and refused to be operated on.

Aggie had a brilliant idea about the census—that he could make the census reports in the Syrian district. To this end she worked for some time, coaching Tufik for the examination, only to have him fail—fail absolutely and without hope. He was staying in the Syrian quarter at that time, on account of Hannah; and he brought us various tempting offers now and then—a fruit stand that could be bought for a hundred dollars; a restaurant for fifty; a tailor's shop for twenty-five. But, as he knew nothing of fruits or restaurants or tailoring, we refused to invest. Tish said that we had been a good while getting to it, but that we were being businesslike at last. We gave the boy nine dollars a week and not a penny more; and we refused to buy any more of his silly linens and crocheted laces. We were quite firm with him.

And now I come to the arriving of Tufik's little sister—not that she was really little. But that comes later.

Tufik had decided at last on what he would be in our so great America. Once or twice, when he was tired or discouraged, Tish had taken him out in her machine, and he had been thrilled—really thrilled. He did not seem able to learn how to crank it—Tish's car is hard to crank—but he learned how to light the lamps and to spot a policeman two blocks away. Several times, when we were going into the country, Tish took him because it gave her a sense of security to have a man along.

Having come from a country where the general travel is by camel, however, he had not the first idea of machinery. He thought Tish made the engine go by pressing on the clutch with her foot, like a sewing machine, and he regarded her strength with awe. And once, when we were filling a tire from an air bottle and the tube burst and struck him, he declared there was a demon in the air bottle and said a prayer in the middle of the road. About that time Tish learned of a school for chauffeurs, and the three of us decided to divide the expense and send him.

"In three months," Tish explained, "we can get him a state license and he can drive a taxicab. It will suit him, because he can sit to do it."

So Tufik went to an automobile school and stood by while some one drew pictures of parts of the engine on a blackboard, and took home lists of words that he translated into Arabic at the library, and learned everything but why and how the engine of an automobile goes. He still thought—at the end of two months—that the driver did it with his foot! But we were ignorant of all that. He would drop round in the evenings, when Hannah was out or in bed, and tell us what "magneto" was in Arabic, and how he would soon be able to care for Tish's car and would not take a cent for it, doing it at night when the taxicab was resting.

At the end of six weeks we bought him a chauffeur's outfit. The next day the sister arrived and Tufik brought her to Aggie's, where we were waiting. We had not told Hannah about the sister; she would not have understood.

Charlie Sands telephoned while we were waiting and asked if he might come over and help receive the girl. We were to greet her and welcome her to America; then she was to go to the home of the Syrian with the large mustache. Charlie Sands came in and shook hands all round, surveying each of us carefully.

"Strange!" he muttered. "Curious is no name for it! What do we know of the vagaries of the human mind? Three minds and one obsession!" he said with the utmost gentleness. "Three maiden ladies who have lived impeccable lives for far be it from me to say how many years; and now—this! Oh, Aunt Tish! Dear Aunt Tish!"

He got out his handkerchief and wiped his eyes. Tish was speechless with rage, but I rose to our defense.

"We don't want to do it and you know it!" I said tartly. "But when the Lord sends want and suffering to one's very door—"

"Want, with large brown eyes and a gentle voice!" he

retorted. "My dear ladies, it's your money; and I dare say it costs you less than bridge at five cents a point, or the Gay White Way. But, for Heaven's sake, my respected but foolish virgins, why not an American that wants a real job? Why let a sticky Oriental pull your legs—"

"Charlie Sands!" cried Tish, rising in her wrath. "I will not endure such vulgarity. And when Tufik takes you out in a taxicab—"

"God forbid!" said Charlie Sands, and sat down to wait for Tufik's sister.

She did not look like Tufik and she was tired and dirty from the journey; but she had big brown eyes and masses of dark hair and she spoke not a single word of English. Tufik's joy was boundless; his soft eyes were snapping with excitement; and Aggie, who is sentimental, was obliged to go out and swallow half a glass of water without breathing to keep from crying. Charlie Sands said nothing, but sat back in a corner and watched us all; and once he took out his notebook and made a memorandum of something. He showed it to us later.

Tufik's sister was the calmest of us all, I believe. She sat on a stiff chair near the door and turned her brown eyes from one to the other. Tish said that proper clothing would make her beautiful; and Aggie, disappearing for a few minutes, came back with her last summer's foulard and a jet bonnet. When the poor thing understood they were for her, she looked almost frightened, the thing being unexpected; and Tufik, in a paroxysm of delight, kissed all our hands and the girl on each cheek.

Tish says our vulgar lip-osculation is unknown in the Orient and that they rub noses by way of greeting.

I think, however, that she is mistaken in this and that the Australians are the nose-rubbers. I recall a returned missionary's telling this, but I cannot remember just where he had been stationed.

Things were very quiet for a couple of weeks. Tufik came round only once—to tell us that, having to pay car fare to get to the automobile school, his nine dollars were not enough. We added a dollar a week under protest; and Tish suggested with some asperity that as he was only busy four hours a day he might find some light employment for the balance of the day. He spread out his hands and drew up his shoulders.

"My friends are angry," he said sadly. "It is not enough that I study? I must also work? Ver' well, I labor. I sell the newspaper. But, to buy newspapers, one must have money—a dollar; two dollars. Ver' leetle; only—I have it not."

We gave him another dollar and he went out smiling and hopeful. It seemed that at last we had solved his problem. Tish recalled one of her Sunday-school scholars who sold papers and saved enough to buy a second-hand automobile and rear a family. But our fond hopes were dashed to the ground when, the next morning, Hannah, opening the door at Tish's to bring in the milk bottles, found a huge stack of the night-before's newspapers and a note on top addressed to Tish, which said:-

Deer Mother Tish: You see now that I am no good. I wish to die! I hav one papier sold, and newsboys kell me on sight. I hav but you and God—and God has forget!

TUFIK.

We were discouraged and so, clearly, was Tufik. For ten days we did not hear from him, except that a flirty little Syrian boy called for the ten dollars on Saturday and brought a pair of Tufik's shoes for us to have resoled. But one day Tish telephoned in some excitement and said that Tufik was there and wanted us to go to a wedding.

"His little sister's wedding!" she explained. "The dear child is all excited. He says it has been going on for two days and this is the day of the ceremony."

Aggie was spending the afternoon with me, and spoke up hastily.

"Ask her if I have time to go home and put on my broadcloth," she said. "I'm not fixed for a wedding."

Tish said there was no time. She would come round with the machine and we were to be ready in fifteen minutes. Aggie hesitated on account of intending to wash her hair that night and so not having put up her crimps; but she finally agreed to go and Tish came for us. Tufik was in the machine. He looked very tidy and wore the shoes we had had repaired, a pink carnation in his buttonhole, and an air of suppressed excitement.

"At last," he said joyously while Tish cranked the car—"at last my friends see my three mothers! They think Tufik only talks—now they see! And the priest will bless my mothers on this so happy day."

Tish having crawled panting from her exertion into the driver's seat and taken the wheel, in sheer excess of boyish excitement he leaned over and kissed the hand nearest him.

The janitor's small boy was on the curb watching, and at that he set up a yell of joy. We left him calling awful things after us and Tish's face was a study; but soon the care of the machine made her forget everything else.

The Syrian quarter was not impressive. It was on a hillside above the Russian Jewish colony, and consisted of a network of cobble-paved alleys, indescribably dirty and incredibly steep. In one or two of these alleys Tish was obliged to turn the car and go up backward, her machine climbing much better on the reverse gear. Crowds of children followed us; dogs got under the wheels and apparently died, judging by the yelps—only to follow us with undiminished energy after they had picked themselves up. We fought and won a battle with a barrel of ashes and came out victorious but dusty; and at last, as Tufik made a lordly gesture, we stopped at an angle of forty-five degrees and Tufik bowed us out of the car. He stood by visibly glowing with happiness, while Tish got a cobblestone and placed it under a wheel, and Aggie and I took in our surroundings.

We were in an alley ten feet wide and paved indiscriminately with stones and tin cans, babies and broken bottles. Before us was a two-story brick house with broken windows and a high, railed wooden stoop, minus two steps. Under the stoop was a door leading into a cellar, and from this cellar was coming a curious stamping noise and a sound as of an animal in its death throes.

Aggie caught my arm. "What's that?" she quavered.

I had no time to reply. Tufik had thrown open the door and stood aside to let us pass.

"They dance," he said gravely. "There is always much dancing before a wedding. The music one hears is of Damascus and he who dances now is a sheik among his people."

Reassured as to the sounds, we stepped down into the

basement. That was at four o'clock in the afternoon.

I have never been fairly clear as to what followed and Aggie's memory is a complete blank. I remember a long, boarded-in and floored cellar, smelling very damp and lighted by flaring gas jets. The center was empty save for a swarthy gentleman in a fez and his shirt-sleeves, wearing a pair of green suspenders and dancing alone—a curious stamping dance that kept time to a drum. I remember the musicians too—three of them in a corner: one playing on a sort of pipes-of-Pan affair of reeds, one on a long-necked instrument that looked like a guitar with zither ambitions, and a drummer who chanted with his eyes shut and kept time to his chants by beating on a sheepskin tied over the mouth of a brass bowl. Round three sides of the room were long, oil cloth-covered tables; and in preparation for the ceremony a little Syrian girl was sweeping up peanut shells, ashes, and beer bottles, with absolute disregard of the guests.

All round the wall, behind rows of beer bottles, dishes of bananas, and plates of raw liver, were men,—soft-eyed Syrians with white teeth gleaming and black hair plastered close and celluloid collars,—gentle-voiced, urbane-mannered Orientals, who came up gravely one by one and shook hands with us; who pressed on us beer and peanuts and raw liver.

Aggie, speaking between sneezes and over the chanting and the drum, bent toward me. "It's a breath of the Orient!" she said ecstatically. "Oh, Lizzie, do you think I could buy that drum for my tabouret?"

"Orient!" observed Tish, coughing. "I'm going out and take the switch-key out of that car. And I wish I'd brought Charlie Sands!"

It was in vain we reminded her that the Syrians are a pastoral people and that they come from the land of the Bible. She looked round her grimly.

"They look like a lot of bandits to me," she sniffed. "And there's always a murder at a wedding of this sort. There isn't a woman here but ourselves!"

She was exceedingly disagreeable and Aggie and I began to get uncomfortable. But when Tufik brought us little thimble-sized glasses filled with a milky stuff and assured us that the women had only gone to prepare the bride, we felt reassured. He said that etiquette demanded that we drink the milky white stuff.

Tish was inclined to demur. "Has it any alcohol in it?" she demanded. Tufik did not understand, but he said it was harmless and given to all the Syrian babies; and while we were still undecided Aggie sniffed it.

"It smells like paregoric, Tish," she said. "I'm sure it's harmless."

We took it then. It tasted sweet and rather spicy, and Aggie said it stopped her sneezing at once. It was very mild and pleasant, and rather medicinal in its flavor. We each had two little glasses—and Tish said she would not bother about the switch-key. The car was insured against theft.

A little later Aggie said she used to do a little jig step when she was a girl, and if they would play slower she would like to see if she had forgotten it. Tish did not hear this—she was talking to Tufik, and a moment later she got up and went out.

Aggie had decided to ask the musicians to play a little slower and I had my hands full with her; so it was with horror that, shortly after, I heard the whirring of the engine and through the cellar window caught a glimpse of Tish's machine starting off up the hill. I rose excitedly, but Tufik was before me, smiling and bowing.

"Miss Tish has gone for the bride," he said softly. "The taxicab hav' not come. Soon the priest arrive, and so great shame—the bride is not here! Miss Tish is my mother, my heart's delight!"

When Aggie realized that Tish had gone, she was rather upset—she depends a great deal on Tish—and she took another of the little glasses of milky stuff to revive her.

I was a little bit nervous with Tish gone and the sun setting and another tub of beer bottles brought in—though the people were orderly enough and Tufik stood near. But Aggie began to feel very strange, and declared that the man with the sheepskin drum was winking at her and that her head was twitching round on her shoulders. And when a dozen or so young Syrians formed a circle, their hands on each other's shoulders, and sang a melancholy chant, stamping to beat time, she wept with sheer sentiment.

"Ha! Hoo! Ta, Ta, Ta!" they chanted in unison; and Tufik bent over us, his soft eyes beaming.

"They are shepherds and the sons of shepherds from Palestine," he whispered. "That is the shepherd's call to his sheep. In my country many are shepherds. Perhaps some day you go with me back to my country, and we hear the shepherd call his sheep—'Ha! Hoo! Ta, Ta, Ta!'—and we hear the sleepy sheep reply: 'Maaaa!'"

"It is too beautiful!" murmured Aggie. "It is the Holy Land all over again! And we should never have known this but for you, Tufik!"

Just then some one near the door clapped his hands

and all the noise ceased. Those who were standing sat down. The little girl with the broom swept the accumulations of the room under a chair and put the broom in a corner. The music became loud and stirring.

Aggie swayed toward me. "I'm sick, Lizzie!" she gasped. "That paregoric stuff has poisoned me. Air!"

I took one arm and Tufik the other, and we got her out and seated on one of the wooden steps. She was a blue-green color and the whites of her eyes were yellow. But I had little time for Aggie. Tufik caught my hand and pointed.

Tish's machine was coming down the alley. Beside her sat Tufik's sister, sobbing at the top of her voice and wearing Aggie's foulard, a pair of cotton gloves, and a lace curtain over her head. Behind in the tonneau were her maid of honor, a young Syrian woman with a baby in her arms and four other black-eyed children about her. But that was not all. In front of the machine, marching slowly and with dignity, were three bearded gentlemen, two in coats and one in a striped vest, blowing on curious double flutes and making a shrill wailing noise. And all round were crowds of women and children, carrying tin pans and paper bags full of parched peas, which they were flinging with all their might.

I caught Tish's eye as the procession stopped, and she looked subdued—almost stunned. The pipers still piped. But the bride refused to move. Instead, her wails rose higher; and Aggie, who had paid no attention so far, but was sitting back with her eyes shut, looked up.

"Lizzhie," she said thickly, "Tish looks about the way I feel." And with that she fell to laughing awful laughter that mingled with the bride's cries and the wail of the pipes.

The bride, after a struggle, was taken by force from the machine and placed on a chair against the wall. Her veil was torn and her wreath crooked, and she observed a sulky silence. To our amazement, Tufik was still smiling, urbane and cheerful.

"It is the custom of my country, my mothers," he said. "The bride leave with tears the home of her good parents or of her friends; and she speak no word—only weep—until she is married. Ah—the priest!"

The rest of the story is short and somewhat blurred. Tish having broken her glasses, Aggie being, as one may say, *hors de combat,* and I having developed a frightful headache in the dust and bad air, the real meaning of what was occurring did not penetrate to any of us. The priest officiated from a table in the center of the room, on which he placed two candles, an Arabic Bible, and a sacred picture, all of which he took out of a brown valise. He himself wore a long black robe and a beard, and looked, as Tish observed, for all the world as if he had stepped from an Egyptian painting. Before him stood Tufik's sister, the maid of honor with her baby, the black-mustached friend who had brought Tufik to us after his tragic attempt at suicide, and Tufik himself.

Everybody held lighted candles, and the heat was frightful. The music ceased, there was much exhorting in Arabic, much reading from the book, many soft replies indiscriminately from the four principals—and then suddenly Tish turned and gripped my arm.

"Lizzie," she said hoarsely, "that little thief and liar has done us again! That isn't his sister at all. He's marrying her—for us to keep!"

Luckily Aggie grew faint again at that moment, and we led her out into the open air. Behind us the ceremony seemed to be over; the drum was beating, the pipes screaming, the lute thrumming.

Tish let in the clutch with a vicious jerk, and the whir of the engine drowned out the beating of the drum and the clapping of the hands. Twilight hid the tin cans and ash-barrels, and the dogs slept on the cool pavements. In the doorways soft-eyed Syrian women rocked their babies to drowsy chants. The air revived Aggie. She leaned forward and touched Tish on the shoulder.

"After all," she said softly, "if he loves her very much, and there was no other way—Do you remember that night she arrived—how he looked at her?"

"Yes," Tish snapped. "And I remember the way he looked at us every time he wanted money. We've been a lot of sheep and we've been sheared good and proper! But we needn't bleat with joy about it!"

As we drew up at my door, Tish pulled out her watch.

"It's seven o'clock," she said brusquely. "I am going to New York on the nine-forty train and I shall take the first steamer outward bound—I need a rest! I'll go anywhere but to the Holy Land!"

We went to Panama.

* * * * *

Two months afterward, in the dusk of a late spring evening, Charlie Sands met us at the station and took us to Tish's in a taxicab. We were homesick, tired, and dirty; and Aggie, who had been frightfully seasick, was clamoring for tea.

As the taxicab drew up at the curb, Tish clutched my arm and Aggie uttered a muffled cry and promptly sneezed. Seated on the doorstep, celluloid collar shining, the brown pasteboard suitcase at his feet, was Tufik. He sat calmly smoking a cigarette, his eyes upturned in placid and Oriental contemplation of the heavens.

"Drive on!" said Tish desperately. "If he sees us we are lost!"

"Drive where?" demanded Charlie.

Tufik's gaze had dropped gradually—another moment and his brown eyes would rest on us. But just then a diversion occurred. A window overhead opened with a slam and a stream of hot water descended. It had been carefully aimed—as if with long practice. Tufik was apparently not surprised. He side-stepped it with a boredom as of many repetitions, and, picking up his suitcase, stood at a safe distance looking up. First, in his gentle voice he addressed the window in Arabic; then from a safer distance in English.

"You ugly old she-wolf!" he said softly. "When my

three old women come back I eat you, skin and bones,—and they shall say nothing! They love me—Tufik! I am their child. Aye! And my child—which comes—will be their grandchild!"

He kissed his fingers to the upper window which closed with a slam. Tufik stooped, picked up his suitcase, and saw the taxi for the first time. Even in the twilight we saw his face change, his brown eyes brighten, his teeth show in his boyish smile. The taxicab driver had stalled his engine and was cranking it.

"Sh!" I said desperately, and we all cowered back into the shadows.

Tufik approached, uncertainty changing to certainty. The engine was started now. Oh, for a second of time! He was at the window now, peering into the darkness.

"Miss Tish!" he said breathlessly. No one answered. We hardly breathed. And then suddenly Aggie sneezed! "Miss Pilk!" he shouted in delight. "My mothers! My so dear friends—"

The machine jerked, started, moved slowly off. He ran beside it, a hand on the door. Tish bent forward to speak, but Charlie Sands put his hand over her mouth.

And so we left him, standing in the street undecided, staring after us wistfully, uncertainly—the suitcase, full of Cluny-lace centerpieces, crocheted lace, silk kimonos, and embroidered bedspreads, in his hand.

That night we hid in a hotel and the next day we started for Europe. We heard nothing from Tufik; but on the anniversary of Mr. Wiggins's death, while we were in Berlin, Aggie received a small package forwarded from home. It was a small lace doily, and pinned to it was a card. It read:—

>   For the sadness, Miss Pilk!
>
>   TUFIK.
>
> Aggie cried over it.

THE SIMPLE LIFERS

I

I suppose there is something in all of us that harks back to the soil. When you come to think of it, what are picnics but outcroppings of instinct? No one really enjoys them or expects to enjoy them, but with the first warm days some prehistoric instinct takes us out into the woods, to fry potatoes over a strangling wood fire and spend the next week getting grass stains out of our clothes. It must be instinct; every atom of intelligence warns us to stay at home near the refrigerator.

Tish is really a child of instinct. She is intelligent enough, but in a contest between instinct and brains, she always follows her instinct. Aggie under the same circumstances follows her heart. As for me, I generally follow Tish and Aggie, and they've led me into some curious places.

This is really a sort of apology, because, whereas usually Tish leads off and we follow her, in the adventure of the Simple Life we were all equally guilty. Tish made the suggestion, but we needed no urging. As you know, this summer two years ago was a fairly good one, as summers go,—plenty of fair weather, only two or three really hot spells, and not a great deal of rain. Charlie Sands, Tish's nephew, went over to England in June to report the visit of the French President to London for his newspaper, and Tish's automobile had been sent to the factory to be gone over. She had been teaching Aggie to drive it, and owing to Aggie's thinking she had her foot on the brake when it was really on the gas, they had leaped a four-foot ditch and gone down into a deep ravine, from which both Tish and Aggie had had to be pulled up with ropes.

Well, with no machine and Charlie Sands away, we hardly knew how to plan the summer. Tish thought at first she would stay at home and learn to ride. She thought her liver needed stirring up. She used to ride, she said, and it was like sitting in a rocking-chair, only perhaps more so. Aggie and I went out to her first lesson; but when I found she had bought a divided skirt and was going to try a man's saddle, I could not restrain my indignation.

"I'm going, Tish," I said firmly, when she had come out of the dressing-room and I realized the situation. "I shan't attempt to restrain you, but I shall not remain to witness your shame."

Tish eyed me coldly. "When you wish to lecture me," she snapped, "about revealing to the public that I have two legs, if I do wear a skirt, don't stand in a sunny doorway in that linen dress of yours. I am going to ride; every woman should ride. It's good for the liver."

I think she rather wavered when they brought the horse, which looked larger than usual and had a Roman nose. The instructor handed Tish four lines and she grabbed them nervously in a bunch.

"Just a moment!" said the instructor, and slipped a line between each two of her fingers.

Tish looked rather startled. "When I used to ride—"

she began with dignity.

But the instructor only smiled. "These two are for the curb," he said—"if he bolts or anything like that, you know. Whoa, Viper! Still, old man!"

"Viper!" Tish repeated, clutching at the lines. "Is—is he—er—nasty?"

"Not a bit of it," said the instructor, while he prepared to hoist her up. "He's as gentle as a woman to the people he likes. His only fault is that he's apt to take a little nip out of the stablemen now and then. He's very fond of ladies."

"Humph!" said Tish. "He's looking at me rather strangely, don't you think? Has he been fed lately?"

"Perhaps he sees that divided skirt," I suggested.

Tish gave me one look and got on the horse. They walked round the ring at first and Tish seemed to like it. Then a stableman put a nickel into a player-piano and that seemed to be a signal for the thing to trot. Tish said afterward that she never hit the horse's back twice in the same place. Once, she says, she came down on his neck, and several times she was back somewhere about his tail. Every time she landed, wherever it might be, he gave a heave and sent her up again. She tried to say "Whoa," but it came out in pieces, so to speak, and the creature seemed to be encouraged by it and took to going faster. By that time, she said, she wasn't coming down at all, but was in the air all the time, with the horse coming up at the rate of fifty revolutions a second. She had presence of mind enough to keep her mouth shut so she wouldn't bite her tongue off.

After four times round the music stopped and the horse did also. They were just in front of us, and Tish looked rather dazed.

"You did splendidly!" said Aggie. "Honestly, Tish, I was frightened at first, but you and that dear horse seemed one piece. Didn't they, Lizzie?"

Tish straightened out the fingers of her left hand with her right and extricated the lines. Then she turned her head slowly from right to left to see if she could.

"Help me down, somebody," she said in a thin voice, "and call an osteopath. There is something wrong with my spine!"

She was in bed three days, having massage and a vibrator and being rubbed with chloroform liniment. At the end of that time she offered me her divided skirt, but I refused.

"Riding would be good for your liver, Lizzie," she said, sitting up in bed with pillows all about her.

"I don't intend to detach it to do it good," I retorted. "What your liver and mine and most of the other livers need these days isn't to be sent out in a divided skirt and beaten to a jelly: they need rest—less food and simpler food. If instead of taking your liver on a horse you'd put it in a tent and feed it nuts and berries, you wouldn't be the color you are to-day, Tish Carberry."

That really started the whole thing, although at the time Tish said nothing. She has a way of getting an idea and letting it simmer on the back of her brain, as you may say, when nobody knows it's been cooking at all, and then suddenly bringing it out cooked and seasoned and ready to serve.

On the day Tish sat up for the first time, Aggie and I went over to see her. Hannah, the maid, had got her out of bed to a window, and Tish was sitting there with books all about her. It is in times of enforced physical idleness that most of Tish's ideas come to her, and

Aggie had reminded me of that fact on the way over.

"You remember, Lizzie," she said, "how last winter when she was getting over the grippe she took up that correspondence-school course in swimming. She's reading, watch her books. It'll probably be suffrage or airships."

Tish always believes anything she reads. She had been quite sure she could swim after six correspondence lessons. She had all the movements exactly, and had worried her trained nurse almost into hysteria for a week by turning on her face in bed every now and then and trying the overhand stroke. She got very expert, and had decided she'd swim regularly, and even had Charlie Sands show her the Australian crawl business so she could go over some time and swim the Channel. It was a matter of breathing and of changing positions, she said, and was up to intelligence rather than muscle.

Then when she was quite strong, she had gone to the natatorium. Aggie and I went along, not that we were any good in emergency, but because Tish had convinced us there would be no emergency. And Tish went in at the deep end of the pool, head first, according to diagram, and *did not come up*.

Well, there seemed to be nothing threatening in what Tish was reading this time. She had ordered some books for Maria Lee's children and was looking them over before she sent them. The "Young Woodsman" was one and "Camper Craft" was another. How I shudder when I recall those names!

Aggie had baked an angel cake and I had brought over a jar of cookies. But Tish only thanked us and asked Hannah to take them out. Even then we were not suspicious. Tish sat back among her pillows and said very little. The conversation was something like this:—

Aggie: Well, you're up again: I hope to goodness it will be a lesson to you. If you don't mind, I'd like Hannah to cut that cake. It fell in the middle.

Tish: Do you know that the Indians never sweetened their food and that they developed absolutely perfect teeth?

Aggie: Well, they never had any automobiles either, but they didn't develop wings.

Lizzie: Don't you want that window closed? I'm in a draft.

Tish:: Air in motion never gave any one a cold. We do not catch cold; we catch heat. It's ridiculous the way we shut ourselves up in houses and expect to remain well.

Aggie: Well, I'b catchig sobethig.

Lizzi (*changing the subject*): Would you like me to help you dress? It might rest your back to have your corset on.

Tish (*firmly*): I shall never wear a corset again.

Aggie (*sneezing*): Why? Didn't the Iddiads wear theb?

Tish is very sensitive to lack of sympathy and she shut up like a clam. She was coldly polite to us for the remainder of our visit, but she did not again refer to the Indians, which in itself was suspicious.

Fortunately for us, or unfortunately, Tish's new scheme was one she could not very well carry out alone. I believe she tried to induce Hannah to go with her, and only when Hannah failed her did she turn to us. Hannah was frightened and came to warn us.

I remember the occasion very well. It was Mr.

Wiggins's birthday anniversary, and we usually dine at Aggie's and have a cake with thirty candles on it. Tish was not yet able to be about, so Aggie and I ate together. She always likes to sit until the last candle is burned out, which is rather dispiriting and always leaves me low in my mind.

Just as it flickered and went out, Hannah came in.

"Miss Tish sent over Mr. Charlie's letter from London," said Hannah, and put it in front of Aggie. Then she sat down on a chair and commenced to cry.

"Why, Hannah!" said Aggie. "What in the world has happened?"

"She's off again!" sniveled Hannah; "and she's worse this time than she's ever been. No sugar, no tea, only nuts and fruit, and her windows open all night, with the curtains getting black. I wisht I had Mr. Charlie by the neck."

I suppose it came over both of us at the same time—the "Young Woodsman," and the "Camper Craft," and no stays, and all that. I reached for Charlie Sands's letter, which was always sent to Tish and meant for all of us. He wrote:—

> *Dear Three of a Kind*: Well, the French President has came and went, and London has taken down all the brilliant flags which greeted him, such tactful bits as bore Cressy and Agincourt, and the pretty little smallpox and "plague here" banners, and has gone back to such innocent diversions as baiting cabinet ministers, blowing up public buildings, or going out into the woods seeking the Simple Life.
>
> The Simple Lifers travel in bands—and little else. They go barefooted, barearmed, bareheaded and

barenecked. They wear one garment, I believe, let their hair hang and their beards grow, eat only what Nature provides, such as nuts and fruits, sleep under the stars, and drink from Nature's pools. Rather bully, isn't it? They're a handsome lot generally, brown as nuts. And I saw a girl yesterday—well, if you do not hear from me for a time it will be because I have discarded the pockets in which I carry my fountain pen and my stamps and am wandering barefoot through the Elysian fields.

Yours for the Simple Life,

CHARLIE SANDS.

As I finished reading the letter aloud, I looked at Aggie in dismay. "That settles it," I said hopelessly. "She had some such idea before, and now this young idiot—" I stopped and stared across the table at Aggie. She was sitting rapt, her eyes fixed on the smouldering wicks of Mr. Wiggins's candles.

"Barefoot through the Elysian fields!" she said.

II

I am not trying to defend myself. I never had the enthusiasm of the other two, but I rather liked the idea. And I did restrain them. It was my suggestion, for instance, that we wear sandals without stockings, instead of going in our bare feet, which was a good thing, for the first day out Aggie stepped into a hornet's nest. And I made out the lists.

The idea, of course, is not how much one can carry, but how little. The "Young Woodsman" told exactly how to manage in the woods if one were lost there and had nothing in the world but a bootlace and a wire hairpin.

With the hairpin one could easily make a fair fish-hook—and with a bootlace or a good hemp cord one could make a rabbit snare.

"So you see," Tish explained, "there's fish and meat with no trouble at all. And there will be berries and nuts. That's a diet for a king."

I was making a list of the necessaries at the time and under bootlaces and hairpins I put down "spade."

"What in Heaven's name is the spade for?" Tish demanded.

"You've got to dig bait, haven't you?"

Tish eyed me with disgust.

"Grasshoppers!" she said tersely.

There was really nothing Tish was not prepared for. I should never have thought of grasshoppers.

"The idea is simply this," observed Tish: "We have surrounded ourselves with a thousand and one things we do not need and would be better without—houses, foolish clothing, electric light, idiotic servants—Hannah, get away from that door!—rich foods, furniture and crowds of people. We've developed and cared for our bodies instead of our souls. What we want is to get out into the woods and think; to forget those pampered bodies of ours and to let our souls grow and assert themselves."

We decided finally to take a blanket apiece, rolled on our shoulders, and Tish and I each took a strong knife. Aggie, instead of the knife, took a pair of scissors. We took a small bottle of blackberry cordial for emergencies, a cake of soap, a salt-cellar for seasoning the fish and rabbits, two towels, a package of court-plaster, Aggie's hay-fever remedy, a bottle of oil of pennyroyal to use against mosquitoes, and a large piece of canvas, light but strong, cut like the diagram.

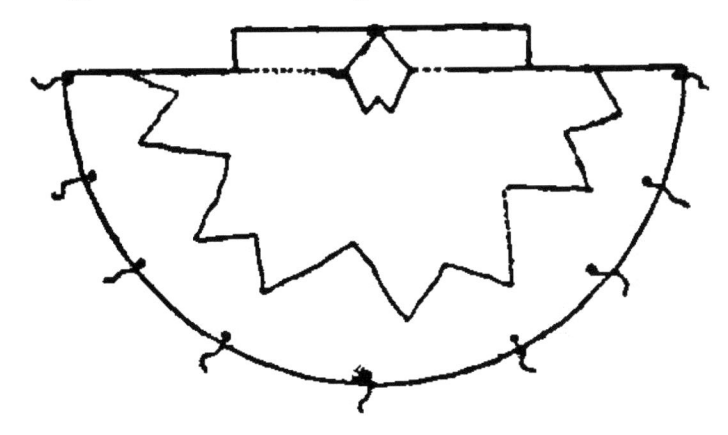

Tish said it was the regulation Indian tepee, and that a squaw could set one up in an hour and have dinner cooked inside it in thirty minutes after. She said she guessed we could do it if an Indian squaw could, and that after we'd cut the poles once, we could carry them with us if we wished to move. She said the tent ought to be ornamented, but she had had no time, and we could paint designs on it with colored clay in the woods when we had nothing more important to do!

It made a largish bundle, but we did not intend to travel much. We thought we could find a good place by a lake somewhere and put up the tent, and set a few snares, and locate the nearest berry-bushes and mushroom-patches, and then, while the rabbits were catching themselves, we should have time to get acquainted with our souls again.

Tish put it in her terse manner most intelligently. "We intend to prove," she stated to Mrs. Ostermaier, the minister's wife, who came to call and found us all sitting on the floor trying to get used to it, for of course there would be no chairs, "we shall prove that the trappings of civilization are a delusion and a snare. We shall bring back 'Mens sana in corpore sano'."

The minister's wife thought this was a disease, for she said, "I hope not, I'm sure," very hastily.

"We shall make our own fire and our own shelter," said Tish from the floor. "We shall wear one garment, loose enough to allow entire freedom of movement. We shall bathe in Nature's pools and come out cleansed. On the Sabbath we shall attend divine service under the Gothic arches of the trees, read sermons in stones, and instead of that whining tenor in the choir we shall listen to the birds singing praise, overhead."

Mrs. Ostermaier looked rather bewildered. "I'm sure I hope so," she said vaguely. "I don't like camping myself. There are so many bugs."

As Tish said, some ideas are so large that the average person cannot see them at all.

We had fixed on Maine. It seemed to combine all the necessary qualities: woods and lakes, rabbits, game and fish, and—solitude. Besides, Aggie's hay fever is better the farther north she gets. On the day we were leaving, Mr. Ostermaier came to see us.

"I—I really must protest, ladies," he said. "That sort of thing may be all right for savages, but—"

"Are we not as intelligent as savages?" Tish demanded.

"Primitive people are inured to hardships, and besides, they have methods of their own. They can make fire—" "So can I," retorted Tish. "Any fool can make a fire with a rubbing-stick. It's been done in thirty-one seconds."

"If you would only take some matches," he wailed, "and a good revolver, Miss Letitia. And—you must pardon this, but I have your well-being at heart—if I could persuade you to take along some—er—flannels and warm clothing!"

"Clothing," said Tish loftily, "is a matter of habit, Mr. Ostermaier."

I think he got the idea from this that we intended to discard clothing altogether, for he went away almost immediately, looking rather upset, and he preached on the following Sunday from "Consider the lilies of the field.... Even Solomon in all his glory was not arrayed like one of these."

We left on Monday evening, and by Tuesday at noon we were at our destination, as far as the railroad was concerned. Tish had a map with the lake we'd picked out, and we had figured that we'd drive out to within ten miles or so of it and then send the driver back. The lake was in an uninhabited neighborhood, with the nearest town twenty-five miles away. We had one suitcase containing our blankets, sandals, short dresses, soap, hairpins, salt-box, knives, scissors, and a compass, and the leather thongs for rabbit snares that we had had cut at a harness shop. In the other suitcase was the tepee.

We ate a substantial breakfast at Tish's suggestion, because we expected to be fairly busy the first day, and there would be no time for hunting. We had to walk ten miles, set up the tent, make a fire and gather nuts and berries. It was about that time, I think, that I happened to recall that it was early for nuts. Still there would be berries, and Tish had added mushrooms to our menu.

We found a man with a spring wagon to drive us out and Tish showed him the map.

"I guess I can get you out that way," he said, "but I

ain't heard of no camp up that direction."

"Who said anything about a camp?" snapped Tish. "How much to drive us fifteen miles in that direction?"

"Fifteen miles! Well, about five dollars, but I think—"

"How much to drive us fifteen miles without thinking?"

"Ten dollars," said the man; and as he had the only wagon in the town we had to pay it.

It was a lovely day, although very warm. The morning sun turned the woods to fairylike glades. Tish sat on the front seat, erect and staring ahead.

Aggie bent over and touched my arm lightly. "Isn't she wonderful!" she whispered; "like some adventurer of old—Balboa discovering the Pacific Ocean, or Joan of Arc leading the what-you-call-'ems."

But somehow my enthusiasm was dying. The sun was hot and there were no berry-bushes to be seen. Aggie's fairy glades in the woods were filled, not with dancing sprites, but with gnats. I wanted a glass of iced tea, and some chicken salad, and talcum powder down my neck. The road was bad, and the driver seemed to have a joke to himself, for every now and then he chuckled, and kept his eyes on the woods on each side, as if he expected to see something. His manner puzzled us all.

"You can trust me not to say anything, ladies," he said at last, "but don't you think you're playing it a bit low down? This ain't quite up to contract, is it?"

"You've been drinking!" said Tish shortly.

After that he let her alone, but soon after he turned round to me and made another venture.

"In case you need grub, lady," he said,"—and them

two suitcases don't hold a lot,—I'll bring out anything you say: eggs and butter and garden truck at market prices. I'm no phylanthropist," he said, glaring at Tish, "but I'd be glad to help the girl, and that's the truth. I been married to this here wife o' mine quite a spell, and to my first one for twenty years, and I'm a believer in married life."

"What girl?" I asked.

He turned right round in the seat and winked at me.

"All right," he said. "I'll not butt in unless you need me. But I'd like to know one thing: He hasn't got a mother, he says, so I take it you're his aunts. Am I on, ladies?"

We didn't know what he was talking about, and we said so. But he only smiled. A mile or so from our destination the horse scared up a rabbit, and Tish could hardly be restrained from running after it with a leather thong. Aggie, however, turned a little pale.

"I'll never be able to eat one, never!" she confided to me. "Did you see its eyes? Lizzie, do you remember Mr. Wiggins's eyes? and the way he used to move his nose, just like that?"

At the end of fifteen miles the driver drew up his horses and took a fresh chew of tobacco.

"I guess this is about right," he said. "That trail there'll take you to the lake. How long do you reckon it'll be before you'll need some fresh eggs?"

"We are quite able to look after ourselves," said Tish with hauteur, and got out of the wagon. She paid him off at once and sat down on her suitcase until he had driven out of sight. He drove slowly, looking back every now and then, and his last view of us must have been impressive—three middle-aged and determined women ready to conquer the wilderness, as Tish put it, and two suitcases.

It was as solitary a place as we could have wished. We had not seen a house in ten miles, and when the last creak of the wagon had died away there was a silence that made our city-broke ears fairly ache. Tish waited until the wagon was out of sight; then she stood up and threw out her arms.

"At last!" she said. "Free to have a lodge in some vast wilderness—to think, to breathe, to expand! Lizzie, do you suppose if we go back we can get that rabbit?"

I looked at my watch. It was one o'clock and there was not a berry-bush in sight. The drive had made me hungry, and I'd have eaten a rabbit that looked like Mr. Wiggins and called me by name if I'd had it. But there was absolutely no use going back for the one we'd seen on our drive.

Aggie was opening her suitcase and getting out her costume, which was a blue calico with short sleeves and a shoe-top skirt.

"Where'll I put it on?" she asked, looking about her.

"Right here!" Tish replied. "For goodness sake, Aggie, try to discard false modesty and false shame. We're here to get close to the great beating heart of Nature. Take off your switch before you do another thing."

None of us looked particularly well, I admit; but it was wonderful how much more comfortable we were. Aggie, who is very thin, discarded a part of her figure, and each of us parted with some pet hypocrisy. But I don't know that I have ever felt better. Only, of course we were hungry.

We packed our things in the suitcases and hid them in a hollow tree, and Tish suggested looking for a spring. She said water was always the first requisite and fire the second.

"Fire!" said Aggie. "What for? We've nothing to cook."

Well, that was true enough, so we sent Aggie to look for water and Tish and I made a rabbit snare. We made a good many snares and got to be rather quick at it. They were all made like this illustration.

First Tish, with her book open in front of her, made a running noose out of one of the buckskin thongs. Next we bent down a sapling and tied the noose to it, and last of all we bound the free part of the thong round a snag and thus held the sapling down. The idea is that a rabbit, bounding along, presumably with his eyes shut, will stick his head through the noose, kick the line clear of the snag and be drawn violently into the air. Tish figured that by putting up half a dozen snares we'd have three or four rabbits at least each day.

It was about three when we finished, and we drew off to a safe distance to watch the rabbit bound to his doom. But no rabbits came along.

I was very empty and rather faint, but Tish said she had never been able to think so clearly, and that we were all overfed and stodgy and would be better for fasting.

Aggie came in at three-thirty with a hornet sting and no water. She said there were no springs, but that she had found a place where a spring had existed before the dry spell, and there was a naked footprint in the mud, quite fresh! We all went to look at it, and Tish was quite positive it was not a man's footprint at all, but only a bear's.

"A bear!" said Aggie.

"What of it?" Tish demanded. "The 'Young Woodsman' says that no bear attacks a human unless he is hungry, and at this time of the year with the woods full of food—"

"Humph!"—I could not restrain myself—"I wish you would show me a little of it. If no rabbit with acute melancholia comes along to commit suicide by hanging on that gallows of yours, I think we'll starve to death."

"There will be a rabbit," Tish said tersely; and we started back to the snare.

I was never so astonished in my life. There was a rabbit! It seems we had struck a runway without knowing it, although Tish said afterward that she had recognized it at once from the rabbit tracks. Anyhow, whether it died of design or curiosity, our supper was kicking at the top of the sapling, and Tish pretended to be calm and to have known all along that we'd get one. But it was not dead.

We got it down somehow or other and I held it by the ears while it kicked and scratched. I was hungry enough to have eaten it alive, but Aggie began to cry.

"You'll be murderers, nothing else," she wailed. "Look at his little white tail and pitiful baby eyes!"

"Good gracious, Aggie," Tish snapped, "get a knife and cut its throat while I make a fire. If it's any help to you, we're not going to eat either its little white tail or its pitiful baby eyes."

As a matter of fact Aggie wouldn't touch the rabbit and I did not care much about it myself. I do not like to kill things. My Aunt Sarah Mackintosh once killed a white hen that lived twenty minutes without its head; two weeks later she dreamed that that same hen, without a head, was sitting on the footboard of the bed, and the next day she got word that her cousin's husband in Sacramento had died of the hiccoughs.

It ended with Tish giving me the fire-making materials and stalking off into the woods with the rabbit in one hand and the knife in the other.

Tish is nothing if not thorough, but she seemed to

me inconsistent. She brought blankets and a canvas tepee and sandals and an aluminum kettle, but she disdained matches. I rubbed with that silly drill and a sort of bow arrangement until my wrists ached, but I did not get even a spark of fire. When Tish came back with the rabbit there was no fire, and Aggie had taken out her watch crystal and was holding it in the sun over a pile of leaves.

Tish got out the "Young Woodsman" from the suitcase. It seems I had followed cuts I and II, but had neglected cut III, which is: Hold the left wrist against the left shin, and the left foot on the fireblock. I had got my feet mixed and was trying to hold my left wrist against my right shin, which is exceedingly difficult. Tish got a fire in fourteen minutes and thirty-one seconds by Aggie's watch, and had to wear a bandage on her hand for a week.

But we had a fire. We cooked the rabbit, which proved to be much older than Aggie had thought, and ate what we could. Personally I am not fond of rabbit, and our enjoyment was rather chastened by the fear that some mushrooms Tish had collected and added to the stew were toadstools *incognito*. To make things worse, Aggie saw some goldenrod nearby and began to sneeze.

It was after five o'clock, but it seemed wisest to move on toward the lake.

"Even if we don't make it," said Tish, "we'll be on our way, and while that bear is likely harmless we needn't thrust temptation in his way."

We carried the fire with us in the kettle and we took turns with the tepee, which was heavy. Our suitcases with our city clothes in them we hid in a hollow tree, and one after the other, with Aggie last, we started on.

The trail, which was a sort of wide wagon road at first, became a footpath; as we went on even that disappeared at times under fallen leaves. Once we lost it entirely, and Aggie, falling over a hidden root, stilled the fire. She became exceedingly disagreeable at about that time, said she was sure Tish's mushrooms were toadstools because she felt very queer, and suddenly gave a yell and said she had seen something moving in the bushes.

We all looked, and the bushes were moving.

III

It was dusk by that time and the path was only a thread between masses of undergrowth. Tish said if it was the bear he would be afraid of the fire, so we put dry leaves in the kettle and made quite a blaze. By its light Tish read that bears in the summer are full fed and really frolicsome and that they are awful cowards. We felt quite cheered and brave, and Tish said if he came near to throw the fire kettle at him and he'd probably die of fright.

It was too late to put up the tepee, so we found a clearing near the path and decided to spend the night there. Aggie still watched the bushes and wanted to spend the night in a tree; but Tish's calmness was a reproach to us both, and after we had emptied the kettle and made quite a fire to keep off animals, we unrolled our blankets and prepared for sleep. I could have slept anywhere, although I was still rather hungry. My last view was of Tish in the firelight grimly bending down a sapling and fastening a rabbit snare to it.

During the night I was wakened by somebody clutching my arm. It was Aggie who lay next to me. When I raised my head she pointed off into the woods to our left. At a height of perhaps four feet from the ground a ghastly red glow was moving rapidly away from us. It was not a torch; it was more a radiance, and it moved not evenly, but jerkily. I could feel the very hair rising on my head and it was all I could do to call Tish. When we had roused her, however, the glow had faded entirely and she said we had had a nightmare.

The snare the next morning contained a skunk, and we moved on as quickly as possible, without attempting to secure the thong, of which we had several. We gathered some puffballs to soak for breakfast and in a clearing I found some blackberry bushes. We were very cheerful that morning, for if we could capture rabbits and skunks, we were sure of other things, also, and soon we would be able to add fish to our menu. True, we had not had much time to commune with our souls, and Aggie's arms were so sunburned that she could not bend them at the elbows. But, as Tish said, we had already proved our contention that we could get along without men or houses or things. Things, she said, were the curse of modern life; we filled our lives with things instead of thoughts.

It was when we were ready to cook the puffballs that we missed the kettle! Tish was very angry; she said it was evident that the bear was mischievous and that all bears were thieves. (See the "Young Woodsman.") But I recalled the glow of the night before, and more than once I caught Aggie's eyes on me, filled with consternation. For we had seen that kettle leaving the camp with some of our fire in it, and bears are afraid of fire!

We reached the lake at noon and it seemed as if we might soon have time to sit down and rest. But there was a great deal to do. Aggie was of no assistance on account of her arms, so Tish and I put up the tent. The "Young Woodsman" said it was easy. First you tied three long poles together near the top and stood them up so they made a sort of triangle. Then you cut about a dozen and filled in between the three. That looked easy, but it took an afternoon, and our first three looked like this first cut.

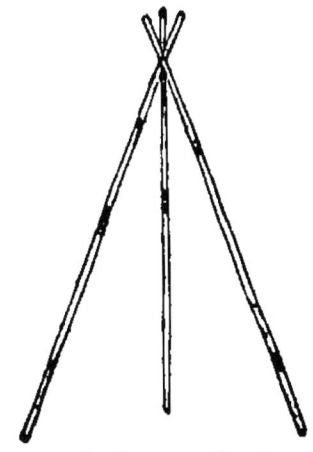

We had caught a rabbit by noon, and Aggie being unfit for other work, and the kettle being gone, Tish set her to roasting it. It was not very good, but we ate some, being ravenous. The method was simplicity itself—two forked sticks in the ground, one across to hang the rabbit to and a fire beneath. It tasted rather smoky.

In the afternoon we finished putting up the tepee, and Tish made a fishhook out of a hairpin and tied it to a strong creeper I had found. But we caught no fish. We had more rabbit for supper, with some puffballs smoked and a few huckleberries. But by that time the very sight of a rabbit sickened me, and Aggie began to talk about broiled beefsteak and fried spring chicken.

We had seen no sign of the bear, or whatever it was, all day, and it seemed likely we were not to be again disturbed. But a most mysterious thing occurred that very night.

As I have said, we had caught no fish. The lake was full of them. We sat on a bank that evening and watched them playing leapfrog, and talked about frying them on red-hot stones, but nothing came near the hairpin. At last Tish made a suggestion.

"We need worms," she said. "A grasshopper loses all his spirit after he's been immersed for an hour, but a worm will keep on wriggling and attracting attention for half a day."

"I wanted to bring a spade," said I.

But Tish had read of a scheme for getting worms that she said the game warden of some place or other had guaranteed officially.

"You stick a piece of wood about two feet into the ground in a likely spot," she said, "and rub a rough piece of bark or plank across the top. This man claims, and it sounds reasonable, that the worms think it is raining and come up for water. All you have to do is to gather them up."

Tish found a pole for the purpose on the beach and set to work, while Aggie and I prepared several hooks and lines. The fish were jumping busily, and it seemed likely we should have more than we could do to haul them in.

The experiment, however, failed entirely, for not a single worm appeared. Tish laid it to the fact that it was very late and that the worms were probably settled down for the night. It may have been that, or it may have been the wrong kind of wood.

The mysterious happening was this: We rose quite early because the tepee did not seem to be well anchored and fell down on us at daybreak. Tish went down to the beach to examine the lines that had been out all night, and found nothing. She was returning rather dispirited to tell us that it would be rabbit again for breakfast, when she saw lying on a flat stone half a dozen beautiful fish, one or two still gasping, in our lost kettle!

Tish said she stood there, opening and shutting her mouth like the fish. Then she gave a whoop and we came running. At first we thought they might have been jumping and leaped out on to the beach by accident, but, as Tish said, they would hardly have landed all together and into a kettle that had been lost for two nights and a day. The queer thing was that they had not been caught with a hook at all. They hadn't a mark on them.

We were so hungry that we ate every one of them for breakfast. It was only when we had eaten, and were sitting gorged and not caring whether the tent was set up again or not, that we fell to wondering about the fish. Tish fancied it might have been the driver of the spring wagon, but decided he'd have sold us the fish at thirty cents a pound live weight.

All day long we watched for a sign of our benefactor, but we saw nothing. Tish set up more rabbit snares; not that she wanted rabbits, but it had become a mania with her, and there were so many of them that as they grew accustomed to us they sat round our camp in a ring and criticized our housekeeping. She thought if she got a good many skins she could have a fur robe made for her automobile. As a matter of fact she found another use for them.

It was that night, then, that we were sitting round the camp-fire on stones that we had brought up from the beach. We had seen nothing more of the bear, and if we had been asked we should have said that the nearest human being was twenty-five miles away.

Suddenly a voice came out of the woods just behind us, a man's voice.

"Please don't be alarmed," said the voice. "But may I have a little of your fire? Mine has gone out again."

"G-g-g-good gracious!" said Aggie. "T-Tish, get your revolver!"

This was for effect. Tish had no revolver.

All of us had turned and were staring into the woods behind, but we could see no one. After Aggie's speech about the revolver it was some time before the voice spoke again.

"Never mind, Aggie," Tish observed, very loud. "The revolver is here and loaded—as nice a little thirty-six as any one needs here in the woods."

She said afterward that she knew all the time there was no thirty-six caliber revolver, but in the excitement she got it mixed with her bust measure. Having replied to Aggie, Tish then turned in the direction of the voice.

"Don't skulk back there," she called. "Come out, where we can see you. If you look reliable, we'll give you some fire, of course."

There was another pause, as if the stranger were hesitating. Then:—

"I think I'd better not," he said with reluctance in his

voice. "Can't you toss a brand this way?"

By that time we had grown accustomed to the darkness, and I thought I could see in the shadow of a tree a lightish figure. Aggie saw it at the same instant and clutched my arm.

"Lizzie!" she gasped.

It was at that moment that Tish tossed the brand. It fell far short, but her movement caught the stranger unawares. He ducked behind the tree, but the flare of light had caught him. With the exception of what looked like a pair of bathing-trunks he was as bare as my hand!

There was a sort of astonished silence. Then the voice called out:—"Why in the world didn't you warn me?" it said, aggrieved. "I didn't know you were going to throw the blamed thing."

We had all turned our backs at once and Tish's face was awful.

"Take it and go," she said, without turning. "Take it and go."

From the crackling of leaves and twigs we judged that he had come out and got the brand, and when he spoke again it was from farther back in the woods.

"You know," he said, "I don't like this any more than you do. I've got forty-two mosquito bites on my left arm."

He waited, as if for a reply; but getting none he evidently retreated. The sound of rustling leaves and crackling twigs grew fainter, fainter still, died away altogether. We turned then with one accord and gazed through the dark arches of the forest. A glowing star was retreating there—a smouldering fire, that seemed to move slowly and with an appearance of dejection.

It was the second time Aggie and I had seen fire thus carried through the wood; but whereas about the kettle there had been a glow and radiance that was almost triumphant, the brand we now watched seemed smouldering, dejected, ashamed. Even Tish felt it.

"The wretch!" she exclaimed. "Daring to come here like that! No wonder he's ashamed."

But Aggie, who is very romantic, sat staring after the distant torch.

"Mr. Wiggins suffered so from mosquitoes," she said softly.

IV

The next morning we found more fish awaiting us, and on the smooth sand of the beach was a message written with a stick:—

> If you will leave a wire hairpin or two on this stone I can get bigger fish. What do you mean to do with all those rabbit skins?
>
> (Signed) P.

Tish was touched by the fish, I think. She smoothed off the sand carefully and wrote a reply:—

> Here are the hairpins. Thank you. Do you want the rabbit skins?
>
> L.C.

All day we were in a state of expectancy. The mosquitoes were very bad, and had it not been for the excitement of the P—— person I should have given up and gone home. I wanted mashed potatoes and lima beans with butter dressing, and a cup of hot tea, and muffins, and ice—in fact, I cannot think of anything I did not want, except rabbits and fish and puffballs and such blackberries as the birds did not fancy. Although we were well enough—almost too well—the better I felt the hungrier I got.

Tish thought the time had now come to rest and invite our souls. She set the example that day by going out on a flat rock in the lake and preparing to think all the things she'd been waiting most of her life to consider.

"I am ready to form my own opinions about some things," she said. "I realize now that all my life the newspapers and stupid people and books have formed my opinions. Now I'm going to think along my own lines. Is there another life after this? Do I really desire the suffrage? Why am I a Baptist?"

Aggie said she would like to invite her soul that day also, not to form any opinions,—Tish always does that for her,—but she had to get some clothes in September and she might as well think them out.

So it happened that I was alone when I met the P—— person's young woman.

I had intended to wander only a short way along the trail, but after I had gone a mile or two it occurred to me as likely that the spring-wagon driver would come back that way before long out of curiosity, and I thought I might leave a message for him to bring out some fresh eggs and leave them there. I could tell Tish I had found a nest, or perhaps, since that would be lying, I could put them in a nest and let her find them. I'd have ordered tea, too, if I could have thought of any way to account for it.

"I'm going to do some meditating myself to-day,"

I remarked, "but I think better when I'm moving. If I don't come back in an hour or so don't imagine I've been kidnaped."

Tish turned on her stone and looked at me.

"You will not be kidnaped," she said shortly. "I cannot imagine any one safer than you are in that costume."

Well, I made my way along the trail as rapidly as I could. It was twenty miles there and back and I've seen the day when two city blocks would send me home to soak my feet in hot water. But the sandals were easy to walk in and my calico skirt was short and light.

I had no paper to write my message on, of course, but on the way I gathered a large white fungus and I scraped a note on it with a pin. With the fungus under my arm I walked briskly along, planning an omelet with the eggs, if we got any, and gathering mushrooms here and there. It was the mushrooms that led me to the discovery of a camping-place that was prehistoric in its primitiveness—a clearing, surrounded by low bushes, and in the center a fireplace of stones with a fire smouldering. At one side a heap of leaves and small twigs for a bed, a stump for a seat, and lying on top of it a sort of stone axe, made by inserting a sharp stone into the cleft of a sapling and tying it into place with a wild-grape tendril. Pegged out on the ground to cure was a rabbit skin, indifferently scraped. It made our aluminum kettle and canvas tepee look like a marble-vestibuled apartment on Riverside Drive.

The whole thing looked pitiful, hungry. I thought of Tish sitting on a stone inviting her soul, while rabbits came from miles round to stick their heads through our nooses and hang themselves for our dinner; and it seemed to me that we should share our plenty. I thought it probable that the gentleman of the woods lived here, and from the appearance of the place he carried all his possessions with him when he wore his bathing-trunks. If I had been in any doubt, the sight of Aggie's wire hairpin, sharpened and bent into a serviceable fishhook, decided me. I scratched a message for him on another fungus and left it:—

> If you need anything come to the Indian tepee at the lake. We have no clothing to spare, but are always glad to help in time of trouble.
> (Signed) ONE OF THE SIMPLE LIFERS.

I went on after that and about noon reached our point of exodus from the wagon. I was tired and hot and I kept thinking of my little dining-room at home, with the electric fan going, and iced cantaloupe, and nobody worrying about her soul or thinking her own thoughts, and no rabbits.

Our suitcases were safe enough in the hollow tree, and I thought the spring wagon had been back already, for there were fresh tracks. This discouraged me and I sat down on a log to rest. It was then that I heard the girl crying.

She was crying softly, but in the woods sounds travel. I found her on her face on the pine needles about twenty yards away, wailing her heart out into a pink automobile veil, and she was so absorbed in her misery that I had to stoop and touch her before she looked up.

"Don't cry," I said. "If you are lost, I can direct you to a settlement."

She looked up at me, and from being very red and suffused she went quite pale. It seems that with my bare legs and sandals and my hair down, which was Tish's idea for making it come in thick and not gray, and what with my being sunburned and stained with berries, she thought I was a wild woman. I realized what was wrong.

"Don't be alarmed," I said somewhat grimly. "I'm rational enough; if I hop about instead of walking, it's because I'm the tomb of more rabbits than I care to remember, but aside from that I'm all right. Are you lost?"

She sat up, still staring, and wiped her eyes.

"No. I have a machine over there among the trees. Are there—are there plenty of rabbits in the woods?"

"Thousands." She was a pretty little thing, very young, and dressed in a white motor coat with white shoes and hat.

"And—and berries?"

"There aren't many berries," I admitted. "The birds eat 'em. We get the ones they don't fancy."

Now I didn't think for a moment that she was worried about my diet, but she was worried about the food supply in the woods, that was sure. So I sat down on a stump and told her about puffballs, and what Tish had read about ants being edible but acid, and that wood mice, roasted and not cooked too dry, were good food, but that Aggie had made us liberate the only ones we had caught, because a man she was once engaged to used to carry a pet mouse in his pocket.

Nothing had really appealed to her until I mentioned Mr. Wiggins. Then unexpectedly she began to cry again. And after that I got the whole story.

It seems she was in love with a young man who was everything a young man ought to be and had money as well. But the money was the barrier really, for the girl's father wouldn't believe that a youth who played polo, and did not have to work for a living, and led cotillons, and paid calls in the afternoon could have really good red blood in him. He had a man in view for her, she said, one who had made his money himself, and had to have his valet lay out his clothes for fear he'd make a mistake. Once the valet had to go to have a tooth pulled and the man had to decline a dinner.

"Father said," finished the little girl tearfully, "that if Percy—that's his name, and it counted against him too—that if Percy was a real man he'd do something. And then he hap-happened on a book of my small brother's, telling how people used to live in the woods, and kill their own food and make their own fire—"

"The 'Young Woodsman,' of course," I put in.

"And how the strong survived, but the weak succumbed, and he said if Percy was a man, and not a t-tailor's dummy, he'd go out in the woods, j-just primitive man, without anything but a pair of bathing trunks, and keep himself alive for a month. If he s-stood the test father was willing to forget the 'Percy.' He said that he knew Mr. Willoughby could do it—that's the other man—and that he'd come in at the end of the time with a deed for the forest and mortgages on all the surrounding camps."

"And Percy agreed?"

"He didn't want to. He said it took mentality and physical endurance as well as some courage to play polo. Father said it did—on the part of the pony. Then s-some of the men heard of it, and there were bets on it—ten to one he wouldn't do it and twenty to one he couldn't do it. So Percy decided to try. Father was so afraid that some of the campers and guides would help him that he had notices sent out at Mr. Willoughby's suggestion offering a reward if Percy could be shown to have asked any assistance. Oh, I know he's sick in there somewhere, or starving or—dead!"

I had had a great light break over me, and now I stooped and patted the girl on the shoulder.

"Dead! Certainly not," I said. "I saw him last night."

"Saw him!"

"Well, not exactly saw him—there wasn't much light. But he's alive and well, and—do you really want him to win?"

"Do I?" She sat up with shining eyes. "I don't care whether he owns anything in the world but the trunks. If I didn't think I'd add to his troubles I'd go into the woods this minute and find him and suffer with him."

"You'd have to be married to him first," I objected, rather startled.

But she looked at me with her cheeks as red strawberries. "Why?" she demanded. "Father's crazy about primitive man—did primitive man take his woman to church to be married, with eight brides maids and a reception after the ceremony? Of course not. He grabbed her and carried her off."

"Good Heavens! You're not in earnest?" "I think I am," she said slowly. "I'd rather live in the woods with Percy and no ceremony than live without him anywhere in the world. And I'll bet primitive man would have been wiped off the earth if he hadn't had primitive woman to add her wits to his strength. If Percy only had a woman to help him!"

"My dear," I said solemnly, "he has! He has, not one,

but three!"

It took me some time to explain that Percy was not supporting a harem in the Maine woods; but when at last she got my idea and that the other two classed with me in beauty and attractiveness, she was overjoyed.

"But Percy promised not to ask for help," she said suddenly.

"He needn't. My dear, go away and stop worrying about Percy—he's all right. When is the time up?"

"In three weeks."

"I suppose father and the Willoughby person will come to meet him?"

"Yes, and all the fellows from the club who have put money up on him. We're going to motor over and father's bringing the physical director of the athletic club. He's not only got to survive, but he's got to be in good condition."

"He'll be in good condition," I said grimly. "Does he drink and smoke?"

"A little, not too much. Oh, yes, I had forgotten!" She opened up a little gold cigarette case, which she took from her pocket, and extracted a handful of cigarettes.

"If you are going to see him," she said, "you might put them where he'll find them?"

"Certainly not."

"But that's not giving them to him."

"My dear child," I said sternly, "Percy is going to come out of these woods so well and strong that he may not have to work, but he'll want to. And he'll not smoke anything stronger than corn-silk, if we're to take charge of this thing."

She understood quickly enough and I must say she was grateful. She was almost radiant with joy when I told her how capable Tish was, and that she was sure to be interested, and about Aggie's hay fever and Mr. Wiggins and the rabbit snares. She leaned over and kissed me impulsively.

"You dear old thing!" she cried. "I know you'll look after him and make him comfortable and—how old is Miss Letitia?"

"Something over fifty and Aggie Pilkington's about the same, although she won't admit it."

She kissed me again at that, and after looking at her wrist watch she jumped to her feet.

"Heavens!" she said. "It's four o'clock and my engine has been running all this time!"

She got a smart little car from somewhere up the road, and the last I saw of her she was smiling back over her shoulder and the car running on the edge of a ditch.

"You are three darlings!" she called back. "And tell Percy I love him—love him—love him!"

I thought I'd never get back to the lake. I was tired to begin with, and after I'd gone about four miles and was limping with a splinter in my heel and no needle to get it out with, I found I still had the fungus message to the spring-wagon person under my arm.

It was dark when I got back and my nerves were rather unstrung, what with wandering from the path here and there, with nothing to eat since morning, and running into a tree and taking the skin off my nose. When I limped into camp at last, I didn't care whether Percy lived or died, and the thought, of rabbit stew made my mouth water.

It was not rabbit, however. Aggie was sitting alone by the fire, waving a brand round her head to keep off mosquitoes, and in front of her, dangling from the spit, were a dozen pairs of frogs' legs in a row.

I ate six pairs without a question and then I asked for Tish.

"Catching frogs," said Aggie laconically, and flourished the brand.

"Where?"

"Pulling them off the trees. Where do you think she gets them?" she demanded.

A large mosquito broke through her guard at that moment and she flung the torch angrily at the fire.

"I'm eaten alive!" she snapped. "I wish to Heaven I had smallpox or something they could all take and go away and die."

The frogs' legs were heavenly, although in a restaurant I loathe the things. I left Aggie wondering if her hay fever wasn't contagious through the blood and hoping the mosquitoes would get it and sneeze themselves to death, and went to find Tish.

She was standing in the margin of the lake up to her knees in water, with a blazing torch in one hand and one of our tent poles in the other. Tied to the end the pole was a grapevine line, and a fishing-hook made of a hairpin was attached to it.

Her method, which it seems she'd heard from Charlie Sands and which was not in the "Young Woodsman," was simple and effectual.

"Don't move," she said tensely when she heard me on the bank. "There's one here as big as a chicken!"

She struck the flare forward, and I could see the frog looking at it and not blinking. He sat in a sort of heavenly ecstasy, like a dog about to bay at the moon, while the hook dangled just at his throat.

"I'm half-ashamed to do it, Lizzie, it's so easy," she said calmly, still tickling the thing's throat with the hook. "Grab him as I throw him at you. They slip off sometimes."

The next instant she jerked the hook up and caught the creature by the lower jaw. It was the neatest thing I have ever seen. Tish came wading over to where I stood and examined the frog.

"If we only had some Tartare sauce!" she said regretfully. "I wish you'd look at my ankle, Lizzie. There's something stuck to it."

The something was a leech. It refused to come off, and so she carried both frog and leech back to the camp. Aggie said on no account to pull a leech off, it left its teeth in and the teeth went on burrowing, or laid eggs or something. One must leave it on until it was full and round and couldn't hold any more, and then it dropped off.

So all night Tish kept getting up and going to the fire to see if it was swelling. But toward morning she fell asleep and it dropped off, and we had a terrible feeling that it was somewhere in our blankets.

But the leech caused less excitement that evening than my story of Percy and the little girl in the white coat. Aggie was entranced, and Tish had made Percy a suit of rabbit skin with a cap to match and outlined a set of exercises to increase his chest measure before I was half through with my story.

But Percy did not appear, although we had an idea that he was not far off in the woods. We could hear a crackling in the undergrowth, but when we called there was no reply. Tish was eating a frog's leg when the idea came to her.

"He'll never come out under ordinary circumstances in that—er—costume," she said. "Suppose we call for help. He'll probably come bounding. Help!" she yelled, between bites, as one may say.

"Help! Fire! Police!"

"Help!" cried Aggie. "Percy, help!" It sounded like "Mercy, help!"

It worked like a charm. The faint cracking became louder, nearer, turned from a suspicion to a certainty and from a certainty to a fact. The bushes parted and Percy stood before us. All he saw was three elderly women eating frogs' legs round a fire under a cloud of mosquitoes. He stopped, dumbfounded, and in that instant we saw that he didn't need the physical exercises, but that, of course, he did need the rabbit-skin suit.

"Great Scott!" he panted. "I thought I heard you calling for help."

"So we did," said Tish, "but we didn't need it. Won't you sit down?"

He looked dazed and backed toward the bushes.

"I—I think," he said, "if there's nothing wrong I'd better not—"

"Fiddlesticks!" Tish snapped. "Are you ashamed of the body the Lord gave you? Don't you suppose we've all got skins? And didn't I thrash my nephew, Charlie Sands, when he was almost as big as you and had less on, for bathing in the river? Sit down, man, and don't be a fool."

He edged toward the fire, looking rather silly, and Aggie passed him a frog's leg on a piece of bark.

"Try this, Percy," she said, smiling.

At the name he looked ready to run. "I guess you've seen the notices," he said, "so you'll understand I cannot accept any food or assistance. I'm very grateful to you, anyhow."

"You may take what food you find, surely," said Aggie. "If you find a roasted frog's leg on the ground—so—there's nothing to prevent you eating it, is there?"

"Nothing at all," said Percy, and picked it up. "Unless, of course—"

"It's not a trap, young man," said Tish. "Eat it and enjoy it. There are lots more where it came from."

He relaxed at that, and on Tish's bringing out a blanket from the tent to throw over his shoulders he became almost easy. He was much surprised to learn that we knew his story, and when I repeated the "love him" message, he seemed to grow a foot taller and his eyes glowed.

"I'm holding out all right," he said. "I'm fit physically. But the thing that gets my goat is that I'm to come out clothed. Dorothea's father says that primitive man, with nothing but his hands and perhaps a stone club, fed himself, made himself a shelter, and clothed himself in skins. Skins! I'm so big that two or three bears would hardly be enough. I did find a hole that I thought a bear or two might fall into, and got almost stung to death robbing a bee tree to bait the thing with honey. But there aren't any bears, and if there were how'd I kill 'em? Wait until they starve to death?"

"Rabbits!" said Tish.

He looked down at himself and he seemed very large in the firelight. "Dear lady," he said, "there aren't enough rabbits in the county to cover me, and how'd I put 'em together? I was a fool to undertake the thing, that's all."

"But aren't you in love with her?" asked Aggie.

"Well, I guess I am. It isn't that, you know. I'm a good bit worse than crazy about her. A man might be crazy about a mint julep or a power boat, but—he'd hardly go into the woods in his skin and live on fish until he's scaly for either of them. If I don't get her, I don't want to live. That's all."

He looked so gloomy and savage that we saw he meant it, and Aggie was perceptibly thrilled. Trish, however, was thinking hard, her eyes on the leech. "Was there anything in the agreement to prevent your accepting any suggestions?"

He pondered. "No, I was to be given no food, drink, shelter, or any weapon. The old man forgot fire—that's how I came to beg some."

"Fire and brains," reflected Tish. "We've given you the first and we've plenty of the second to offer. Now, young man, this is my plan. We'll give you nothing but suggestions. If now and then you find a cooked meal under that tree, that's accident, not design, and you'd better eat it. Can you sew?"

"I'm like the Irishman and the fiddle—I never tried, but I guess I can." He was much more cheerful.

"Do you have to be alone?"

"I believe he took that for granted, in this costume."

"Will it take you long to move over here?"

"I think I can move without a van," he said, grinning. "My sole worldly possessions are a stone hatchet and a hairpin fishhook."

"Get them and come over," commanded Tish. "When you leave this forest at the end of the time you are going to be fed and clothed and carry a tent; you will have with you smoked meat and fish; you will carry under your arm an Indian clock or sundial; you will have a lamp—if we can find a clamshell or a broken bottle—and you will have a fire-making outfit with your monogram on it."

"But, my dear friend," he said, "I am not supposed to have any assistance and—"

"Assistance!" Tish snapped. "Who said assistance? I'm providing the brains, but you'll do it all yourself."

He moved over an hour or so later and Tish and I went into the tent to bed. Somewhat later, when she limped to the fire to see how the leech was filling up, he and Aggie were sitting together talking, he of Dorothea and Aggie of Mr. Wiggins. Tish said they were both talking at the same time, neither one listening to the other, and that it sounded like this:—"She's so sweet and trusting and honest—well, I'd believe what she said if she—"

"—fell off a roof on a rainy day and was picked up by a man with a horse and buggy quite unconscious."

V

The next three weeks were busy times for Percy. He wore Tish's blanket for two days, and then, finding it in the way, he discarded it altogether. Seen in daylight it was easy to understand why little Dorothea was in love with him. He was a handsome young giant, although much bitten by mosquitoes and scratched with briers.

The arrangement was a good one all round. He knew of things in the wood we'd never heard of—wild onions and artichokes, and he had found a clump of wild cherry trees. He made snares of the fibers of tree bark, and he brought in turtles and made plates out of the shells. And all the time he was working on his outfit, curing rabbit skins and sewing them together with fibers under my direction.

When he'd made one sleeve of his coat we had a sort of celebration. He'd found an empty bottle somewhere in the woods, and he had made a wild-cherry decoction that he declared was cherry brandy, keeping it in the sun to ferment. Well, he insisted on opening the brandy that day and passing it round. We had cups made of leaves and we drank to his sleeve, although the stuff was villainous. He had put the sleeve on, and it looked rather inadequate. "Here's fun," he said joyously. "If my English tailor could see this sleeve he'd die of envy. A sleeve's not all of a coat, but what's a coat without a sleeve? Look at it—grace, ease of line, and beauty of material."

Aggie lifted her leaf.

"To Dorothea!" she said. "And may the sleeve soon be about her."

Tish thought this toast was not delicate, but Percy was enchanted with it.

It was on the evening of the fourth day of Percy's joining our camp that the Willoughby person appeared. It happened at a most inauspicious time. We had eaten supper and were gathered round the camp-fire and Tish had put wet leaves on the blaze to make a smudge that would drive the mosquitoes away. We were sitting there, Tish and I coughing and Aggie sneezing in the smoke, when Percy came running through the woods and stopped at the foot of a tree near by.

"Bring a club, somebody," he yelled. "I've treed the back of my coat."

Tish ran with one of the tent poles. A tepee is inconvenient for that reason. Every time any one wants a fishing-pole or a weapon, the tent loses part of its bony structure and sags like the face of a stout woman who has reduced. And it turned out that Percy had treed a coon. He climbed up after it, taking Tish's pole with him to dislodge it, and it was at that moment that a man rode into the clearing and practically fell off his horse. He was dirty and scratched with brambles, and his once immaculate riding-clothes were torn. He was about to take off his hat when he got a good look at us and changed his mind.

"Have you got anything to eat?" he asked. "I've been lost since noon yesterday and I'm about all in."

The leaves caught fire suddenly and sent a glow into Percy's tree. I shall never forget Aggie's agonized look or the way Tish flung on more wet leaves in a hurry.

"I'm sorry," she said, "but supper's over."

"But surely a starving man—"

"You won't starve inside of a week," Tish snapped. "You've got enough flesh on you for a month."

He stared at her incredulously.

"But, my good woman," he said, "I can pay for my food. Even you itinerant folk need money now and then, don't you? Come, now, cook me a fish; I'll pay for it. My name is Willoughby—J.K. Willoughby. Perhaps you've heard of me."

Tish cast a swift glance into the tree. It was in shadow again and she drew a long breath. She said afterward that the whole plan came to her in the instant of that breath.

"We can give you something," she said indifferently. "We have a stewed rabbit, if you care for it."

There was a wild scramble in the tree at that moment, and we thought all was over. We learned later that Percy had made a move to climb higher, out of the firelight, and the coon had been so startled that he almost fell out. But instead of looking up to investigate, the stranger backed toward the fire.

"Only a wildcat," said Tish. "They'll not come near the fire."

"Near!" exclaimed Mr. Willoughby. "If they came any nearer, they'd have to get into it!"

"I think," said Tish, "that if you are afraid of them—although you are safe enough if you don't get under the trees; they jump down, you know—that you would better stay by the fire to-night. In the morning we'll start you toward a road."

All night with Percy in the tree! I gave her a savage glance, but she ignored me.

The Willoughby looked up nervously, and of course there were trees all about.

"I guess I'll stay," he agreed. "What about that rabbit?"

I did not know Tish's plan at that time, and while Aggie was feeding the Willoughby person and he was grumbling over his food, I took Tish aside.

"Are you crazy?" I demanded. "Just through your idiocy Percy will have to stay in that tree all night—and he'll go to sleep, likely, and fall out."

Tish eyed me coldly.

"You are a good soul, Lizzie," she observed, "but don't overwork your mind. Go back and do something easy—let the Willoughby cross your palm with silver, and tell his fortune. If he asks any questions I'm queen of the gypsies, and give him to understand that we're in temporary hiding from the law. The worse he thinks of us the better. Remember, we haven't seen Percy."

"I'm not going to lie," I said sternly.

"Pooh!" Tish sneered. "That wretch came into the woods to gloat over his rival's misery. The truth's too good for him."

I did my best, and I still have the silver dollar he gave me. I told him I saw a small girl, who loved him but didn't realize it yet, and there was another man.

"Good gracious," I said, "there must be something wrong with your palm. I see the other man, but he seems to be in trouble. His clothing has been stolen, for he has none, and he is hungry, very hungry."

"Ha!" said Mr. Willoughby, looking startled. "You old gypsies beat the devil! Hungry, eh? Is that all?"

The light flared up again and I could see clearly the pale spot in the tree, which was Percy. But Mr. Willoughby's eyes were on his palm.

"He has about decided to give up something—I cannot see just what," I said loudly. "He seems to be in the air, in a tree, perhaps. If he wishes to be safe he should go higher."

Percy took the hint and moved up, and I said that was all there was in the palm. Soon after that Mr. Willoughby stretched out on the ground by the fire, and before long he was asleep.

During the night I heard Tish moving stealthily about in the tepee and she stepped on my ankle as she went out. I fell asleep again as soon as it stopped aching. Just at dawn Tish came back and touched me on the shoulder.

"Where's the blackberry cordial?" she whispered I sat up instantly.

"Has Percy fallen out of the tree?"

"No. Don't ask any questions, Lizzie. I want it for

myself. That dratted horse fell on me."

She refused to say any more and lay down groaning. But I was too worried to sleep again. In the morning Percy was gone from the tree. Mr. Willoughby had more rabbit and prepared to leave the forest. He offered Tish a dollar for the two meals and a bed, and Tish, who was moving about stiffly, said that she and her people took no money for their hospitality. Telling fortunes was one thing, bread and salt was another. She looked quite haughty, and the Willoughby person apologized and went into the woods to get his horse.

The horse was gone!

It was rather disagreeable for a time. He plainly thought we'd taken it, although Tish showed him that the end of the strap had been chewed partly through and then jerked free.

"If the creature smelled a wildcat," she said, "nothing would hold it. None of my people ever bring a horse into this part of the country."

"Humph!" said Mr. Willoughby. "Well, I'll bet they take a few out!"

He departed on foot shortly after, very disgusted and suspicious. We showed him the trail, and the last we saw of him he was striding along, looking up now and then for wildcats.

When he was well on his way, Percy emerged from the bushes. I had thought that he had helped Tish to take the Willoughby horse, but it seems he had not, and he was much amazed when Tish came through the wood leading the creature by the broken strap.

"I'll turn it loose," she said to Percy, "and you can capture it. It will make a good effect for you to emerge from the forest on horseback, and anyhow, what with the rabbit skin, the tent, and the sundial and the other things, you have a lot to carry. You can say you found it straying in the woods and captured it."

Percy looked at her with admiration not unmixed with reverence. "Miss Letitia," he said solemnly, "if it were not for Dorothea, I should ask you to marry me. I'd like to have you in my family."

* * * * *

I am very nearly to the end of my narrative.

Toward the last Percy was obliged to work far into the night, for of course we could not assist him. He made a full suit of rabbit skins sewed with fibers, and a cap and shoes of coonskin to match. The shoes were cut from a bedroom-slipper pattern that Tish traced in the sand on the beach, and the cap had an eagle feather in it. He made a birch-bark knapsack to hold the fish he smoked and a bow and arrow that looked well but would not shoot. When he had the outfit completed, he put it on, with the stone hatchet stuck into a grapevine belt and the bow and arrow over his shoulder, and he looked superb.

"The question is," he reflected, trying to view himself in the edge of the lake: "Will Dorothea like it? She's very keen about clothes. And gee, how she hates a beard!"

"You could shave as the Indians do," Tish said.

"How?"

"With a clamshell."

He looked dubious, but Tish assured him it was feasible. So he hunted a clamshell, a double one, Tish requested, and brought it into camp.

"I'd better do it for you," said Tish. "It's likely to be slow, but it is sure."

He was eyeing the clamshell and looking more and more uneasy.

"You're not going to scrape it off?" he asked anxiously. "You know, pumice would be better for that, but somehow I don't like the idea."

"Nothing of the sort," said Tish. "The double clamshell merely forms a pair of Indian nippers. I'm going to pull it out."

But he made quite a fuss about it, and said he didn't care whether the Indians did it or not, he wouldn't. I think he saw how disappointed Tish was and was afraid she would attempt it while he slept, for he threw the Indian nippers into the lake and then went over and kissed her hand.

"Dear Miss Tish," he said; "no one realizes more than I your inherent nobility of soul and steadfastness of purpose. I admire them both. But if you attempt the Indian nipper business, or to singe me like a chicken while I sleep, I shall be—forgive me, but I know my impulsiveness of disposition—I shall be really vexed with you."

Toward the last we all became uneasy for fear hard work was telling on him physically. He used to sit cross-legged on the ground, sewing for dear life and singing Hood's "Song of the Shirt" in a doleful tenor.

"You know," he said, "I've thought once or twice I'd like to do something—have a business like other fellows. But somehow dressmaking never occurred to me. Don't you think the expression of this right pant is good? And shall I make this gore bias or on the selvage?"

He wanted to slash one trouser leg.

"Why not?" he demanded when Tish frowned him

down. "It's awfully fetching, and beauty half-revealed, you know. Do you suppose my breastbone will ever straighten out again? It's concave from stooping."

It was after this that Tish made him exercise morning and evening and then take a swim in the lake. By the time he was to start back, he was in wonderful condition, and even the horse looked saucy and shiny, owing to our rubbing him down each day with dried grasses.

The actual leave-taking was rather sad. We'd grown to think a lot of the boy and I believe he liked us. He kissed each one of us twice, once for himself and once for Dorothea, and flushed a little over doing it, and Aggie's eyes were full of tears.

He rode away down the trail like a mixture of Robinson Crusoe and Indian brave, his rubbing-fire stick, his sundial with burned figures, and his bow and arrow jingling, his eagle feather blowing back in the wind, and his moccasined feet thrust into Mr. Willoughby's stirrups, and left us desolate. Tish watched him out of sight with set lips and Aggie was whimpering on a bank.

"Tish," she said brokenly, "does he recall anything to you?"

"Only my age," said Tish rather wearily, "and that I'm an elderly spinster teaching children to defy their parents and committing larceny to help them."

"To me," said Aggie softly, "he is young love going out to seek his mate. Oh, Tish, do you remember how Mr. Wiggins used to ride by taking his work horses to be shod!"

* * * * *

We went home the following day, which was the

time the spring-wagon man was to meet us. We started very early and were properly clothed and hatted when we saw him down the road.

The spring-wagon person came on without hurry and surveyed us as he came.

"Well, ladies," he said, stopping before us, "I see you pulled it off all right."

"We've had a very nice time, thank you," said Tish, drawing on her gloves. "It's been rather lonely, of course."

The spring-wagon person did not speak again until he had reached the open road. Then he turned round.

"The horse business was pretty good," he said. "You ought to hev seen them folks when he rode out of the wood. Flabbergasted ain't the word. They was ding-busted."

Tish whispered to us to show moderate interest and to say as little as possible, except to protest our ignorance. And we got the story at last like this:—

It seems the newspapers had been full of the attempt Percy was to make, and so on the day before quite a crowd had gathered to see him come out of the wood.

"Ten of these here automobiles," said the spring-wagon person, "and a hay-wagon full of newspaper fellows from the city with cameras, and about half the village back home walked out or druv and brought their lunches—sort of a picnic. I kep' my eye on the girl and on a Mr. Willoughby.

"The story is that Willoughby who was the father's choice—Willoughby was pale and twitching and kep' moving about all the time. But the girl, she just kep' her eyes on the trail and waited. Noon was the time set, or as near it as possible.

"The father talked to the newspaper men mostly. 'I don't think he'll do it, boys!' he said. 'He's as soft as milk and he's surprised me by sticking it out as long as he has. But mark my words, boys,' he said, 'he's been living on berries and things he could pick up off the ground, and if his physical condition's bad he loses all bets!'"

It seems that, just as he said it, somebody pulled out a watch and announced "noon." And on the instant Percy was seen riding down the trail and whistling. At first they did not know it was he, as they had expected him to arrive on foot, staggering with fatigue probably. He rode out into the sunlight, still whistling, and threw an unconcerned glance over the crowd.

He looked at the trees, and located north by the moss on the trunks, the S.-W.P. said, and unslinging his Indian clock he held it in front of him, pointing north and south. It showed exactly noon. It was then, and not until then, that Percy addressed the astonished crowd.

"Twelve o'clock, gentlemen," he said. "My watch is quite accurate."

Nobody said anything, being, as the S.-W.P. remarked, struck dumb. But a moment afterward the hay-wagon started a cheer and the machines took it up. Even the father "let loose," as we learned, and the little girl sat back in her motor car and smiled through her tears.

But Willoughby was furious. It seems he had recognized the horse. "That's my horse," he snarled. "You stole it from me."

"As a matter of fact," Percy retorted, "I found the beast wandering loose among the trees and I'm perfectly willing to return him to you. I brought him out for a purpose."

"To make a Garrison finish!"

"Not entirely. To prove that you violated the contract by going into the forest to see if you could find me and gloat over my misery. Instead you found—By the way, Willoughby, did you see any wild-cats?"

"Those three hags are in this!" said Willoughby furiously. "Are you willing to swear you made that silly outfit?"

"I am, but not to you."

"And at that minute, if you'll believe me," said the S.-W.P., "the girl got out of her machine and walked right up to the Percy fellow. I was standing right by and I heard what she said. It was, curious, seeing he'd had no help and had gone in naked, as you may say, and came out clothed head to foot, with a horse and weapons and a watch, and able to make fire in thirty-one seconds, and a tent made of about a thousand rabbit skins."

Tish eyed him coldly.

"What did she say?" she demanded severely. "She said: 'Those three dear old things!'" replied the S.-W.P. "And she said: 'I hope you kissed them for me.'"

"He did indeed," said Aggie dreamily, and only roused when Tish nudged her in a rage.

* * * * *

Charlie Sands came to have tea with us yesterday at Tish's. He is just back from England and full of the subject.

"But after all," he said, "the Simple Lifers take the palm. Think of it, my three revered and dearly beloved spinster friends; think of the peace, the holy calm of it! Now, if you three would only drink less tea and once in a while would get back to Nature a bit, it would be good for you. You're all too civilized."

"Probably," said Tish, pulling down her sleeves to hide her sunburned hands. "But do you think people have so much time in the—er—woods?"

"Time!" he repeated. "Why, what is there to do?"

Just then the doorbell rang and a huge box was carried in. Tish had a warning and did not wish to open it, but Charlie Sands insisted and cut the string. Inside were three sets of sable furs, handsomer than any in the church, Tish says, and I know I've never seen any like them.

Tish and I hid the cards, but Aggie dropped hers and Charlie Sands pounced on it.

"'The sleeve is now about Dorothea,'" he read aloud, and then, turning, eyed us all sternly.

"Now, then," said Charlie Sands, "out with it! What have you been up to this time?"

Tish returned his gaze calmly. "We have been in the Maine woods in the holy calm," she said. "As for those furs, I suppose a body may buy a set of furs if she likes." This, of course, was not a lie. "As for that card, it's a mistake." Which it was indeed.

"But—Dorothea!" persisted Charlie Sands.

"Never in my life knew anybody named Dorothea. Did you, Aggie?"

"Never," said Aggie firmly.

Charlie Sands apologized and looked thoughtful. On Tish's remaining rather injured, he asked us all out to dinner that night, and almost the first thing he ordered was frogs' legs. Aggie got rather white about the lips.

"I—I think I'll not take any," she said feebly. "I—I

keep thinking of Tish tickling their throats with the hairpin, and how Percy—"

We glared at her, but it was too late. Charlie Sands drew up his chair and rested his elbows on the table.

"So there was a Percy as well as a Dorothea!" he said cheerfully. "I might have known it. Now we'll have the story!"

TISH'S SPY

The Adventure of the Red-Headed Detective, The Lady Chauffeur, and the Man Who Could Not Tell The Truth

I

It is easy enough, of course, to look back on our Canadian experience and see where we went wrong. What I particularly resent is the attitude of Charlie Sands.

I am writing this for his benefit. It seems to me that a clean statement of the case is due to Tish, and, in less degree, to Aggie and myself.

It goes back long before the mysterious cipher. Even the incident of our abducting the girl in the pink tam-o'-shanter was, after all, the inevitable result of the series of occurrences that preceded it.

It is my intention to give this series of occurrences in their proper order and without bias. Herbert Spencer says that every act of one's life is the unavoidable result of every act that has preceded it.

Naturally, therefore, I begin with the engagement by Tish of a girl as chauffeur; but even before that there were contributing causes. There was the faulty rearing of the McDonald youth, for instance, and Tish's aesthetic dancing. And afterward there was Aggie's hay fever, which made her sneeze and let go of a rope at a critical moment. Indeed, Aggie's hay fever may be said to be one of the fundamental causes, being the reason we went to Canada.

It was like this: Along in June of the year before last, Aggie suddenly announced that she was going to spend the summer in Canada.

"It's the best thing in the world for hay fever," she said, avoiding Tish's eye. "Mrs. Ostermaier says she never sneezed once last year. The Northern Lights fill the air with ozone, or something like that."

"Fill the air with ozone!" Tish scoffed. "Fill Mrs. Ostermaier's skull with ozone, instead of brains, more likely!"

Tish is a good woman—a sweet woman, indeed; but she has a vein of gentle irony, which she inherited from her maternal grandfather, who was on the Supreme Bench of his country. However, that spring she was inclined to be irritable. She could not drive her car, and that was where the trouble really started.

Tish had taken up aesthetic dancing in Mareb, wearing no stays and a middy blouse and short skirt; and during a fairy dance, where she was to twirl on her right toes, keeping the three other limbs horizontal, she twisted her right lower limb severely. Though not incapacitated, she could not use it properly; and, failing one day to put on the brake quickly, she drove into an open-front butter-and-egg shop.

[This was the time one of the newspapers headed the article: "Even the Eggs Scrambled."]

When Tish decided to have a chauffeur for a time she advertised. There were plenty of replies, but all of the applicants smoked cigarettes—a habit Tish very properly deplores. The idea of securing a young woman was, I must confess, mine.

"Plenty of young women drive cars," I said, "and drive well. And, at least, they don't light a cigarette every time one stops to let a train go by."

"Huh!" Tish commented. "And have a raft of men about all the time!"

Nevertheless, she acted on the suggestion, advertising for a young woman who could drive a car and had no followers. Hutchins answered.

She was very pretty and not over twenty; but, asked about men, her face underwent a change, almost a hardening. "You'll not be bothered with men," she said briefly. "I detest them!"

And this seemed to be the truth. Charlie Sands, for instance, for whose benefit this is being written, absolutely failed to make any impression on her. She met his overtures with cold disdain. She was also adamant to the men at the garage, succeeding in having the gasoline filtered through a chamois skin to take out the water, where Tish had for years begged for the same thing without success.

Though a dashing driver, Hutchins was careful. She sat on the small of her back and hurled us past the traffic policemen with a smile.

[Her name was really Hutchinson; but it took so long to say it at the rate she ran the car that Tish changed it to Hutchins.]

Really the whole experiment seemed to be an undoubted success, when Aggie got the notion of

Canada into her head. Now, as it happened, owing to Tish's disapproval, Aggie gave up the Canada idea in favor of Nantucket, some time in June; but she had not reckoned with Tish's subconscious self. Tish was interested that spring in the subconscious self.

You may remember that, only a year or so before, it had been the fourth dimension.

[She became convinced that if one were sufficiently earnest one could go through closed doors and see into solids. In the former ambition she was unsuccessful, obtaining only bruises and disappointment; but she did develop the latter to a certain extent, for she met the laundress going out one day and, without a conscious effort, she knew that she had the best table napkins pinned to her petticoat. She accused the woman sternly—and she had six!]

"Nantucket!" said Tish. "Why Nantucket?"

"I have a niece there, and you said you hated Canada."

"On the contrary," Tish replied, with her eyes partly shut, "I find that my subconscious self has adopted and been working on the Canadian suggestion. What a wonderful thing is this buried and greater ego! Worms, rifles, fishing-rods, 'The Complete Angler,' mosquito netting, canned goods, and sleeping-bags, all in my mind and in orderly array!"

"Worms!" I said, with, I confess, a touch of scorn in my voice. "If you will tell me, Tish Carberry—"

"Life preservers," chanted Tish's subconscious self, "rubber blankets, small tent, folding camp-beds, a camp-stove, a meat-saw, a wood-saw, and some beads and gewgaws for placating the Indians." Then she opened her eyes and took up her knitting. "There are no worms in Canada, Lizzie, just as there are no snakes in Ireland. They were all destroyed during the glacial period."

"There are plenty of worms in the United States," I said with spirit. "I dare say they could crawl over the border—unless, of course, they object to being British subjects."

She ignored me, however, and, getting up, went to one of her bureau drawers. We saw then that her subconscious self had written down lists of various things for the Canadian excursion. There was one headed Foodstuffs. Others were: Necessary Clothing; Camp Outfit; Fishing-Tackle; Weapons of Defense: and Diversions. Under this last heading it had placed binoculars, yarn and needles, life preservers, a prayer-book, and a cribbage-board.

"Boats," she said, "we can secure from the Indians, who make them, I believe, of hollow logs. And I shall rent a motor boat. Hutchins says she can manage one. When she's not doing that she can wash dishes."

[We had been rather chary of motor boats, you may remember, since the time on Lake Penzance, when something jammed on our engine, and we had gone madly round the lake a number of times, with people on various docks trying to lasso us with ropes.]

Considering that it was she who had started the whole thing, and got Tish's subconscious mind to working, Aggie was rather pettish.

"Huh!" she said. "I can't swim, and you know it, Tish. Those canoe things turn over if you so much as sneeze in them."

"You'll not sneeze," said Tish. "The Northern Lights fill the air with ozone."

Aggie looked at me helplessly; but I could do nothing. Only the year before, Tish, as you may recall, had taken us out into the Maine woods without any outfit at all, and we had lived on snared rabbits, and things that no Christian woman ought to put into her stomach. This time we were at least to go provisioned and equipped.

"Where are we going?" Aggie asked.

"Far from a white man," said Tish. "Away from milk wagons and children on velocipedes and the grocer calling up every morning for an order. We'll go to the Far North, Aggie, where the red man still treads his native forests; we'll make our camp by some lake, where the deer come at early morning to drink and fish leap to see the sunset."

Well, it sounded rather refreshing, though I confess that, until Tish mentioned it, I had always thought that fish leaped in the evening to catch mosquitoes.

We sent for Hutchins at once. She was always respectful, but never subservient. She stood in the doorway while Tish explained.

"How far north?" she said crisply. Tish told her. "We'll have no cut-and-dried destination," she said. "There's a little steamer goes up the river I have in mind. We'll get off when we see a likely place."

"Are you going for trout or bass?"

Tish was rather uncertain, but she said bass on a chance, and Hutchins nodded her approval.

"If it's bass, I'll go," she said. "I'm not fond of trout-fishing."

"We shall have a motor boat. Of course I shall not take the car."

Hutchins agreed indifferently. "Don't you worry

about the motor boat," she said. "Sometimes they go, and sometimes they don't. And I'll help round the camp; but I'll not wash dishes."

"Why not?" Tish demanded.

"The reason doesn't really matter, does it? What really concerns you is the fact."

Tish stared at her; but instead of quailing before Tish's majestic eye she laughed a little.

"I've camped before," she said. "I'm very useful about a camp. I like to cook; but I won't wash dishes. I'd like, if you don't mind, to see the grocery order before it goes."

Well, Aggie likes to wash dishes if there is plenty of hot water; and Hannah, Tish's maid, refusing to go with us on account of Indians, it seemed wisest to accept Hutchins's services.

Hannah's defection was most unexpected. As soon as we reached our decision, Tish ordered beads for the Indians; and in the evenings we strung necklaces, and so on, while one of us read aloud from the works of Cooper. On the second evening thus occupied, Hannah, who is allowed to come into Tish's sitting-room in the evening and knit, suddenly burst into tears and refused to go.

"My scalp's as good to me as it is to anybody, Miss Tish," she said hysterically; and nothing would move her.

She said she would run no risk of being cooked over her own camp-fire; and from that time on she would gaze at Tish for long periods mournfully, as though she wanted to remember how she looked when she was gone forever.

Except for Hannah, everything moved smoothly.

Tish told Charlie Sands about the plan, and he was quite enthusiastic.

"Great scheme!" he said. "Eat a broiled black bass for me. And take the advice of one who knows: don't skimp on your fishing-tackle. Get the best. Go light on the canned goods, if necessary; but get the best reels and lines on the market. Nothing in life hurts so much," he said impressively, "as to get a three-pound bass to the top of the water and have your line break. I've had a big fellow get away like that and chase me a mile with its thumb on its nose." This last, of course, was purely figurative.

He went away whistling. I wish he had been less optimistic. When we came back and told him the whole story, and he sat with his mouth open and his hair, as he said, crackling at the roots, I reminded him with some bitterness that he had encouraged us. His only retort was to say that the excursion itself had been harmless enough; but that if three elderly ladies, church members in good standing, chose to become freebooters and pirates the moment they got away from a corner policeman, they need not blame him.

The last thing he said that day in June was about fishing-worms.

"Take 'em with you," he said. "They charge a cent apiece for them up there, assorted colors, and there's something stolid and British about a Canadian worm. The fish aren't crazy about 'em. On the other hand, our worms here are—er—vivacious, animated. I've seen a really brisk and on-to-its-job United States worm reach out and clutch a bass by the gills."

I believe it was the next day that Tish went to the library and read about worms. Aggie and I had spent the day buying tackle, according to Charlie Sands's advice. We got some very good rods with nickel-plated reels for two dollars and a quarter, a dozen assorted hooks for each person, and a dozen sinkers. The man wanted to sell us what he called a "landing net," but I took a good look at it and pinched Aggie.

"I can make one out of a barrel hoop and mosquito netting," I whispered; so we did not buy it.

Perhaps he thought we were novices, for he insisted on showing us all sorts of absurd things—trolling-hooks, he called them; gaff hooks for landing big fish and a spoon that was certainly no spoon and did not fool us for a minute, being only a few hooks and a red feather. He asked a dollar and a quarter for it!

[I made one that night at home, using a bit of red feather from a duster. It cost me just three cents. Of that, as of Hutchins, more later.]

Aggie, whose idea of Canada had been the Hotel Frontenac, had grown rather depressed as our preparations proceeded. She insisted that night on recalling the fact that Mr. Wiggins had been almost drowned in Canada.

"He went with the Roof and Gutter Club, Lizzie," she said, "and he was a beautiful swimmer; but the water comes from the North Pole, freezing cold, and the first thing he knew—"

The telephone bell rang just then. It was Tish.

"I've just come from the library, Lizzie," she said. "We'd better raise the worms. We've got a month to do it in. Hutchins and I will be round with the car at eight o'clock to-night. Night is the time to get them."

She refused to go into details, but asked us to have an electric flash or two ready and a couple of wooden pails. Also she said to wear mackintoshes and rubbers. Just before she rang off, she asked me to see that there was a package of oatmeal on hand, but did not explain. When I told Aggie she eyed me miserably.

"I wish she'd be either more explicit or less," she said. "We'll be arrested again. I know it!"

[Now and then Tish's enthusiasms have brought us into collision with the law—not that Tish has not every respect for law and order, but that she is apt to be hasty and at times almost unconventional.]

"You remember," said Aggie, "that time she tried to shoot the sheriff, thinking he was a train robber? She started just like this—reading up about walking-tours, and all that. I—I'm nervous, Lizzie."

I was staying with Aggie for a few days while my apartment was being papered. To soothe Aggie's nerves I read aloud from Gibbon's "Rome" until dinner-time, and she grew gradually calmer.

"After all, Lizzie," she said, "she can't get us into mischief with two wooden pails and a package of oatmeal."

Tish and Hutchins came promptly at eight and we got into the car. Tish wore the intent and dreamy look that always preceded her enterprises. There was a tin sprinkling-can, quite new, in the tonneau, and we placed our wooden pails beside it and the oatmeal in it. I confess I was curious, but to my inquiries Tish made only one reply:—

"Worms!"

Now I do not like worms. I do not like to touch them. I do not even like to look at them. As the machine went along I began to have a creepy loathing of them. Aggie must have been feeling the same way, for when my hand touched hers she squealed.

Over her shoulder Tish told her plan. She said it was easy to get fishing-worms at night and that Hutchins knew of a place a few miles out of town where the family was away and where there would be plenty.

"We'll put them in boxes of earth," she said, "and feed them coffee or tea grounds one day and oatmeal water the next. They propagate rapidly. We'll have a million to take with us. If we only have a hundred thousand at a cent apiece, that's a clear saving of a thousand dollars."

"We could sell some," I suggested sarcastically; for Tish's enthusiasms have a way of going wrong.

But she took me seriously. "If there are any fishing clubs about," she said, "I dare say they'll buy them; and we can turn the money over to Mr. Ostermaier for the new organ."

Tish had bought the organ and had an evening concert with it before we turned off the main road into a private drive.

"This is the place," Hutchins said laconically.

Tish got out and took a survey. There was shrubbery all round and a very large house, quite dark, in the foreground.

"Drive onto the lawn, Hutchins," she said. "When the worms come up, the lamps will dazzle them and they'll be easy to capture."

We bumped over a gutter and came to a stop in the middle of the lawn.

"It would be better if it was raining," Tish said. "You know, yourself, Lizzie, how they come up during a gentle rain. Give me the sprinkling-can."

I do not wish to lay undue blame on Hutchins, who

was young; but it was she who suggested that there would probably be a garden hose somewhere and that it would save time. I know she went with Tish round the corner of the house, and that they returned in ten minutes or so, dragging a hose.

"I broke a tool-house window," Tish observed, "but I left fifty cents on the sill to replace it. It's attached at the other end. Run back, Hutchins, and turn on the water; but not too much. We needn't drown the little creatures."

Well, I have never seen anything work better. Aggie, who had refused to put a foot out of the car, stood up in it and held the hose. As fast as she wet a bit of lawn, we followed with the pails. I spread my mackintosh out and knelt on it.

The thing took skill. The worms had a way of

snapping back into their holes like lightning.

Tish got about three to my one, and talked about packing them in moss and ice, and feeding them every other day. Hutchins, however, stood on the lawn, with her hands in her pockets, and watched the house.

Suddenly, without warning, Aggie turned the hose directly on my left ear and held it there.

"There's somebody coming!" she cried. "Merciful Heavens, what'll I do with the hose?"

"You can turn it away from me!" I snapped.

So she did, and at that instant a young man emerged from the shrubbery.

He did not speak at once. Probably he could not. I happened to look at Hutchins, and, for all her usual *savoir-faire*, as Charlie Sands called it, she was clearly uncomfortable.

Tish, engaged in a struggle at that moment and sitting back like a robin, did not see him at once.

"Well!" said the young man; and again: "Well, upon my word!"

He seemed out of breath with surprise; and he took off his hat and mopped his head with a handkerchief. And, of course, as though things were not already bad enough, Aggie sneezed at that instant, as she always does when she is excited; and for just a second the hose was on him.

It was unexpected and he almost staggered. He looked at all of us, including Hutchins, and ran his handkerchief round inside his collar. Then he found his voice.

"Really," he said, "this is awfully good of you. We do need rain—don't we?"

Tish was on her feet by that time, but she could not

think of anything to say.

"I'm sorry if I startled you," said the young man. "I—I'm a bit startled myself."

"There is nothing to make a fuss about!" said Hutchins crisply. "We are getting worms to go fishing."

"I see," said the young man. "Quite natural, I'm sure. And where are you going fishing?"

Hutchins surprised us all by rudely turning her back on him. Considering we were on his property and had turned his own hose on him, a little tact would have been better.

Tish had found her voice by that time. "We broke a window in the tool-house," she said; "but I put fifty cents on the sill."

"Thank you," said the young man.

Hutchins wheeled at that and stared at him in the most disagreeable fashion; but he ignored her.

"We are trespassing," said Tish; "but I hope you understand. We thought the family was away."

"I just happened to be passing through," he explained. "I'm awfully attached to the place—for various reasons. Whenever I'm in town I spend my evenings wandering through the shrubbery and remembering—er—happier days."

"I think the lamps are going out," said Hutchins sharply. "If we're to get back to town—"

"Ah!" he broke in. "So you have come out from the city?"

"Surely," said Hutchins to Tish, "it is unnecessary to give this gentleman any information about ourselves! We have done no damage—"

"Except the window," he said.

"We've paid for that," she said in a nasty tone; and to

Tish: "How do we know this place is his? He's probably some newspaper man, and if you tell him who you are this whole thing will be in the morning paper, like the eggs."

"I give you my word of honor," he said, "that I am nothing of the sort; in fact, if you will give me a little time I'd—I'd like to tell all about myself. I've got a lot to say that's highly interesting, if you'll only listen."

Hutchins, however, only gave him a cold glance of suspicion and put the pails in the car. Then she got in and sat down.

"I take it," he said to her, "that you decline either to give or to receive any information."

"Absolutely!"

He sighed then, Aggie declares.

"Of course," he said, "though I haven't really the slightest curiosity, I could easily find out, you know. Your license plates—"

"Are under the cushion I'm sitting on," said Hutchins, and started the engine.

"Really, Hutchins," said Tish, "I don't see any reason for being so suspicious. I have always believed in human nature and seldom have I been disappointed. The young man has done nothing to justify rudeness. And since we are trespassing on his place—"

"Huh!" was all Hutchins said.

The young man sauntered over to the car, with his hands thrust into this coat pockets. He was nice-looking, especially then, when he was smiling.

"Hutchins!" he said. "Well, that's a clue anyhow. It—it's an uncommon name. You didn't happen to notice a large 'No-Trespassing!' sign by the gate, did you?"

Hutchins only looked ahead and ignored him. As

Tish said afterward, we had a good many worms, anyhow; and, as the young man and Hutchins had clearly taken an awful dislike to each other at first sight, the best way to avoid trouble was to go home. So she got into the car. The young man helped her and took off his hat.

"Come out any time you like," he said affably. "I'm not here at all in the daytime, and the grounds are really rather nice. Come out and get some roses. We've some pretty good ones—English importations. If you care to bring some children from the tenements out for a picnic, please feel free to do it. We're not selfish."

Hutchins rudely started the car before he had finished; but he ignored her and waved a cordial farewell to the rest of us.

"Bring as many as you like," he called. "Sunday is a good day. Ask Miss—Miss Hutchins to come out and bring some friends along."

We drove back at the most furious rate. Tish was at last compelled to remonstrate with Hutchins.

"Not only are we going too fast," she said, "but you were really rude to that nice young man."

"I wish I had turned the hose on him and drowned him!" said Hutchins between her teeth.

II

Hutchins brought a newspaper to Tish the next morning at breakfast, and Tish afterwards said her expression was positively malevolent in such a young and pretty woman.

The newspaper said that an attempt had been made to rob the Newcomb place the night before, but that the thieves had apparently secured nothing but a package of oatmeal and a tin sprinkling-can, which they had abandoned on the lawn. Some color, however, was lent to the fear that they had secured an amount of money, from the fact that a silver half-dollar had been found on the window sill of a tool-house. The Newcomb family was at its summer home on the Maine coast.

"You see," Hutchins said to Tish, "that man didn't belong there at all. He was just impertinent and—laughing in his sleeve."

Tish was really awfully put out, having planned to take the Sunday school there for a picnic. She was much pleased, however, at Hutchins's astuteness.

"I shall take her along to Canada," she said to me. "The girl has instinct, which is better than reason. Her subconsciousness is unusually active."

Looking back, as I must, and knowing now all that was in her small head while she whistled about the car, or all that was behind her smile, one wonders if women really should have the vote. So many of them are creatures of sex and guile. A word from her would have cleared up so much, and she never spoke it!

Well, we spent most of July in getting ready to go. Charlie Sands said the mosquitoes and black flies would be gone by August, and we were in no hurry.

We bought a good tent, with a diagram of how to put it up, some folding camp-beds, and a stove. The day we bought the tent we had rather a shock, for as we left the shop the suburban youth passed us. We ignored him completely, but he lifted his hat. Hutchins, who was waiting in Tish's car, saw him, too, and went quite white with fury.

Shortly after that, Hannah came in one night and said that a man was watching Tish's windows. We thought it was imagination, and Tish gave her a dose of sulphur and molasses—her liver being sluggish.

"Probably an Indian, I dare say," was Tish's caustic comment.

In view of later developments, however, it is a pity we did not investigate Hannah's story; for Aggie, going home from Tish's late one night in Tish's car, had a similar experience, declaring that a small machine had followed them, driven by a heavy-set man with a mustache. She said, too, that Hutchins, swerving sharply, had struck the smaller machine a glancing blow and almost upset it.

It was about the middle of July, I believe, that Tish received the following letter:—

> *Madam*: Learning that you have decided to take a fishing-trip in Canada, I venture to offer my services as guide, philosopher, and friend. I know Canada thoroughly; can locate bass, as nearly as it lies in a mortal so to do; can manage a motor launch; am thoroughly at home in a canoe; can shoot, swim, and cook—the last indifferently well; know the Indian mind and my own—and will carry water and chop wood.
>
> I do not drink, and such smoking as I do will, if I am engaged, be done in the solitude of the woods.
>
> I am young and of a cheerful disposition. My object is not money, but only expenses paid and a chance to forget a recent and still poignant grief. I hope you will see the necessity for such an addition to your party, and allow me to subscribe myself, madam,
>
> Your most obedient servant,
>
> J. UPDIKE.

Tish was much impressed; but Hutchins, in whose

judgment she began to have the greatest confidence, opposed the idea.

"I wouldn't think of it," she said briefly.

"Why? It's a frank, straightforward letter."

"He likes himself too much. And you should always be suspicious of anything that's offered too cheap."

So the Updike application was refused. I have often wondered since what would have been the result had we accepted it!

The worms were doing well, though Tish found that Hannah neglected them, and was compelled to feed them herself. On the day before we started, we packed them carefully in ice and moss, and fed them. That was the day the European war was declared.

"Canada is at war," Tish telephoned. "The papers say the whole country is full of spies, blowing up bridges and railroads."

"We can still go to the seashore," I said. "The bead things will do for the missionary box to Africa."

"Seashore nothing!" Tish retorted. "We're going, of course,—just as we planned. We'll keep our eyes open; that's all. I'm not for one side or the other, but a spy's a spy."

Later that evening she called again to say there were rumors that the Canadian forests were bristling with German wireless outfits.

"I've a notion to write J. Updike, Lizzie, and find out whether he knows anything about wireless telegraphy," she said, "only there's so little time. Perhaps I can find a book that gives the code."

[This is only pertinent as showing Tish's state of mind. As a matter of fact, she did not write to Updike at all.]

Well, we started at last, and I must say they let us over the border with a glance; but they asked us whether we had any firearms. Tish's trunk contained a shotgun and a revolver; but she had packed over the top her most intimate personal belongings, and they were not disturbed.

"Have you any weapons?" asked the inspector.

"Do we look like persons carrying weapons?" Tish demanded haughtily. And of course we did not. Still, there was an untruth of the spirit and none of us felt any too comfortable. Indeed, what followed may have been a punishment on us for deceit and conspiracy.

Aggie had taken her cat along—because it was so fond of fish, she said. And, between Tish buying ice for the worms and Aggie getting milk for the cat, the journey was not monotonous; but on returning from one of her excursions to the baggage-car, Tish put a heavy hand on my shoulder.

"That boy's on the train, Lizzie!" she said. "He had the impudence to ask me whether I still drive with the license plates under a cushion. English roses—importations!" said Tish, and sniffed. "You don't suppose he went into that tent shop and asked about us?"

"He might," I retorted; "but, on the other hand, there's no reason why our going to Canada should keep the rest of the United States at home!"

However, the thing did seem queer, somehow. Why had he told us things that were not so? Why had he been so anxious to know who we were? Why, had he asked us to take the Sunday-school picnic to a place that did not belong to him?

"He may be going away to forget some trouble.

You remember what he said about happier days," said Tish.

"That was Updike's reason too," I relied. "Poignant grief!"

For just a moment our eyes met. The same suspicion had occurred to us both. Well, we agreed to say nothing to Aggie or Hutchins, for fear of upsetting them, and the next hour or so was peaceful.

Hutchins read and Aggie slept. Tish and I strung beads for the Indians, and watched the door into the next car. And, sure enough, about the middle of the afternoon he appeared and stared in at us. He watched us for quite a time, smoking a cigarette as he did so. Then he came in and bent down over Tish.

"You didn't take the children out for the picnic, did you?" he said.

"I did not!" Tish snapped.

"I'm sorry. Never saw the place look so well!"

"Look here," Tish said, putting down her beads; "what were you doing there that night anyhow? You don't belong to the family."

He looked surprised and then grieved.

"You've discovered that, have you?" he said. "I did, you know—word of honor! They've turned me off; but I love the old place still, and on summer nights I wander about it, recalling happier days."

Hutchins closed her book with a snap, and he sighed.

"I perceive that we are overheard," he said. "Some time I hope to tell you the whole story. It's extremely sad. I'll not spoil the beginning of your holiday with it."

All the time he had been talking he held a piece of

paper in his hand. When he left us Tish went back thoughtfully to her beads.

"It just shows, Lizzie," she said, "how wrong we are to trust to appearances. That poor boy—"

I had stooped into the aisle and was picking up the piece of paper which he had accidentally dropped as he passed Hutchins. I opened it and read aloud to Tish and Aggie, who had wakened:—

"'Afraid you'll not get away with it! The red-haired man in the car behind is a plain-clothes man.'"

Tish has a large fund of general knowledge, gained through Charlie Sands; so what Aggie and I failed to understand she interpreted at once.

"A plain-clothes man," she explained, "is a detective dressed as a gentleman. It's as plain as pikestaff! The boy's received this warning and dropped it. He has done something he shouldn't and is escaping to Canada!"

I do not believe, however, that we should have thought of his being a political spy but for the conductor of the train. He proved to be a very nice person, with eight children and a toupee; and he said that Canada was honeycombed with spies in the pay of the German Government.

"They're sending wireless messages all the time, probably from remote places," he said. "And, of course, their play now is to blow up the transcontinental railroads. Of course the railroads have an army of detectives on the watch."

"Good Heavens!" Aggie said, and turned pale.

Well, our pleasure in the journey was ruined. Every time the whistle blew on the engine we quailed, and Tish wrote her will then and there on the back of an envelope. It was while she was writing that the truth came to her.

"That boy!" she said. "Don't you see it all? That note was a warning to him. He's a spy and the red-haired man is after him."

None of us slept that night though Tish did a very courageous thing about eleven o'clock, when she was ready for bed. I went with her. We had put our dressing-gowns over our nightrobes, and we went back to the car containing the spy.

He had not retired, but was sitting alone, staring ahead moodily. The red-haired man was getting ready for bed, just opposite. Tish spoke loudly, so the detective should hear.

"I have come back," Tish said, "to say that we know everything. A word to the wise, Mister Happier Days! Don't try any of your tricks!"

He sat, with his mouth quite open, and stared at us: but the red-haired man pretended to hear nothing and took off his other shoe.

None of us slept at all except Hutchins. Though we had told her nothing, she seemed inherently to distrust the spy. When, on arriving at the town where we were to take the boat, he offered to help her off with Aggie's cat basket, which she was carrying, she snubbed him.

"I can do it myself," she said coldly; "and if you know when you're well off you'll go back to where you came from. Something might happen to you here in the wilderness."

"I wish it would," he replied in quite a tragic manner.

[As Tish said then, a man is probably often forced by circumstances into hateful situations. No spy can really want to be a spy with every brick wall suggesting, as it must, a firing-squad.]

Well, to make a long story short, we took the little steamer that goes up the river three times a week to take groceries and mail to the logging-camps, and the spy and the red-haired detective went along. The spy seemed to have quite a lot of luggage, but the detective had only a suitcase.

Tish, watching the detective, said his expression grew more and more anxious as we proceeded up the river. Cottages gave place to logging-camps and these to rocky islands, with no sign of life; still, the spy stayed on the steamer, and so, of course, did the detective.

Tish went down and examined the luggage. She reported that the spy was traveling under the name of McDonald and that the detective's suitcase was unmarked. Mr. McDonald had some boxes and a green canoe. The detective had nothing at all. There were no other passengers.

We let Aggie's cat out on the boat and he caught a mouse almost immediately, and laid it in the most touching manner at the detective's feet; but he was in a very bad humor and flung it over the rail. Shortly after that he asked Tish whether she intended to go to the Arctic Circle.

"I don't know that that's any concern of yours," Tish said. "You're not after me, you know."

He looked startled and muttered something into his mustache.

"It's perfectly clear what's wrong with him," Tish said. "He's got to stick to Mr. McDonald, and he hasn't got a tent in that suitcase, or even a blanket. I don't suppose he knows where his next meal's coming from."

She was probably right, for I saw the crew of the boat packing a box or two of crackers and an old comfort into a box; and Aggie overheard the detective say to the captain that if he would sell him some fishhooks he would not starve anyhow.

Tish found an island that suited her about three o'clock that afternoon, and we disembarked. Mr. McDonald insisted on helping the crew with our stuff, which they piled on a large flat rock; but the detective stood on the upper deck and scowled down at us. Tish suggested that he was a woman-hater.

"They know so many lawbreaking women," she said, "it's quite natural."

Having landed us, the boat went across to another island and deposited Mr. McDonald and the green canoe. Tish, who had talked about a lodge in some vast wilderness, complained at that; but when the detective got off on a little tongue of the mainland, in sight of both islands, she said the place was getting crowded and she had a notion to go farther.

The first thing she did was to sit on a box and open a map. The Canadian Pacific was only a few miles away through the woods!

Hutchins proved herself a treasure. She could work all round the three of us; she opened boxes and a can of beans for supper with the same hatchet, and had tea made and the beans heated while Tish was selecting a site for the tent.

But—and I remembered this later—she watched the river at intervals, with her cheeks like roses from the exertion. She was really a pretty girl—only, when no one was looking, her mouth that day had a way of setting itself firmly, and she frowned at the water.

We, Hutchins and I, set up the stove against a large rock, and when the teakettle started to boil it gave the river front a homey look. Sitting on my folding-chair beside the stove, with a cup of tea in my hand and a plate of beans on a doily on a packing-box beside me, I was entirely comfortable. Through the glasses I could see the red-haired man on the other shore sitting on a rock, with his head in his hands; but Mr. McDonald had clearly located on the other side of his island and was not in sight.

Aggie and Tish were putting up the tent, and Hutchins was feeding the tea grounds to the worms, which had traveled comfortably, when I saw a canoe coming up the river. I called to Tish about it.

"An Indian!" she said calmly. "Get the beads, Aggie; and put my shotgun on that rock, where he can see it." She stood and watched him. "Primitive man, every inch of him!" she went on. "Notice his uncovered head. Notice the freedom, almost the savagery, of the way he uses that paddle. I wish he would sing. You remember, in Hiawatha, how they sing as they paddle along?"

She got the beads and went to the water's edge; but the Indian stooped just then and, picking up a Panama hat, put it on his head.

"I have called," he said, "to see whether I can interest you in a set of books I am selling. I shall detain you only a moment. Sixty-three steel engravings by well-known artists; best hand-made paper; and the work itself is of high educational value."

Tish suddenly put the beads behind her back and said we did not expect to have any time to read. We had come into the wilderness to rest our minds.

"You are wrong, I fear," said the Indian. "Personally

I find that I can read better in the wilds than anywhere else. Great thoughts in great surroundings! I take Nietzsche with me when I go fishing."

Tish had the wretched beads behind her all the time; and, to make conversation, more than anything else, she asked about venison. He shrugged his shoulders. J. Fenimore Cooper had not prepared us for an Indian who shrugged his shoulders.

"We Indians are allowed to kill deer," he said; "but I fear you are prohibited. I am not even permitted to sell it."

"I should think," said Tish sharply, "that, since we are miles from a game warden, you could safely sell us a steak or two."

He gazed at her disapprovingly. "I should not care to break the law, madam," he said.

Then he picked up his paddle and took himself and his scruples and his hand-made paper and his sixty-three steel engravings down the river.

"Primitive man!" I said to Tish, from my chair. "Notice the freedom, almost the savagery, with which he swings that paddle."

We had brought a volume of Cooper along, not so much to read as to remind us how to address the Indians. Tish said nothing, but she got the book and flung it far out into the river.

There were a number of small annoyances the first day or two. Hutchins was having trouble with the motor launch, which the steamer had towed up the day we came, and which she called the "Mebbe." And another civilized Indian, with a gold watch and a cigarette case, had rented us a leaky canoe for a dollar a day.

[We patched the leak with chewing gum, which

Aggie always carried for indigestion; and it did fairly well, so long as the gum lasted.]

Then, on the second night, there was a little wind, and the tent collapsed on us, the ridgepole taking Aggie across the chest. It was that same night, I think, when Aggie's cat found a porcupine in the woods, and came in looking like a pincushion.

What with chopping firewood for the stove, and carrying water, and bailing out the canoe, and with the motor boat giving one gasp and then dying for every hundred times somebody turned over the engine, we had no time to fish for two days.

The police agent fished all day from a rock, for, of course, he had no boat; but he seemed to catch nothing. At times we saw him digging frantically, as though for worms. What he dug with I do not know; but, of course, he got no worms. Tish said if he had been more civil she would have taken something to him and a can of worms; but he had been rude, especially to Aggie's cat, and probably the boat would bring him things.

What with getting settled and everything, we had not much time to think about the spy. It was on the third day, I believe, that he brought his green canoe to the open water in front of us and anchored there, just beyond earshot.

He put out a line and opened a book; and from that time on he was a part of the landscape every day from 10 A.M. to 4 P.M. At noon he would eat some sort of a lunch, reading as he ate.

He apparently never looked toward us, but he was always there. It was the most extraordinary thing. At first we thought he had found a remarkable fishing-place; but he seemed to catch very few fish. It was Tish,

I think, who found the best explanation.

"He's providing himself with an alibi," she stated. "How can he be a spy when we see him all day long? Don't you see how clever it is?"

It was the more annoying because we had arranged a small cove for soap-and-water bathing, hanging up a rod for bath-towels and suspending a soap-dish and a sponge-holder from an overhanging branch. The cove was well shielded by brush and rocks from the island, but naturally was open to the river.

It was directly opposite this cove that Mr. McDonald took up his position.

This compelled us to bathe in the early morning, while the water was still cold, and resulted in causing Aggie a most uncomfortable half-hour on the fourth morning of our stay.

She was the last one in the pool, and Tish absent-mindedly took her bathrobe and slippers back to the camp when she went. Tish went out in the canoe shortly after. She was learning to use one, with a life preserver on—Tish, of course, not the canoe. And Mr. McDonald arriving soon after, Aggie was compelled to sit in the water for two hours and twenty minutes. When Hutchins found her she was quite blue.

This was the only disagreement we had all summer: Aggie's refusing to speak to Tish that entire day. She said Mr. McDonald had seen her head and thought it was some sort of swimming animal, and had shot at her.

Mr. McDonald said afterward he knew her all the time, and was uncertain whether she was taking a cure for something or was trying to commit suicide. He said he spent a wretched morning. At five o'clock that evening we began to hear a curious tapping noise from the spy's island. It would last for a time, stop, and go on.

Hutchins said it was woodpeckers; but Tish looked at me significantly.

"Wireless!" she said. "What did I tell you?"

That decided her next move, for that evening she put some tea and canned corn and a rubber blanket into the canoe; and in fear and trembling I went with her.

"It's going to rain, Lizzie," she said, "and after all, that detective may be surly; but he's doing his duty by his country. It's just as heroic to follow a spy up here, and starve to death watching him, as it is to storm a trench—and less showy. And I've something to tell him."

The canoe tilted just then, and only by heroic effort, were we able to calm it.

"Then why not go comfortably in the motor boat?"

Tish stopped, her paddle in the air. "Because I can't make that dratted engine go," she said, "and because I believe Hutchins would drown us all before she'd take any help to him. It's my belief that she's known him somewhere. I've seen her sit on a rock and look across at him with murder in her eyes."

A little wind had come up, and the wretched canoe was leaking, the chewing gum having come out. Tish was paddling; so I was compelled to sit over the aperture, thus preventing water from coming in. Despite my best efforts, however, about three inches seeped in and washed about me. It was quite uncomfortable.

The red-haired man was asleep when we landed. He had hung the comfort over a branch, like a tent, and built a fire at the end of it. He had his overcoat on, buttoned to the chin, and his head was on his suit-case. He sat up and looked at us, blinking.

"We've brought you some tea and some canned corn," Tish said; "and a rubber blanket. It's going to rain."

He slid out of the tent, feet first, and got up; but when he tried to speak he sneezed. He had a terrible cold.

"I might as well say at once," Tish went on, "that we know why you are here—"

"The deuce you do!" he said hoarsely.

"We do not particularly care about you, especially since the way you acted to a friendly and innocent cat—one can always judge a man by the way he treats dumb animals; but we sympathize with your errand. We'll even help if we can."

"Then the—the person in question has confided in you?"

"Not at all," said Tish loftily. "I hope we can put two and two together. Have you got a revolver?"

He looked startled at that. "I have one," he said; "but I guess I'll not need it. The first night or two a skunk hung round; two, in fact—mother and child—but I think they're gone."

"Would you like some fish?"

"My God, no!"

This is a truthful narrative. That is exactly what he said.

"I'll tell you what I do need, ladies," he went on: "If you've got a spare suit of underwear over there, I could use it. It'd stretch, probably. And I'd like a pen and some ink. I must have lost my fountain pen out of my pocket stooping over the bank to wash my face."

"Do you know the wireless code?" Tish asked suddenly.

"Wireless?"

"I have every reason to believe," she said impressively, "that one of the great trees on that island conceals a wireless outfit."

"I see!" He edged back a little from us both.

"I should think," Tish said, eyeing him, "that a knowledge of the wireless code would be essential to you in your occupation."

"We—we get a smattering of all sorts of things," he said; but he was uneasy—you could see that with half an eye.

He accompanied us down to the canoe; but once, when Tish turned suddenly, he ducked back as though he had been struck and changed color. He thanked us for the tea and corn, and said he wished we had a spare razor—but, of course, he supposed not. Then:—

"I suppose the—the person in question will stay as long as you do?" he asked, rather nervously.

"It looks like it," said Tish grimly. "I've no intention of being driven away, if that's what you mean. We'll stay as long as the fishing's good."

He groaned under his breath. "The whole d—d river is full of fish," he said. "They crawled up the bank last night and ate all the crackers I'd saved for to-day. Oh, I'll pay somebody out for this, all right! Good gracious, ladies, your boat's full of water!"

"It has a hole in it," Tish replied and upturned it to empty it.

When he saw the hole his eyes stuck out. "You can't go out in that leaky canoe! It's suicidal!"

"Not at all," Tish assured him. "My friend here will sit on the leak. Get in quick, Lizzie. It's filling."

The last we saw of the detective that night he was standing on the bank, staring after us. Afterward, when a good many things were cleared up, he said he decided that he'd been asleep and dreamed the whole thing—the wireless, and my sitting on the hole in the canoe, and the wind tossing it about, and everything—only, of course, there was the tea and the canned corn!

We did our first fishing the next day. Hutchins had got the motor boat going, and I put over the spoon I had made from the feather duster. After going a mile or so slowly I felt a tug, and on drawing my line in I found I had captured a large fish. I wrapped the line about a part of the engine and Tish put the barrel hoop with the netting underneath it. The fish was really quite large—about four feet, I think—and it broke through the netting. I wished to hit it with the oar, but Hutchins said that might break the fin and free it. Unluckily we had not brought Tish's gun, or we might have shot it.

At last we turned the boat round and went home, the fish swimming alongside, with its mouth open. And there Aggie, who is occasionally almost inspired, landed the fish by the simple expedient of getting out of the boat, taking the line up a bank and wrapping it round a tree. By all pulling together we landed the fish successfully. It was forty-nine inches by Tish's tape measure.

Tish did not sleep well that night. She dreamed that the fish had a red mustache and was a spy in disguise. When she woke she declared there was somebody prowling round the tent.

She got her shotgun and we all sat up in bed for an

hour or so.

Nothing happened, however, except that Aggie cried out that there was a small animal just inside the door of the tent. We could see it, too, though faintly. Tish turned the shotgun on it and it disappeared; but the next morning she found she had shot one of her shoes to pieces.

III

It was the day Tish began her diary that we discovered the red-haired man's signal. Tish was compelled to remain at home most of the day, breaking in another pair of shoes, and she amused herself by watching the river and writing down interesting things. She had read somewhere of the value of such records of impressions:—

10 A.M. Gull on rock. Very pretty. Frightened away by the McDonald person, who has just taken up his customary position. Is he reading or watching this camp?

10.22. Detective is breakfasting—through glasses, he is eating canned corn. Aggie—pickerel, from bank.

10.40. Aggie's cat, beside her, has caught a small fish. Aggie declares that the cat stole one of her worms and held it in the water. I think she is mistaken.

11. Most extraordinary thing—Hutchins has asked permission to take pen and ink across to the detective! Have consented.

11.20. Hutchins is still across the river. If I did not know differently I should say she and the detective are quarreling. He is whittling something. Through glasses, she appears to stamp her foot.

11.30. Aggie has captured a small sunfish. Hutchins is still across the river. He seems to be appealing to her for something—possibly the underwear. We have none to spare.

11.40. Hutchins is an extraordinary girl. She hates men, evidently. She has had some sort of quarrel with the detective and has returned flushed with battle. Mr. McDonald called to her as she passed, but she ignored him.

12. NOON. Really, there is something mysterious about all this. The detective was evidently whittling a flagpole. He has erected it now, with a red silk handkerchief at end. It hangs out over the water. Aggie—bass, but under legal size.

1.15 P.M. The flag puzzles Hutchins. She is covertly watching it. It is evidently a signal—but to whom? Are the secret-service men closing in on McDonald?

1. Aggie—pike!
2. On consulting map find unnamed lake only a few miles away. Shall investigate to-morrow.
3. Steamer has just gone. Detective now has canoe, blue in color. Also food. He sent off his letter.
4. Fed worms. Lizzie thinks they know me. How kindness is its own reward! Mr. McDonald is drawing in his anchor, which is a large stone fastened to a rope. Shall take bath.

Tish's notes ended here. She did not take the bath after all, for Mr. McDonald made us a call that afternoon.

He beached the green canoe and came up the rocks calmly and smilingly. Hutchins gave him a cold glance and went on with what she was doing, which was chopping a plank to cook the fish on. He bowed cheerfully to all of us and laid a string of fish on a rock.

"I brought a little offering," he said, looking at Hutchins's back. "The fishing isn't what I expected but if the young lady with the hatchet will desist, so I can make myself heard, I've found a place where there are fish! This biggest fellow is three and a quarter pounds."

Hutchins chopped harder than ever, and the plank flew up, striking her in the chest; but she refused all assistance, especially from Mr. McDonald, who was really concerned. He hurried to her and took the hatchet out of her hand, but in his excitement he was almost uncivil.

"You obstinate little idiot!" he said. "You'll kill yourself yet."

To my surprise, Hutchins, who had been entirely unemotional right along, suddenly burst into tears and went into the tent. Mr. McDonald took a hasty step or two after her, realizing, no doubt, that he had said more than he should to a complete stranger; but she closed the fly of the tent quite viciously and left him standing, with his arms folded, staring at it.

It was at that moment he saw the large fish, hanging from a tree. He stood for a moment staring at it and we could see that he was quite surprised.

"It is a fish, isn't it?" he said after a moment. "I—I thought for a moment it was painted on something."

He sat down suddenly on one of our folding-chairs and looked at the fish, and then at each of us in turn.

"You know," he said, "I didn't think there were such fish! I—you mustn't mind my surprise." He wiped his forehead with his handkerchief. "Just kick those things I brought into the river, will you? I apologize for them."

"Forty-nine inches," Tish said. "We expect to do better when we really get started. This evening we shall go after its mate, which is probably hanging round."

"Its mate?" he said, rather dazed. "Oh, I see. Of course!"

He still seemed to doubt his senses, for he went over and touched it with his finger. "Ladies," he said, "I'm not going after the—the mate. I couldn't land it if I did get it. I am going to retire from the game—except for food; but I wish, for the sake of my reason, you'd tell me what you caught it with."

Well, you may heartily distrust a person; but that is no reason why you should not answer a simple question. So I showed him the thing I had made—and he did not believe me!

"You're perfectly right," he said. "Every game has its secrets. I had no business to ask. But you haven't caught me with that feather-duster thing any more than you caught that fish with it. I don't mind your not telling me. That's your privilege. But isn't it rather rubbing it in to make fun of me?"

"Nothing of the sort!" Aggie said angrily. "If you had caught it—"

"My dear lady," he said, "I couldn't have caught it. The mere shock of getting such a bite would have sent me out of my boat in a swoon." He turned to Tish. "I have only one disappointment," he said, "that it wasn't one of *our* worms that did the work."

Tish said afterward she was positively sorry for him, he looked so crestfallen. So, when he started for his canoe she followed him.

"Look here," she said; "you're young, and I don't

want to see you get into trouble. Go home, young man! There are plenty of others to take your place."

He looked rather startled. "That's it exactly," he said, after a moment. "As well as I can make out there are about a hundred. If you think," he said fiercely, raising his voice, "that I'm going to back out and let somebody else in, I'm not. And that's flat."

"It's a life-and-death matter," said Tish.

"You bet it's a life-and-death matter."

"And—what about the—the red-headed man over there?"

His reply amazed us all. "He's harmless," he said. "I don't like him, naturally; but I admire the way he holds on. He's making the best of a bad business."

"Do you know why he's here?"

He looked uneasy for once.

"Well, I've got a theory," he replied; but, though his voice was calm, he changed color.

"Then perhaps you'll tell me what that signal means?"

Tish gave him the glasses and he saw the red flag. I have never seen a man look so unhappy.

"Holy cats!" he said, and almost dropped the glasses. "Why, he—he must be expecting somebody!"

"So I should imagine," Tish commented dryly. "He sent a letter by the boat to-day."

"The h—l he did!" And then: "That's ridiculous! You're mistaken. As a—as a matter of fact, I went over there the other night and commandeered his fountain pen."

So it had not fallen out of his pocket!

"I'll be frank, ladies," he said. "It's my object just now to keep that chap from writing letters. It doesn't matter why, but it's vital."

He was horribly cast down when we told him about Hutchins and the pen and ink.

"So that's it!" he said gloomily. "And the flag's a signal, of course. Ladies, you have done it out of the kindness of your hearts, I know; but I think you have wrecked my life."

He took a gloomy departure and left us all rather wrought up. Who were we, as Tish said, to imperil a fellow man? And another thing—if there was a reward on him, why should we give it to a red-haired detective, who was rude to harmless animals and ate canned corn for breakfast?

With her customary acumen Tish solved the difficulty that very evening.

"The simplest thing," she said, "of course, would be to go over during the night and take the flag away; but he may have more red handkerchiefs. Then, too, he seems to be a light sleeper, and it would be awkward to have him shoot at us."

She sat in thought for quite a while. Hutchins was watching the sunset, and seemed depressed and silent. Tish lowered her voice.

"There's no reason why we shouldn't have a red flag, too," she said. "It gives us an even chance to get in on whatever is about to happen. We can warn Mr. McDonald, for one thing, if any one comes here. Personally I think he is unjustly suspected."

[But Tish was to change her mind very soon.]

We made the flag that night, by lantern light, out of Tish's red silk petticoat. Hutchins was curious, I am sure; but we explained nothing. And we fastened it obliquely over the river, like the one on the other side.

Tish's change of heart, which occurred the next morning, was due to a most unfortunate accident that happened to her at nine o'clock. Hutchins, who could swim like a duck, was teaching Tish to swim, and she was learning nicely. Tish had put a life-preserver on, with a clothes-line fastened to it, and Aggie was sitting on the bank holding the rope while she went through the various gestures.

Having completed the lesson Hutchins went into the woods for red raspberries, leaving Tish still practicing in the water with Aggie holding the rope. Happening to sneeze, the line slipped out of her hand, and she had the agonizing experience of seeing Tish carried away by the current.

I was washing some clothing in the river a few yards down the stream when Tish came floating past. I shall never forget her expression or my own sense of absolute helplessness.

"Get the canoe," said Tish, "and follow. I'm heading

for Island Eleven."

She was quite calm, though pale; but, in her anxiety to keep well above the water, she did what was almost a fatal thing—she pushed the life-preserver lower down round her body. And having shifted the floating center, so to speak, without warning her head disappeared and her feet rose in the air.

For a time it looked as though she would drown in that position; but Tish rarely loses her presence of mind. She said she knew at once what was wrong. So, though somewhat handicapped by the position, she replaced the cork belt under her arms and emerged at last.

Aggie had started back into the woods for Hutchins; but, with one thing and another, it was almost ten before they returned together. Tish by that time was only a dot on the horizon through the binocular, having missed Island Eleven, as she explained later, by the rope being caught on a submerged log, which deflected her course.

We got into the motor boat and followed her, and, except for a most unjust sense of irritation that I had not drowned myself by following her in the canoe, she was unharmed. We got her into the motor boat and into a blanket, and Aggie gave her some blackberry cordial at once. It was some time before her teeth ceased chattering so she could speak. When she did it was to announce that she had made a discovery.

"He's a spy, all right!" she said. "And that Indian is another. Neither of them saw me as I floated past. They were on Island Eleven. Mr. McDonald wrote something and gave it to the Indian. It wasn't a letter or he'd have sent it by the boat. He didn't even put it in an envelope, so far as I could see. It's probably in cipher."

Well, we took her home, and she had a boiled egg at dinner.

The rest of us had fish. It is one of Tish's theories that fish should only be captured for food, and that all fish caught must be eaten. I do not know when I have seen fish come as easy. Perhaps it was the worms, which had grown both long and fat, so that one was too much for a hook; and we cut them with scissors, like tape or ribbon. Aggie and I finally got so sick of fish that while Tish's head was turned we dropped in our lines without bait. But, even at that, Aggie, reeling in her line to go home, caught a three-pound bass through the gills and could not shake it off.

We tried to persuade Tish to lie down that afternoon, but she refused.

"I'm not sick," she said, "even if you two idiots did try to drown me. And I'm on the track of something. If that was a letter, why didn't he send it by the boat?"

Just then her eye fell on the flagpole, and we followed her horrified gaze. The flag had been neatly cut away!

Tish's eyes narrowed. She looked positively dangerous; and within five minutes she had cut another flag out of the back breadth of the petticoat and flung it defiantly in the air. Who had cut away the signal—McDonald or the detective? We had planned to investigate the nameless lake that afternoon, Tish being like Colonel Roosevelt in her thirst for information, as well as in the grim pugnacity that is her dominant characteristic; but at the last minute she decided not to go.

"You and Aggie go, Lizzie," she said. "I've got something on hand."

"Tish!" Aggie wailed. "You'll drown yourself or something."

"Don't be a fool!" Tish snapped. "There's a portage, but you and Lizzie can carry the canoe across on your heads. I've seen pictures of it. It's easy. And keep your eyes open for a wireless outfit. There's one about, that's sure!"

"Lots of good it will do to keep our eyes open," I said with some bitterness, "with our heads inside the canoe!"

We finally started and Hutchins went with us. It was Hutchins, too, who voiced the way we all felt when we had crossed the river and were preparing for what she called the portage.

"She wants to get us out of the way, Miss Lizzie," she said. "Can you imagine what mischief she's up to?"

"That is not a polite way to speak of Miss Tish, Hutchins," I said coldly. Nevertheless, my heart sank.

Hutchins and I carried the canoe. It was a hot day and there was no path. Aggie, who likes a cup of hot tea at five o'clock, had brought along a bottle filled with tea, and a small basket containing sugar and cups.

Personally I never had less curiosity about a lake. As a matter of fact I wished there was no lake. Twice—being obliged, as it were, to walk blindly and the canoe being excessively heavy—I, who led the way, ran the front end of the thing against the trunk of a tree, and both Hutchins and I sat down violently, under the canoe as a result of the impact.

To add to the discomfort of the situation Aggie declared that we were being followed by a bear, and at the same instant stepped into a swamp up to her knees. She became calm at once, with the calmness of despair.

"Go and leave me, Lizzie!" she said. "He is just behind those bushes. I may sink before he gets me—that's one comfort."

Hutchins found a log and, standing on it, tried to pull her up; but she seemed firmly fastened. Aggie went quite white; and, almost beside myself, I poured her a cup of hot tea, which she drank. I remember she murmured Mr. Wiggins's name, and immediately after she yelled that the bear was coming.

It was, however, the detective who emerged from the bushes. He got Aggie out with one good heave, leaving both her shoes gone forever; and while she collapsed, whimpering, he folded his arms and stared at all of us angrily.

"What sort of damnable idiocy is this?" he demanded in a most unpleasant tone.

Aggie revived and sat upright.

"That's our affair, isn't it?" said Hutchins curtly.

"Not by a blamed sight!" was his astonishing reply.

"The next time I am sinking in a morass, let me sink," Aggie said, with simple dignity.

He did not speak another word, but gave each of us a glance of the most deadly contempt, and finished up with Hutchins.

"What I don't understand," he said furiously, "is why you have to lend yourself to this senile idiocy. Because some old women choose to sink themselves in a swamp is no reason why you should commit suicide!"

Aggie said afterward only the recollection that he had saved her life prevented her emptying the tea on him. I should hardly have known Hutchins.

"Naturally," she said in a voice thick with fury, "you

are in a position to insult these ladies, and you do. But I warn you, if you intend to keep on, this swamp is nothing. We like it here. We may stay for months. I hope you have your life insured."

Perhaps we should have understood it all then. Of course Charlie Sands, for whom I am writing this, will by this time, with his keen mind, comprehend it all; but I assure you we suspected nothing.

How simple, when you line it up: The country house and the garden hose; the detective, with no camp equipment; Mr. McDonald and the green canoe; the letter on the train; the red flag; the girl in the pink tam-o'-shanter—who has not yet appeared, but will shortly; Mr. McDonald's incriminating list—also not yet, but soon.

How inevitably they led to what Charlie Sands has called our crime!

The detective, who was evidently very strong, only glared at her. Then he swung the canoe up on his head and, turning about, started back the way we had come. Though Hutchins and Aggie were raging, I was resigned. My neck was stiff and my shoulders ached. We finished our tea in silence and then made our way back to the river.

I have now reached Tish's adventure. It is not my intention in this record to defend Tish. She thought her conclusions were correct. Charlie Sands says she is like Shaw—she has got a crooked point of view, but she believes she is seeing straight. And, after a while, if you look her way long enough you get a sort of mental astigmatism.

So I shall confess at once that, at the time, I saw nothing immoral in what she did that afternoon while we were having our adventure in the swamp.

I was putting cloths wrung out of arnica and hot water on my neck when she came home, and Hutchins was baking biscuit—she was a marvelous cook, though Aggie, who washed the dishes, objected to the number of pans she used.

Tish ignored both my neck and the biscuits, and, marching up the bank, got her shotgun from the tent and loaded it.

"We may be attacked at any time," she said briefly; and, getting the binocular, she searched the river with a splendid sweeping glance. "At any time. Hutchins, take these glasses, please, and watch that we are not disturbed."

"I'm baking biscuit, Miss Letitia."

"Biscuit!" said Tish scornfully. "Biscuit in times like these?"

She walked up to the camp stove and threw the oven door open; but, though I believe she had meant to fling them into the river, she changed her mind when she saw them.

"Open a jar of honey, Hutchins," she said, and closed the oven; but her voice was abstracted. "You can watch the river from the stove, Hutchins," she went on. "Miss Aggie and Miss Lizzie and I must confer together."

So we went into the tent, and Tish closed and fastened it.

"Now," she said, "I've got the papers."

"Papers?"

"The ones Mr. McDonald gave that Indian this morning. I had an idea he'd still have them. You can't hurry an Indian. I waited in the bushes until he went in swimming. Then I went through his pockets."

"Tish Carberry!" cried Aggie.

"These are not times to be squeamish," Tish said loftily. "I'm neutral; of course; but Great Britain has had this war forced on her and I'm going to see that she has a fair show. I've ordered all my stockings from the same shop in London, for twenty years, and squarer people never lived. Look at these—how innocent they look, until one knows!"

She produced two papers from inside her waist. I must confess that, at first glance, I saw nothing remarkable.

"The first one looks," said Tish, "like a grocery order. It's meant to look like that. It's relieved my mind of one thing—McDonald's got no wireless or he wouldn't be sending cipher messages by an Indian."

It was written on a page torn out of a pocket notebook and the page was ruled with an inch margin at the left. This was the document:—

    1 Dozen eggs.
    20 Yards fishing-line.
    1 pkg. Needles—anything to sew a button on.
    1 doz. A B C bass hooks.
    3 lbs. Meat—anything so it isn't fish.
    1 bot. Ink for fountain pen.
    3 Tins sardines.
    1 Extractor.

Well, I could not make anything of it; but, of course, I have not Tish's mind. Aggie was almost as bad.

"What's an extractor?" she asked.

"Exactly!" said Tish. "What is an extractor? Is the fellow going to pull teeth? No! He needed an *e* so he made up a word."

She ran her finger down the first letters of the second

column. "D-y-n-a-m-i-t-e!" she said triumphantly. "Didn't I tell you?"

IV

Well, there it was—staring at us. I felt positively chilled. He looked so young and agreeable, and, as Aggie said, he had such nice teeth. And to know him for what he was—it was tragic! But that was not all.

"Add the numbers!" said Tish. "Thirty-one tons, perhaps, of dynamite! And that's only part," said Tish. "Here's the most damning thing of all—a note to his accomplice!"

"Damning" is here used in the sense of condemnatory. We are none of us addicted to profanity.

We read the other paper, which had been in a sealed envelope, but without superscription. It is before me as I write, and I am copying it exactly:—

> I shall have to see you. I'm going crazy! Don't you realize that this is a matter of life and death to me? Come to Island Eleven to-night, won't you? And give me a chance to talk, anyhow. Something has got to be done and done soon. I'm desperate!

Aggie sneezed three times in sheer excitement; for anyone can see how absolutely incriminating the letter was. It was not signed, but it was in the same writing as the list.

Tish, who knows something about everything, said the writing denoted an unscrupulous and violent nature.

"The *y* is especially vicious," she said. "I wouldn't trust a man who made a *y* like that to carry a sick child to the doctor!"

The thing, of course, was to decide at once what measures to take. The boat would not come again for two days, and to send a letter by it to the town marshal or sheriff, or whatever the official is in Canada who takes charge of spies, would be another loss of time.

"Just one thing," said Tish. "I'll plan this out and find some way to deal with the wretch; but I wouldn't say anything to Hutchins. She's a nice little thing, though she is a fool about a motor boat. There's no case in scaring her."

For some reason or other, however, Hutchins was out of spirits that night.

"I hope you're not sick, Hutchins?" said Tish.

"No, indeed, Miss Tish."

"You're not eating your fish."

"I'm sick of fish," she said calmly. "I've eaten so much fish that when I see a hook I have a mad desire to go and hang myself on it."

"Fish," said Tish grimly, "is good for the brain. I do not care to boast, but never has my mind been so clear as it is to-night."

Now certainly, though Tish's tone was severe, there was nothing in it to hurt the girl; but she got up from the cracker box on which she was sitting, with her eyes filled with tears.

"Don't mind me. I'm a silly fool," she said; and went down to the river and stood looking out over it.

It quite spoiled our evening. Aggie made her a hot lemonade and, I believe, talked to her about Mr. Wiggins, and how, when he was living, she had had fits of weeping without apparent cause. But if the girl was in love, as we surmised, she said nothing about it. She insisted that it was too much fish and nervous strain about the Mebbe.

"I never know," she said, "when we start out whether we're going to get back or be marooned and starve to death on some island."

Tish said afterward that her subconscious self must have taken the word "marooned" and played with it; for in ten minutes or so her plan popped into her head.

"'Full-panoplied from the head of Jove,' Lizzie," she said. "Really, it is not necessary to think if one only has faith. The supermind does it all without effort. I do not dislike the young man; but I must do my duty."

Tish's plan was simplicity itself. We were to steal his canoe.

"Then we'll have him," she finished. "The current's too strong there for him to swim to the mainland."

"He might try it and drown," Aggie objected. "Spy or no spy, he's somebody's son."

"War is no time to be chicken-hearted," Tish replied.

I confess I ate little all that day. At noon Mr. McDonald came and borrowed two eggs from us.

"I've sent over to a store across country, by my Indian guide, philosopher, and friend," he said, "for some things I needed; but I dare say he's reading Byron somewhere and has forgotten it."

"Guide, philosopher, and friend!" I caught Tish's eye. McDonald had written the Updike letter! McDonald had meant to use our respectability to take him across the border!

We gave him the eggs, but Tish said afterward she was not deceived for a moment.

"The Indian has told him," she said, "and he's allaying our suspicions. Oh, he's clever enough! 'Know the Indian mind and my own!'" she quoted from the Updike letter. "'I know Canada thoroughly.' 'My object is not money.' I should think not!"

Tish stole the green canoe that night. She put on the life preserver and we tied the end of the rope that Aggie had let slip to the canoe. The life-preserver made it difficult to paddle, Tish said, but she felt more secure. If she struck a rock and upset, at least she would not drown; and we could start after her at dawn with the Mebbe.

"I'll be somewhere down the river," she said, "and safe enough, most likely, unless there are falls."

Hutchins watched in a puzzled way, for Tish did not leave until dusk.

"You'd better let me follow you with the launch, Miss Tish," she said. "Just remember that if the canoe sinks you're tied to it."

"I'm on serious business to-night, Hutchins," Tish said ominously. "You are young, and I refuse to trouble your young mind; but your ears are sharp. If you hear any shooting, get the boat and follow me."

The mention of shooting made me very nervous. We watched Tish as long as we could see her; then we returned to the tent, and Aggie and I crocheted by the hanging lantern. Two hours went by. At eleven o'clock Tish had not returned and Hutchins was in the motor boat, getting it ready to start.

"I like courage, Miss Lizzie," she said to me; "but this thing of elderly women, with some sort of bug, starting out at night in canoes is too strong for me. Either she's going to stay in at night or I'm going home."

"Elderly nothing!" I said, with some spirit. "She is in the prime of life. Please remember, Hutchins, that you are speaking of your employer. Miss Tish has no bug, as you call it."

"Oh, she's rational enough," Hutchins retorted: "but she is a woman of one idea and that sort of person is dangerous."

I was breathless at her audacity.

"Come now, Miss Lizzie," she said, "how can I help when I don't know what is being done? I've done my best up here to keep you comfortable and restrain Miss Tish's recklessness; but I ought to know something."

She was right; and, Tish or no Tish, then and there I told her. She was more than astonished. She sat in the motor boat, with a lantern at her feet, and listened.

"I see," she said slowly. "So the—so Mr. McDonald is a spy and has sent for dynamite to destroy the railroad! And—and the red-haired man is a detective! How do you know he is a detective?"

I told her then about the note we had picked up from beside her in the train, and because she was so much interested she really seemed quite thrilled. I brought the cipher grocery list and the other note down to her.

"It's quite convincing, isn't it?" she said. "And—and exciting! I don't know when I've been so excited."

She really was. Her cheeks were flushed. She looked exceedingly pretty.

"The thing to do," she said, "is to teach him a lesson. He's young. He mayn't always have had to stoop to such—such criminality. If we can scare him thoroughly, it might do him a lot of good."

I said I was afraid Tish took a more serious view of things and would notify the authorities. And at that moment there came two or three shots—then silence.

I shall never forget the ride after Tish and how we

felt when we failed to find her; for there was no sign of her. The wind had come up, and, what with seeing Tish tied to that wretched canoe and sinking with it or shot through the head and lying dead in the bottom of it, we were about crazy. As we passed Island Eleven we could see the spy's camp-fire and his tent, but no living person.

At four in the morning we gave up and started back, heavy-hearted. What, therefore, was our surprise to find Tish sitting by the fire in her bathrobe, with a cup of tea in her lap and her feet in a foot-tub of hot water! Considering all we had gone through and that we had obeyed orders exactly, she was distinctly unjust. Indeed, at first she quite refused to speak to any of us.

"I do think, Tish," Aggie said as she stood shivering by the fire, "that you might at least explain where you have been. We have been going up and down the river for hours, burying you over and over."

Tish took a sip of tea, but said nothing.

"You said," I reminded her, "that if there was shooting, we were to start after you at once. When we heard the shots, we went, of course."

Tish leaned over and, taking the teakettle from the fire, poured more water into the foot-tub. Then at last she turned to speak.

"Bring some absorbent cotton and some bandages, Hutchins," she said. "I am bleeding from a hundred wounds. As for you"—she turned fiercely on Aggie and me—"the least you could have done was to be here when I returned, exhausted, injured, and weary; but, of course, you were gallivanting round the lake in an upholstered motor boat."

Here she poured more water into the foot-tub and

made it much too hot. This thawed her rather, and she explained what was wrong. She was bruised, scratched to the knees, and with a bump the size of an egg on her forehead, where she had run into a tree.

The whole story was very exciting. It seems she got the green canoe without any difficulty, the spy being sound asleep in his tent; but about that time the wind came up and Tish said she could not make an inch of progress toward our camp.

The chewing gum with which we had repaired our canoe came out at that time and the boat began to fill, Tish being unable to sit over the leak and paddle at the same time. So, at last, she gave up and made for the mainland.

"The shooting," Tish said with difficulty, "was by men from the Indian camp firing at me. I landed below the camp, and was making my way as best I could through the woods when they heard me moving. I believe they thought it was a bear."

I think Tish was more afraid of the Indians, in spite of their sixty-three steel engravings and the rest of it, than she pretended, though she said she would have made herself known, but at that moment she fell over a fallen tree and for fifteen minutes was unable to speak a word. When at last she rose the excitement was over and they had gone back to their camp.

"Anyhow," she finished, "the green canoe is hidden a couple of miles down the river, and I guess Mr. McDonald is safe for a time. Lizzie, you can take a bath to-morrow safely."

Tish sat up most of the rest of the night composing a letter to the authorities of the town, telling them of Mr. McDonald and enclosing careful copies of the incriminating documents she had found.

During the following morning the river was very quiet. Through the binocular we were able to see Mr. McDonald standing on the shore of his island and looking intently in our direction, but naturally we paid no attention to him.

The red-haired man went in swimming that day and necessitated our retiring to the tent for an hour and a half; but at noon Aggie's naturally soft heart began to assert itself.

"Spy or no spy," she said to Tish, "we ought to feed him."

"Huh!" was Tish's rejoinder. "There is no sense is wasting good food on a man whose hours are numbered."

We were surprised, however, to find that Hutchins, who had detested Mr. McDonald, was rather on Aggie's side.

"The fact that he has but a few more hours," she said to Tish, "is an excellent reason for making those hours as little wretched as possible."

It was really due to Hutchins, therefore, that Mr. McDonald had a luncheon. The problem of how to get it to him was a troublesome one, but Tish solved it with her customary sagacity.

"We can make a raft," she said, "a small one, large enough to hold a tray. By stopping the launch some yards above the island we can float his luncheon to him quite safely."

That was the method we ultimately pursued and it worked most satisfactorily.

Hutchins baked hot biscuits; and, by putting a cover over the pan, we were enabled to get them to him before they cooled.

We prepared a really appetizing luncheon of hot biscuits, broiled ham, marmalade, and tea, adding, at Aggie's instructions, a jar of preserved peaches, which she herself had put up.

Tish made the raft while we prepared the food, and at exactly half-past twelve o'clock we left the house. Mr. McDonald saw us coming and was waiting smilingly at the upper end of the island.

"Great Scott!" he said. "I thought you were never going to hear me. Another hour and I'd have made a swim for it, though it's suicidal with this current. I'll show you where you can come in so you won't hit a rock."

Hutchins had stopped the engine of the motor boat and we threw out the anchor at a safe distance from the shore.

"We are not going to land," said Tish, "and I think you know perfectly well the reason why."

"Oh, now," he protested; "surely you are going to land! I've had an awfully uncomfortable accident—my canoe's gone."

"We know that," Tish said calmly. "As a matter of fact, we took it."

Mr. McDonald sat down suddenly on a log at the water's edge and looked at us.

"Oh!" he said.

"You may not believe it," Tish said, "but we know everything—your dastardly plot, who the red-haired man is, and all the destruction and wretchedness you are about to cause."

"Oh, I say!" he said feebly. "I wouldn't go as far as that. I'm—I'm not such a bad sort."

"That depends on the point of view," said Tish grimly.

Aggie touched her on the arm then and reminded her that the biscuits were getting cold; but Tish had a final word with him.

"Your correspondence has fallen into my hands, young man," she said, "and will be turned over to the proper authorities."

"It won't tell them anything they don't know," he said doggedly. "Look here, ladies: I am not ashamed of this thing. I—I am proud of it. I am perfectly willing to yell it out loud for everybody to hear. As a matter of fact, I think I will."

Mr. McDonald stood up suddenly and threw his head back; but here Hutchins, who had been silent, spoke for the first time.

"Don't be an idiot!" she said coldly. "We have something here for you to eat if you behave yourself."

He seemed to see her then for the first time, for he favored her with a long stare.

"Ah!" he said. "Then you are not entirely cold and heartless?"

She made no reply to this, being busy in assisting Aggie to lower the raft over the side of the boat.

"Broiled ham, tea, hot biscuits, and marmalade," said Aggie gently. "My poor fellow, we are doing what we consider our duty; but we want you to know that it is hard for us—very hard."

When he saw our plan, Mr. McDonald's face fell; but he stepped out into the water up to his knees and caught the raft as it floated down.

Before he said "Thank you" he lifted the cover of the pan and saw the hot biscuits underneath.

"Really," he said, "it's very decent of you. I sent off a grocery order yesterday, but nothing has come."

Tish had got Hutchins to start the engine by that time and we were moving away. He stood there, up to his knees in water, holding the tray and looking after us. He was really a pathetic figure, especially in view of the awful fate we felt was overtaking him.

He called something after us. On account of the noise of the engine, we could not be certain, but we all heard it the same way.

"Send for the whole d—d outfit!" was the way it sounded to us. "It won't make any difference to me."

V

The last thing I recall of Mr. McDonald that day is seeing him standing there in the water, holding the tray, with the teapot steaming under his nose, and gazing after us with an air of bewilderment that did not deceive us at all.

As I look back, there is only one thing we might have noticed at the time. This was the fact that Hutchins, having started the engine, was sitting beside it on the floor of the boat and laughing in the cruelest possible manner. As I said to Aggie at the time: "A spy is a spy and entitled to punishment if discovered; but no young woman should laugh over so desperate a situation."

I come now to the denouement of this exciting period. It had been Tish's theory that the red-haired man should not be taken into our confidence. If there was a reward for the capture of the spy, we ourselves intended to have it.

The steamer was due the next day but one. Tish was in favor of not waiting, but of at once going in the motor boat to the town, some thirty miles away, and telling of our capture; but Hutchins claimed there was not sufficient gasoline for such an excursion. That afternoon we went in the motor launch to where Tish had hidden the green canoe and, with a hatchet, rendered it useless.

The workings of the subconscious mind are marvelous. In the midst of chopping, Tish suddenly looked up.

"Have you noticed," she said, "that the detective is always watching our camp?"

"That's all he has to do," Aggie suggested.

"Stuff and nonsense! Didn't he follow you into the swamp? Does Hutchins ever go out in the canoe that he doesn't go out also? I'll tell you what has happened: She's young and pretty, and he's fallen in love with her."

I must say it sounded reasonable. He never bothered about the motor boat, but the instant she took the canoe and started out he was hovering somewhere near.

"She's noticed it," Tish went on. "That's what she was quarreling about with him yesterday."

"How are we to know," said Aggie, who was gathering up the scraps of the green canoe and building a fire under them—"how are we to know they are not old friends, meeting thus in the wilderness? Fate plays strange tricks, Tish. I lived in the same street with Mr. Wiggins for years, and never knew him until one day when my umbrella turned wrong side out in a gust of wind."

"Fate fiddlesticks!" said Tish. "There's no such thing as fate in affairs of this sort. It's all instinct—the instinct of the race to continue itself."

This Aggie regarded as indelicate and she was rather cool to Tish the balance of the day.

Our prisoner spent most of the day at the end of the island toward us, sitting quietly, as we could see through the glasses. We watched carefully, fearing at any time to see the Indian paddling toward him.

[Tish was undecided what to do in such an emergency, except to intercept him and explain, threatening him also with having attempted to carry the incriminating papers. As it happened, however, the entire camp had gone for a two-days' deer hunt, and before they returned the whole thing had come to its surprising end.]

Late in the afternoon Tish put her theory of the red-haired man to the test.

"Hutchins," she said, "Miss Lizzie and I will cook the dinner if you want to go in the canoe to Harvey's Bay for water-lilies."

Hutchins at once said she did not care a rap for water-lilies; but, seeing a determined glint in Tish's eye, she added that she would go for frogs if Tish wanted her out of the way.

"Don't talk like a child!" Tish retorted. "Who said I wanted you out of the way?"

It is absolutely true that the moment Hutchins put her foot into the canoe the red-haired man put down his fishing-rod and rose. And she had not taken three strokes with the paddle before he was in the blue canoe.

Hutchins saw him just then and scowled. The last we saw of her she was moving rapidly up the river and the detective was dropping slowly behind. They both disappeared finally into the bay and Tish drew a long breath.

"Typical!" she said curtly. "He's sent here to watch a dangerous man and spends his time pursuing the young woman who hates the sight of him. When women achieve the suffrage they will put none but married men in positions of trust."

Hutchins and the detective were still out of sight when supper-time came. The spy's supper weighed on us, and at last Tish attempted to start the motor launch. We had placed the supper and the small raft aboard, and Aggie was leaning over the edge untying the painter,—not a man, but a rope,—when unexpectedly the engine started at the first revolution of the wheel.

It darted out to the length of the rope, where it was checked abruptly, the shock throwing Aggie entirely out and into the stream. Tish caught the knife from the supper tray to cut us loose, and while Tish cut I pulled Aggie in, wet as she was. The boat was straining and panting, and, on being released, it sprang forward like a dog unleashed.

Aggie had swallowed a great deal of water and was most disagreeable; but the Mebbe was going remarkably well, and there seemed to be every prospect that we should get back to the camp in good order. Alas, for human hopes! Mr. McDonald was not very agreeable.

"You know," he said as he waited for his supper to float within reach, "you needn't be so blamed radical about everything you do! If you object to my hanging round, why not just say so? If I'm too obnoxious I'll clear out."

"Obnoxious is hardly the word," said Tish. "How long am I to be a prisoner?"

"I shall send letters off by the first boat."

He caught the raft just then and examined the supper

with interest.

"Of course things might be worse," he said; "but it's dirty treatment, anyhow. And it's darned humiliating. Somebody I know is having a good time at my expense. It's heartless! That's what it is—heartless!"

Well, we left him, the engine starting nicely and Aggie being wrapped in a tarpaulin; but about a hundred yards above the island it began to slow down, and shortly afterward it stopped altogether. As the current caught us, we luckily threw out the anchor, for the engine refused to start again. It was then we saw the other canoes.

The girl in the pink tam-o'-shanter was in the first one.

They glanced at us curiously as they passed, and the P.T.S.—that is the way we grew to speak of the pink tam-o'-shanter—raised one hand in the air, which is a form of canoe greeting, probably less upsetting to the equilibrium than a vigorous waving of the arm.

It was just then, I believe, that they saw our camp and headed for it. The rest of what happened is most amazing. They stopped at our landing and unloaded their canoes. Though twilight was falling, we could see them distinctly. And what we saw was that they calmly took possession of the camp.

"Good gracious!" Tish cried. "The girls have gone into the tent! And somebody's working at the stove. The impertinence!"

Our situation was acutely painful. We could do nothing but watch. We called, but our voices failed to reach them. And Aggie took a chill, partly cold and partly fury. We sat there while they ate the entire supper!

They were having a very good time. Now and then somebody would go into the tent and bring something out, and there would be shrieks of laughter.

[We learned afterward that part of the amusement was caused by Aggie's false front, which one of the wretches put on as a beard.]

It was while thus distracted that Aggie suddenly screamed, and a moment later Mr. McDonald climbed over the side and into the boat, dripping.

"Don't be alarmed!" he said. "I'll go back and be a prisoner again just as soon as I've fired the engine. I couldn't bear to think of the lady who fell in sitting here indefinitely and taking cold." He was examining the engine while he spoke. "Have visitors, I see," he observed, as calmly as though he were not dripping all over the place.

"Intruders, not visitors!" Tish said angrily. "I never saw them before."

"Rather pretty, the one with the pink cap. May I examine the gasoline supply?" There was no gasoline. He shrugged his shoulders. "I'm afraid no amount of mechanical genius I intended to offer you will start her," he said; "but the young lady—Hutchins is her name, I believe?—will see you here and come after you, of course."

Well, there was no denying that, spy or no spy, his presence was a comfort. He offered to swim back to the island and be a prisoner again, but Tish said magnanimously that there was no hurry. On Aggie's offering half of her tarpaulin against the wind, which had risen, he accepted.

"Your Miss Hutchins is reckless, isn't she?" he said when he was comfortably settled. "She's a strong swimmer; but a canoe is uncertain at the best."

"She's in no danger," said Tish. "She has a devoted admirer watching out for her."

"The deuce she has!" His voice was quite interested. "Why, who on earth—"

"Your detective," said Aggie softly. "He's quite mad about her. The way he follows her and the way he looks at her—it's thrilling!"

Mr. McDonald said nothing for quite a while. The canoe party had evidently eaten everything they could find, and somebody had brought out a banjo and was playing.

Tish, unable to vent her anger, suddenly turned on Mr. McDonald. "If you think," she said, "that the grocery list fooled us, it didn't!"

"Grocery list?"

"That's what I said."

"How did you get my grocery list?"

So she told him, and how she had deciphered it, and how the word "dynamite" had only confirmed her early suspicions.

His only comment was to say, "Good Heavens!" in a smothered voice.

"It was the extractor that made me suspicious," she finished. "What were you going to extract? Teeth?"

"And so, when my Indian was swimming, you went through his things! It's the most astounding thing I ever—My dear lady, an extractor is used to get the hooks out of fish. It was no cipher, I assure you. I needed an extractor and I ordered it. The cipher you speak of is only a remarkable coincidence."

"Huh!" said Tish. "And the paper you dropped in the train—was that a coincidence?"

"That's not my secret," he said, and turned sulky at once.

"Don't tell me," Tish said triumphantly, "that any young man comes here absolutely alone without a purpose!"

"I had a purpose, all right; but it was not to blow up a railroad train."

Apparently he thought he had said too much, for he relapsed into silence after that, with an occasional muttering.

It was eight o'clock when Hutchins's canoe came into sight. She was paddling easily, but the detective was far behind and moving slowly.

She saw the camp with its uninvited guests, and then she saw us. The detective, however, showed no curiosity; and we could see that he made for his landing and stumbled exhaustedly up the bank. Hutchins drew up beside us. "He'll not try that again, I think," she said in her crisp voice. "He's out of training. He panted like a motor launch. Who are our visitors?"

Here her eyes fell on Mr. McDonald and her face set in the dusk.

"You'll have to go back and get some gasoline, Hutchins."

"What made you start out without looking?"

"And send the vandals away. If they wait until I arrive, I'll be likely to do them some harm. I have never been so outraged."

"Let me go for gasoline in the canoe," said Mr. McDonald. He leaned over the thwart and addressed Hutchins. "You're worn out," he said. "I promise to come back and be a perfectly well-behaved prisoner again."

"Thanks, no."

"I'm wet. The exercise will warm me."

"Is it possible," she said in a withering tone that was lost on us at the time, "that you brought no dumb-bells with you?"

If we had had any doubts they should have been settled then; but we never suspected. It is incredible, looking back.

The dusk was falling and I am not certain of what followed. It was, however, something like this: Mr. McDonald muttered something angrily and made a motion to get into the canoe. Hutchins replied that she would not have help from him if she died for it. The next thing we knew she was in the launch and the canoe was floating off on the current. Aggie squealed; and Mr. McDonald, instead of swimming after the thing, merely folded his arms and looked at it.

"You know," he said to Hutchins, "you have so unpleasant a disposition that somebody we both know of is better off than he thinks he is!"

Tish's fury knew no bounds, for there we were marooned and two of us wet to the skin. I must say for Hutchins, however, that when she learned about Aggie she was bitterly repentant, and insisted on putting her own sweater on her. But there we were and there we should likely stay.

It was quite dark by that time, and we sat in the launch, rocking gently. The canoeing party had lighted a large fire on the beach, using the driftwood we had so painfully accumulated.

We sat in silence, except that Tish, who was watching our camp, said once bitterly that she was glad there were three beds in the tent. The girls of the canoeing party would be comfortable.

After a time Tish turned on Mr. McDonald sharply. "Since you claim to be no spy," she said, "perhaps you will tell us what brings you alone to this place? Don't tell me it's fish—I've seen you reading, with a line out. You're no fisherman."

He hesitated. "No," he admitted. "I'll be frank, Miss Carberry. I did not come to fish."

"What brought you?"

"Love," he said, in a low tone. "I don't expect you to believe me, but it's the honest truth."

"Love!" Tish scoffed.

"Perhaps I'd better tell you the story," he said. "It's long and—and rather sad."

"Love stories," Hutchins put in coldly, "are terribly stupid, except to those concerned."

"That," he retorted, "is because you have never been in love. You are young and—you will pardon the liberty?—attractive; but you are totally prosaic and unromantic."

"Indeed!" she said, and relapsed into silence.

"These other ladies," Mr. McDonald went on, "will understand the strangeness of my situation when I explain that the—the young lady I care for is very near; is, in fact, within sight."

"Good gracious!" said Aggie. "Where?"

"It is a long story, but it may help to while away the long night hours; for I dare say we are here for the night. Did any one happen to notice the young lady in the first canoe, in the pink tam-o'-shanter?"

We said we had—all except Hutchins, who, of course, had not seen her. Mr. McDonald got a wet cigarette from his pocket and, finding a box of matches on the seat, made an attempt to dry it over the flames; so his story was told in the flickering light of one match after another.

VI

"I am," Mr. McDonald said, as the cigarette steamed, "the son of poor but honest parents. All my life I have been obliged to labor. You may say that my English is surprisingly pure, under such conditions. As a matter of fact, I educated myself at night, using a lantern in the top of my father's stable."

"I thought you said he was poor," Hutchins put in nastily. "How did he have a stable?"

"He kept a livery stable. Any points that are not clear I will explain afterward. Once the thread of a narrative is broken, it is difficult to resume, Miss Hutchins. Near us, in a large house, lived the lady of my heart."

"The pink tam-o'-shanter girl!" said Aggie. "I begin to understand."

"But," he added, "near us also lived a red-headed boy. She liked him very much, and even in the long-ago days I was fiercely jealous of him. It may surprise you to know that in those days I longed—fairly longed—for red hair and a red mustache."

"I hate to interrupt," said Hutchins; "but did he have a mustache as a boy?"

He ignored her. "We three grew up together. The girl is beautiful—you've probably noticed that—and amiable. The one thing I admire in a young woman is amiability. It would not, for instance, have occurred to her to isolate an entire party on the bosom of a northern and treacherous river out of pure temper."

"To think," said Aggie softly, "that she is just over

there by the camp-fire! Don't you suppose, if she loves you, she senses your nearness?"

"That's it exactly," he replied in a gloomy voice, "if she loves me! But does she? In other words, has she come up the river to meet me or to meet my rival? She knows we are here. Both of us have written her. The presence of one or the other of us is the real reason for this excursion of hers. But again the question is—which?"

Here the match he was holding under the cigarette burned his fingers and he flung it overboard with a violent gesture.

"The detective, of course," said Tish. "I knew it from the beginning of your story."

"The detective," he assented. "You see his very profession attracts. There's an element of romance in it. I myself have kept on with my father and now run the—er—livery stable. My business is a handicap from a romantic point of view.

"I am aware," Mr. McDonald went on, "that it is not customary to speak so frankly of affairs of this sort; but I have two reasons. It hurts me to rest under unjust suspicion. I am no spy, ladies. And the second reason is even stronger. Consider my desperate position: In the morning my rival will see her; he will paddle his canoe to the great rock below your camp and sing his love song from the water. In the morning I shall sit here helpless—ill, possibly—and see all that I value in life slip out of my grasp. And all through no fault of my own! Things are so evenly balanced, so little will shift the weight of her favor, that frankly the first one to reach her will get her."

I confess I was thrilled. And even Tish was touched;

but she covered her emotion with hard common sense.

"What's her name?" she demanded.

"Considering my frankness I must withhold that. Why not simply refer to her as the pink tam-o'-shanter—or, better still and more briefly, the P.T.S.? That may stand for pink tam-o'-shanter, or the Person That Smiles,—she smiles a great deal,—or—or almost anything."

"It also stands," said Hutchins, with a sniff, "for Pretty Tall Story."

Tish considered her skepticism unworthy in one so young, and told her so; on which she relapsed into a sulky silence.

In view of what we knew, the bonfire at our camp and the small figure across the river took on a new significance.

As Aggie said, to think of the red-haired man sleeping calmly while his lady love was so near and his rival, so to speak, *hors de combat!* Shortly after finishing his story, Mr. McDonald went to the stern of the boat and lifted the anchor rope.

"It is possible," he said, "that the current will carry us to my island with a little judicious management. Even though we miss it, we'll hardly be worse off than we are."

It was surprising we had not thought of it before, for the plan succeeded admirably. By moving a few feet at a time and then anchoring, we made slow but safe progress, and at last touched shore. We got out, and Mr. McDonald built a large fire, near which we put Aggie to steam. His supper, which he had not had time to eat, he generously divided, and we heated the tea. Hutchins, however, refused to eat.

Warmth and food restored Tish's mind to its usual keenness. I recall now the admiration in Mr. McDonald's eyes when she suddenly put down the sandwich she was eating and exclaimed:—

"The flags, of course! He told her to watch for a red flag as she came up the river; so when the party saw ours they landed. Perhaps they still think it is his camp and that he is away overnight."

"That's it, exactly," he said. "Think of the poor wretch's excitement when he saw your flag!"

Still, on looking back, it seems curious that we overlooked the way the red-headed man had followed Hutchins about. True, men are polygamous animals, Tish says, and are quite capable of following one woman about while they are sincerely in love with somebody else. But, when you think of it, the detective had apparently followed Hutchins from the start, and had gone into the wilderness to be near her, with only a suitcase and a mackintosh coat; which looked like a mad infatuation.

[Tish says she thought of this at the time, and that; from what she had seen of the P.T.S., Hutchins was much prettier. But she says she decided that men often love one quality in one girl and another in another; that he probably loved Hutchins's beauty and the amiability of the P.T.S. Also, she says, she reflected that the polygamy of the Far East is probably due to this tendency in the male more than to a preponderance of women.]

Tish called me aside while Mr. McDonald was gathering firewood. "I'm a fool and a guilty woman, Lizzie," she said. "Because of an unjust suspicion I have possibly wrecked this poor boy's life."

I tried to soothe her. "They might have been wretchedly unhappy together, Tish," I said; "and, anyhow, I doubt whether he is able to support a wife. There's nothing much in keeping a livery stable nowadays."

"There's only one thing that still puzzles me," Tish observed: "granting that the grocery order was a grocery order, what about the note?"

We might have followed this line of thought, and saved what occurred later, but that a new idea suddenly struck Tish. She is curious in that way; her mind works very rapidly at times, and because I cannot take her mental hurdles, so to speak, she is often impatient.

"Lizzie," she said suddenly, "did you notice that when the anchor was lifted, we drifted directly to this island? Don't stare at me like that. Use your wits."

When I failed instantly to understand, however, she turned abruptly and left me, disappearing in the shadows.

For the next hour nothing happened. Tish was not in sight and Aggie slept by the fire. Hutchins sat with her chin cupped in her hands, and Mr. McDonald gathered driftwood.

Hutchins only spoke once. "I'm awfully sorry about the canoe, Miss Lizzie," she said; "it was silly and—and selfish. I don't always act like a bad child. The truth is, I'm rather upset and nervous. I hate to be thwarted—I'm sorry I can't explain any further."

I was magnanimous. "I'm sure, until to-night, you've been perfectly satisfactory," I said; "but it seems extraordinary that you should dislike men the way you do."

She only eyed me searchingly.

It is my evening custom to prepare for the night by taking my switch off and combing and braiding my hair; so, as we seemed to be settled for the night, I asked Mr. McDonald whether the camp afforded an extra comb. He brought out a traveling-case at once from the tent and opened it.

"Here's a comb," he said. "I never use one. I'm sorry this is all I can supply."

My eyes were glued to the case. It was an English traveling-case, with gold-mounted fittings. He saw me staring at it and changed color.

"Nice bag, isn't it?" he said. "It was a gift, of course. The—the livery stable doesn't run much to this sort of thing."

But the fine edge of suspicion had crept into my mind again.

* * * * *

Tish did not return to the fire for some time. Before she came back we were all thoroughly alarmed. The island was small, and a short search convinced us that she was not on it!

We wakened Aggie and told her, and the situation was very painful. The launch was where we had left it. Mr. McDonald looked more and more uneasy.

"My sane mind tells me she's perfectly safe," he said. "I don't know that I've ever met a person more able to take care of herself; but it's darned odd—that's all I can say."

Just as he spoke a volley of shots sounded from up the river near our camp, two close together and then one; and somebody screamed.

It was very dark. We could see lanterns flashing at

our camp and somebody was yelling hoarsely. One lantern seemed to run up and down the beach in mad excitement, and then, out of the far-off din, Aggie, whose ears are sharp, suddenly heard the splash of a canoe paddle.

I shall tell Tish's story of what happened as she told it to Charlie Sands two weeks or so later.

"It is perfectly simple," she said, "and it's stupid to make such a fuss over it. Don't talk to me about breaking the law! The girl came; I didn't steal her."

Charlie Sands, I remember, interrupted at that moment to remind her that she had shot a hole in the detective's canoe; but this only irritated her.

"Certainly I did," she snapped; "but it's perfectly idiotic of him to say that it took off the heel of his shoe. In that stony country it's always easy to lose a heel."

But to return to Tish's story:—

"It occurred to me," she said, "that, if the launch had drifted to Mr. McDonald's island, the canoe might have done so too; so I took a look round. I'd been pretty much worried about having called the boy a spy when he wasn't, and it worried me to think that he couldn't get away from the place. I never liked the red-haired man. He was cruel to Aggie's cat—but we've told you that.

"I knew that in the morning the detective would see the P.T.S., as we called her, and he could get over and propose before breakfast. But when I found the canoe—yes, I found it—I didn't intend to do anything more than steal the detective's boat."

"Is that all?" said Charlie Sands sarcastically. "You disappoint me, Aunt Letitia! With all the chances you had—to burn his pitiful little tent, for instance, or steal his suitcase—"

"But on my way," Tish went on with simple dignity, "it occurred to me that I could move things a step farther by taking the girl to Mr. McDonald and letting him have his chance right away. Things went well from the start, for she was standing alone, looking out over the river. It was dark, except for the starlight, and I didn't know it was she. I beached the canoe and she squealed a little when I spoke to her."

"Just what," broke in Charlie Sands, "does one say under such circumstances? Sometime I may wish to abduct a young woman and it is well to be prepared."

"I told her the young man she had expected was on Island Eleven and had sent me to get her. She was awfully excited. She said they'd seen his signal, but nothing of him. And when they'd found a number of feminine things round they all felt a little—well, you can understand. She went back to get a coat, and while she was gone I untied the canoes and pushed them out into the river. I'm thorough, and I wasn't going to have a lot of people interfering before we got things fixed."

It was here, I think, that Charlie Sands gave a low moan and collapsed on the sofa. "Certainly!" he said in a stifled voice. "I believe in being thorough. And, of course, a few canoes more or less do not matter."

"Later," Tish said, "I knew I'd been thoughtless about the canoes; but, of course, it was too late then."

"And when was it that you assaulted the detective?"

"He fired first," said Tish. "I never felt more peaceable in my life. It's absurd for him to say that he was watching our camp, as he had every night we'd been there. Who asked him to guard us? And the idea of his saying he thought we were Indians stealing things, and that he fired into the air! The bullets sang past me. I had hardly time to get my revolver out of my stocking."

"And then?" asked Charlie Sands.

"And then," said Tish, "we went calmly down the river to Island Eleven. We went rapidly, for at first the detective did not know I had shot a hole in his canoe, and he followed us. It stands to reason that if I'd shot his heel off he'd have known there was a hole in the boat. Luckily the girl was in the bottom of the canoe when she fainted or we might have been upset."

It was at this point, I believe, that Charlie Sands got his hat and opened the door.

"I find," he said, "that I cannot stand any more at present, Aunt Tish. I shall return when I am stronger."

* * * * *

So I shall go back to my own narrative. Really my justification is almost complete. Any one reading to this point will realize the injustice of the things that have been said about us.

We were despairing of Tish, as I have said, when we heard the shots and then the approach of a canoe. Then Tish hailed us.

"Quick, somebody!" she said. "I have a cramp in my right leg."

[The canoeing position, kneeling as one must, had been always very trying for her. She frequently developed cramps, which only a hot footbath relieved.]

Mr. McDonald waded out into the water. Our beach fire illuminated the whole scene distinctly, and when he saw the P.T.S. huddled in the canoe he stopped as though he had been shot.

"How interesting!" said Hutchins from the bank, in

her cool voice.

I remember yet Tish, stamping round on her cramped limb and smiling benevolently at all of us. The girl, however, looked startled and unhappy, and a little dizzy. Hutchins helped her to a fallen tree.

"Where—where is he?" said the P.T.S.

Tish stared at her. "Bless the girl!" she said. "Did you think I meant the other one?"

"I—What other one?"

Tish put her hand on Mr. McDonald's arm. "My dear girl," she said, "this young man adores you. He's all that a girl ought to want in the man she loves. I have done him a grave injustice and he has borne it nobly. Come now—let me put your hand in his and say you will marry him."

"Marry him!" said the P.T.S. "Why, I never saw him in my life before!"

We had been so occupied with this astounding scene that none of us had noticed the arrival of the detective. He limped rapidly up the bank—having lost his heel, as I have explained—and, dripping with water, confronted us. When a red-haired person is pale, he is very pale. And his teeth showed.

He ignored all of us but the P.T.S., who turned and saw him, and went straight into his arms in the most unmaidenly fashion.

"By Heaven," he said, "I thought that elderly lunatic had taken you off and killed you!"

He kissed her quite frantically before all of us; and then, with one arm round her, he confronted Tish.

"I'm through!" he said. "I'm done! There isn't a salary in the world that will make me stay within gunshot of you another day." He eyed her fiercely. "You are a dangerous woman, madam," he said. "I'm going to bring a charge against you for abduction and assault with intent to kill. And if there's any proof needed I'll show my canoe, full of water to the gunwale."

Here he kissed the girl again.

"You—you know her?" gasped Mr. McDonald, and dropped on a tree-trunk, as though he were too weak to stand.

"It looks like it, doesn't it?"

Here I happened to glance at Hutchins, and she was convulsed with mirth! Tish saw her, too, and glared at her; but she seemed to get worse. Then, without the slightest warning, she walked round the camp-fire and kissed Mr. McDonald solemnly on the top of his head.

"I give it up!" she said. "Somebody will have to marry you and take care of you. I'd better be the person."

* * * * *

"But why was the detective watching Hutchins?" said Charlie Sands. "Was it because he had heard of my Aunt Letitia's reckless nature? I am still bewildered."

"You remember the night we got the worms?"

"I see. The detective was watching all of you because you stole the worms."

"Stole nothing!" Tish snapped. "That's the girl's house. She's the Miss Newcomb you read about in the papers. Now do you understand?"

"Certainly I do. She was a fugitive from justice because the cat found dynamite in the woods. Or—perhaps I'm a trifle confused, but—Now I have it! She had stolen a gold-mounted traveling-bag and given it to McDonald. Lucky chap! I was crazy about Hutchins myself. You might tip her the word that I'm badly off for a traveling-case myself. But what about the P.T.S.? How did she happen on the scene?"

"She was engaged to the detective, and she was camping down the river. He had sent her word where he was. The red flag was to help her find him."

Tish knows Charlie Sands, so she let him talk. Then:—

"Mr. McDonald was too wealthy, Charlie," she said; "so when she wanted him to work and be useful, and he refused, she ran off and got a situation herself to teach him a lesson. She could drive a car. But her people heard about it, and that wretched detective was responsible for her safety. That's why he followed her about."

"I should like to follow her about myself," said Charlie Sands. "Do you think she's unalterably decided to take McDonald, money and all? He's still an idler. Lend me your car, Aunt Tish. There's a theory there; and—who knows?"

"He is going to work for six months before she marries him," Tish said. "He seems to like to work, now he has started."

She rang the bell and Hannah came to the door.

"Hannah," said Tish calmly, "call up the garage and tell McDonald to bring the car round. Mr. Sands is going out."

MY COUNTRY TISH OF THEE—

We had meant to go to Europe this last summer, and Tish would have gone anyhow, war or no war, if we had not switched her off onto something else. "Submarines fiddlesticks!" she said. "Give me a good life preserver, with a bottle of blackberry cordial fastened to it, and the sea has no terrors for me."

She said the proper way to do, in case the ship was torpedoed, was to go up on an upper deck, and let the vessel sink under one.

"Then without haste," she explained, "as the water rises about one, strike out calmly. The life-belt supports one, but swim gently for the exercise. It will prevent chilling. With a waterproof bag of crackers, and mild weather, one could go on comfortably for a day or two."

I still remember the despairing face Aggie turned to me. It was December then, and very cold.

However, she said nothing more until January. Early in that month Charlie Sands came to Tish's to Sunday dinner, and we were all there. The subject came up then.

It was about the time Tish took up vegetarianism, I remember that, because the only way she could induce Charlie Sands to come to dinner was to promise to have two chops for him. Personally I am not a vegetarian. I am not and never will be. I took a firm stand except when at Tish's home. But Aggie followed Tish's lead, of course, and I believe lived up to it as far as possible, although it is quite true that, stopping in one day unexpectedly to secure a new crochet pattern, I smelled broiling steak. But Aggie explained that she merely intended to use the juice from a small portion, having had one of her weak spells, the balance to go to the janitor's dog.

However, this is a digression.

"Europe!" said Charlie Sands. "Forget it! What in the name of the gastric juice is this I'm eating?"

It was a mixture of bran, raisins, and chopped nuts, as I recall it, moistened with water and pressed into a compact form. It was Tish's own invention. She called it "Bran-Nut," and was talking of making it in large quantities for sale.

Charlie Sands gave it up with a feeble gesture. "I'm sorry, Aunt Letitia," he said at last; "I'm a strong man ordinarily, but by the time I've got it masticated I'm too weak to swallow it. If—if one could have a stream of water playing on it while working, it would facilitate things."

"The Ostermaiers," said Aggie, "are going West."

"Good for the Ostermaiers," said Charlie Sands. "Great idea. See America first. 'My Country Tish of Thee,' etc. Why don't you three try it?"

Tish relinquished Europe slowly.

"One would think," Charlie Sands said, "that you were a German being asked to give up Belgium."

"What part of the West?" she demanded. "It's all civilized, isn't it?"

"The Rocky Mountains," said Charlie Sands, "will

never be civilized."

Tish broke off a piece of Bran-Nut, and when she thought no one was looking poured a little tea over it. There was a gleam in her eye that Aggie and I have learned to know.

"Mountains!" she said. "That ought to be good for Aggie's hay fever."

"I'd rather live with hay fever," Aggie put in sharply, "than cure it by falling over a precipice."

"You'll have to take a chance on that, of course," Charlie Sands said. "I'm not sure it will be safe, but I am sure it will be interesting."

Oh, he knew Tish well enough. Tell her a thing was dangerous, and no power could restrain her.

I do not mind saying that I was not keen about the thing. I had my fortune told years ago, and the palmist said that if a certain line had had a bend in it I should have been hanged. But since it did not, to be careful of high places.

"It's a sporting chance," said Charlie Sands, although I was prodding him under the table. "With some good horses and a bag of this—er—concentrated food, you would have the time of your young lives."

This was figurative. We are all of us round fifty.

"The—the Bran-Nut," he said, "would serve for both food and ammunition. I can see you riding along, now and then dropping a piece of it on the head of some unlucky mountain goat, and watching it topple over into eternity. I can see—"

"Riding!" said Aggie. "Then I'm not going. I have never been on a horse and I never intend to be."

"Don't be a fool," Tish snapped. "If you've never been on a horse, it's time and to spare you got on one."

Hannah had been clearing the table with her lips shut tight. Hannah is an old and privileged servant and has a most unfortunate habit of speaking her mind. So now she stopped beside Tish.

"You take my advice and go, Miss Tish," she said. "If you ride a horse round some and get an appetite, you'll go down on your knees and apologize to your Maker for the stuff we've been eating the last four weeks." She turned to Charlie Sands, and positively her chin was quivering. "I'm a healthy woman," she said, "and I work hard and need good nourishing food. When it's come to a point where I eat the cat's meat and let it go hungry," she said, "it's time either I lost my appetite or Miss Tish went away."

Well, Tish dismissed Hannah haughtily from the room, and the conversation went on. None of us had been far West, although Tish has a sister-in-law in, Toledo, Ohio. But owing to a quarrel over a pair of andirons that had been in the family for a time, she had never visited her.

"You'll like it, all of you," Charlie Sands said as we waited for the baked apples. "Once get started with a good horse between your knees, and—"

"I hope," Tish interrupted him, "that you do not think we are going to ride astride!"

"I'm darned sure of it."

That was Charlie Sands's way of talking. He does not mean to be rude, and he is really a young man of splendid character. But, as Tish says, contact with the world, although it has not spoiled him, has roughened his speech.

"You see," he explained, "there are places out there where the horses have to climb like goats. It's only fair to them to distribute your weight equally. A side saddle is likely to turn and drop you a mile or two down a crack."

Aggie went rather white and sneezed violently.

But Tish looked thoughtful. "It sounds reasonable," she said. "I've felt for along time that I'd be glad to discard skirts. Skirts," she said, "are badge of servitude, survivals of the harem, reminders of a time when nothing was expected of women but parasitic leisure."

I tried to tell her that she was wrong about the skirts. Miss MacGillicuddy, our missionary in India, had certainly said that the women in harems wore bloomers. But Tish left the room abruptly, returning shortly after with a volume of the encyclopaedia, and looked up the Rocky Mountains.

I remember it said that the highest ranges were, as compared with the size and shape of the earth, only as the corrugations on the skin of an orange. Either the man who wrote that had never seen an orange or he had never seen the Rocky Mountains. Orange, indeed! If he had said the upper end of a pineapple it would have been more like it. I wish the man who wrote it would go to Glacier Park. I am not a vindictive woman, but I know one or two places where I would like to place him and make him swallow that orange. I'd like to see him on a horse, on the brink of a canon a mile deep, and have his horse reach over the edge for a stray plant or two, or standing in a cloud up to his waist, so that, as Aggie so plaintively observed, "The lower half of one is in a snowstorm while the upper part is getting sunburned."

For we went. Oh, yes, we went. It is not the encyclopaedia's fault that we came back. But now that we are home, and nothing wrong except a touch of lumbago that Tish got from sleeping on the ground, and, of course, Aggie's unfortunate experience with her teeth, I look back on our various adventures with pleasure. I even contemplate a return next year, although Aggie says she will die first. But even that is not to be taken as final. The last time I went to see her, she had bought a revolver from the janitor and was taking lessons in loading it.

The Ostermaiers went also. Not with us, however. The congregation made up a purse for the purpose, and Tish and Aggie and I went further, and purchased a cigar-case for Mr. Ostermaier and a quantity of cigars. Smoking is the good man's only weakness.

I must say, however, that it is absurd to hear Mrs. Ostermaier boasting of the trip. To hear her talk, one would think they had done the whole thing, instead of sitting in an automobile and looking up at the mountains. I shall never forget the day they were in a car passing along a road, and we crossed unexpectedly ahead of them and went on straight up the side of a mountain.

Tish had a sombrero on the side of her head, and was resting herself in the saddle by having her right leg thrown negligently over the horse's neck. With the left foot she was kicking our pack-horse, a creature so scarred with brands that Tish had named her Jane, after a cousin of hers who had had so many operations that Tish says she is now entirely unfurnished.

Mr. Ostermaier's face was terrible, and only two days ago Mrs. Ostermaier came over to ask about putting an extra width in the skirt to her last winter's suit. But it is my belief that she came to save Tish's soul, and nothing else.

"I'm so glad wide skirts have come in," she said. "They're so modest, aren't they, Miss Tish?"

"Not in a wind," Tish said, eying her coldly.

"I do think, dear Miss Tish," she went on with her eyes down, "that to—to go about in riding-breeches before a young man is—well, it is hardly discreet, is it?"

I saw Tish glancing about the room. She was pretty angry, and I knew perfectly well what she wanted. I put my knitting-bag over Charlie Sands's tobacco-pouch.

Tish had learned to roll cigarettes out in Glacier Park. Not that she smoked them, of course, but she said she might as well know how. There was no knowing when it would come in handy. And when she wishes to calm herself she reaches instinctively for what Bill used to call, strangely, "the makings."

"If," she said, her eye still roving,—"if it was any treat to a twenty-four-year-old cowpuncher to see three elderly women in riding-breeches, Mrs. Ostermaier,—and it's kind of you to think so,—why, I'm not selfish."

Mrs. Ostermaier's face was terrible. She gathered up her skirt and rose. "I shall not tell Mr. Ostermaier what you have just said," she observed with her mouth set hard. "We owe you a great deal, especially the return of my earrings. But I must request, Miss Tish, that you do not voice such sentiments in the Sunday school."

Tish watched her out. Then she sat down and rolled eleven cigarettes for Charlie Sands, one after the other. At last she spoke.

"I'm not sure," she said tartly, "that if I had it to do over again I'd do it. That woman's not a Christian. I was thinking," she went on, "of giving them a part of the reward to go to Asbury Park with. But she'd have to wear blinders on the bathing-beach, so I'll not do it."

However, I am ahead of my recital.

For a few days Tish said nothing more, but one Sunday morning, walking home from church, she turned to me suddenly and said:—

"Lizzie, you're fat."

"I'm as the Lord made me," I replied with some spirit.

"Fiddlesticks!" said Tish. "You're as your own sloth and overindulgence has made you. Don't blame the Good Man for it."

Now, I am a peaceful woman, and Tish is as my own sister, and indeed even more so. But I was roused to anger by her speech.

"I've been fleshy all my life," I said. "I'm no lazier than most, and I'm a dratted sight more agreeable than some I know, on account of having the ends of my nerves padded."

But she switched to another subject in her characteristic manner.

"Have you ever reflected, either of you," she observed, "that we know nothing of this great land of ours? That we sing of loving 'thy rocks and rills, thy woods and templed hills'—although the word 'templed' savors of paganism and does not belong in a national hymn? And that it is all balderdash?"

Aggie took exception to this and said that she loved her native land, and had been south to Pinehurst and west to see her niece in Minneapolis, on account of the baby having been named for her.

But Tish merely listened with a grim smile. "Travel from a car window," she observed, "is no better than travel in a nickelodeon. I have done all of that I am going to. I intend to become acquainted with my native land, closely acquainted. State by State I shall wander over it, refreshing soul and body and using muscles too long unused."

"Tish!" Aggie quavered. "You are not going on another walking-tour?"

Only a year or two before Tish had read Stevenson's "Travels with a Donkey," and had been possessed to follow his example. I have elsewhere recorded the details of that terrible trip. Even I turned pale, I fear, and cast a nervous eye toward the table where Tish keeps her reading-matter.

Tish is imaginative, and is always influenced by the latest book she has read. For instance, a volume on "Nursing at the Front" almost sent her across to France, although she cannot make a bed and never could, and turns pale at the sight of blood; and another time a book on flying machines sent her up into the air, mentally if not literally. I shall never forget the time she secured some literature on the Mormon Church, and the difficulty I had in smuggling it out under my coat.

Tish did not refute the walking-tour at once, but fell into a deep reverie.

It is not her custom to confide her plans to us until they are fully shaped and too far on to be interfered with, which accounts for our nervousness.

On arriving at her apartment, however, we found a map laid out on the table and the Rocky Mountains marked with pins. We noticed that whenever she straightened from the table she grunted.

"What we want," Tish said, "is isolation. No people. No crowds. No servants. If I don't get away from Hannah soon I'll murder her."

"It wouldn't hurt to see somebody now and then, Tish," Aggie objected.

"Nobody," Tish said firmly. "A good horse is companion enough." She forgot herself and straightened completely, and she groaned.

"We might meet some desirable people, Tish," I put in firmly. "If we do, I don't intend to run like a rabbit."

"Desirable people!" Tish scoffed. "In the Rocky Mountains! My dear Lizzie, every desperado in the country takes refuge in the Rockies. Of course, if you want to take up with that class—"

Aggie sneezed and looked wretched. As for me, I made up my mind then and there that if Letitia Carberry was going to such a neighborhood, she was not going alone. I am not much with a revolver, but mighty handy with a pair of lungs.

Well, Tish had it all worked out. "I've found the very place," she said. "In the first place, it's Government property. When our country puts aside a part of itself as a public domain we should show our appreciation. In the second place, it's wild. I'd as soon spend a vacation in Central Park near the Zoo as in the Yellowstone. In the third place, with an Indian reservation on one side and a national forest on the other, it's bound to be lonely. Any tourist," she said scornfully, "can go to the Yosemite and be photographed under a redwood tree."

"Do the Indians stay on the reservation?" Aggie asked feebly.

"Probably not," Tish observed coldly. "Once for all, Aggie—if you are going to run like a scared deer every time you see an Indian or a bear, I wish you would go to Asbury Park."

She forgot herself then and sat down quickly, an action which was followed by an agonized expression.

"Tish," I said sharply, "you have been riding a horse!

"Only in a cinder ring," she replied with unwonted docility. "The teacher said I would be a trifle stiff."

"How long did you ride?"

"Not more than twenty minutes," she said. "The lesson was to be an hour, but somebody put a nickel in a mechanical piano, and the creature I was on started going sideways."

Well, she had fallen off and had to be taken home in a taxicab. When Aggie heard it she simply took the pins out of the map and stuck them in Tish's cushion. Her mouth was set tight.

"I didn't really fall," Tish said. "I sat down, and it was cinders, and not hard. It has made my neck stiff, that's all."

"That's enough," said Aggie. "If I've got to seek pleasure by ramming my spinal column up into my skull and crowding my brains, I'll stay at home."

"You can't fall out of a Western saddle," Tish protested rather bitterly. "And if I were you, Aggie, I wouldn't worry about crowding my brains."

However, she probably regretted this speech, for she added more gently: "A high altitude will help your hay fever, Aggie."

Aggie said with some bitterness that her hay fever did not need to be helped. That, as far as she could see, it was strong and flourishing. At that matters rested, except for a bit of conversation just before we left. Aggie had put on her sweater vest and her muffler and the jacket of her winter suit and was getting into her fur coat, when Tish said: "Soft as mush, both of you!"

"If you think, Tish Carberry," I began, "that I—"

"Apple dumplings!" said Tish. "Sofa pillows! Jellyfish! Not a muscle to divide between you!"

I drew on my woolen tights angrily.

"Elevators!" Tish went on scornfully. "Street cars and taxicabs! No wonder your bodies are mere masses of protoplasm, or cellulose, or whatever it is."

"Since when," said Aggie, "have you been walking to develop yourself, Tish? I must say—"

Here anger brought on one of her sneezing attacks, and she was unable to finish.

Tish stood before us oracularly. "After next September," she said, "you will both scorn the sloth of civilization. You will move about for the joy of moving about. You will have cast off the shackles of the flesh and be born anew. That is, if a plan of mine goes through. Lizzie, you will lose fifty pounds!"

Well, I didn't want to lose fifty pounds. After our summer in the Maine woods I had gone back to find that my new tailor-made coat, which had fitted me exactly, and being stiffened with haircloth kept its shape off and looked as if I myself were hanging to the hook, had caved in on me in several places. Just as I had gone to the expense of having it taken in I began to put on flesh again, and had to have it let out. Besides, no woman over forty should ever reduce, at least not violently. She wrinkles. My face that summer had fallen into accordion plaits, and I had the curious feeling of having enough skin for two.

Aggie had suggested at that time that I have my cheeks filled out with paraffin, which I believe cakes and gives the appearance of youth. But Mrs. Ostermaier knew a woman who had done so, and being hit on one side by a snowball, the padding broke in half, one part moving up under her eye and the second lodging at the angle of her jaw. She tried lying on a hot-water bottle to melt the pieces and bring them together again, but they did not remain fixed, having developed a wandering habit and slipping unexpectedly now and then. Mrs. Ostermaier says it is painful to watch her holding them in place when she yawns.

Strangely enough, however, a few weeks later Tish's enthusiasm for the West had apparently vanished. When several weeks went by and the atlas had disappeared from her table, and she had given up vegetarianism for Swedish movements, we felt that we were to have a quiet summer after all, and Aggie wrote to a hotel in Asbury Park about rooms for July and August.

There was a real change in Tish. She stopped knitting abdominal bands for the soldiers in Europe, for one thing, although she had sent over almost a dozen very tasty ones. In the evenings, when we dropped in to chat with her, she said very little and invariably dozed in her chair.

On one such occasion, Aggie having inadvertently stepped on the rocker of her chair while endeavoring by laying a hand on Tish's brow to discover if she was feverish, the chair tilted back and Tish wakened with a jerk.

She immediately fell to groaning and clasped her hands to the small of her back, quite ignoring poor

Aggie, whom the chair had caught in the epigastric region, and who was compelled for some time to struggle for breath.

"Jumping Jehoshaphat!" said Tish in an angry tone. It is rare for Tish to use the name of a Biblical character in this way, but she was clearly suffering. "What in the world are you doing, Aggie?"

"T-t-trying to breathe," poor Aggie replied.

"Then I wish," Tish said coldly, "that you would make the effort some place else than on the rocker of my chair. You jarred me, and I am in no state to be jarred."

But she refused to explain further, beyond saying, in reply to a question of mine, that she was not feverish and that she had not been asleep, having merely closed her eyes to rest them. Also she affirmed that she was not taking riding-lessons. We both noticed however, that she did not leave her chair during the time we were there, and that she was sitting on the sofa cushion I had made her for the previous Christmas, and on which I had embroidered the poet Moore's beautiful words: "Come, rest in this bosom."

As Aggie was still feeling faint, I advised her to take a mouthful of blackberry cordial, which Tish keeps for emergencies in her bathroom closet. Immediately following her departure the calm of the evening was broken by a loud shriek.

It appeared, on my rushing to the bathroom, while Tish sat heartlessly still, that Aggie, not seeing a glass, had placed the bottle to her lips and taken quite a large mouthful of liniment, which in color resembled the cordial. I found her sitting on the edge of the bathtub in a state of collapse.

"I'm poisoned!" she groaned. "Oh, Lizzie, I am not fit to die!"

I flew with the bottle to Tish, who was very calm and stealthily rubbing one of her ankles.

"Do her good," Tish said. "Take some of the stiffness out of her liver, for one thing. But you might keep an eye on her. It's full of alcohol."

"What's the antidote?" I asked, hearing Aggie's low groans.

"The gold cure is the only thing I can think of at the moment," said Tish coldly, and started on the other ankle.

I merely record this incident to show the change in Tish. Aggie was not seriously upset, although dizzy for an hour or so and very talkative, especially about Mr. Wiggins.

Tish was changed. Her life, which mostly had been an open book to us, became filled with mystery. There were whole days when she was not to be located anywhere, and evenings, as I have stated, when she dozed in her chair.

As usual when we are worried about Tish, we consulted her nephew, Charlie Sands. But like all members of the masculine sex he refused to be worried.

"She'll be all right," he observed. "She takes these spells. But trust the old lady to come up smiling."

"It's either Christian Science or osteopathy," Aggie said dolefully. "She's not herself. The fruit cake she sent me the other day tasted very queer, and Hannah thinks she put ointment in instead of butter."

"Ointments!" observed Charlie thoughtfully. "And salves! By George, I wonder—I'll tell you," he said: "I'll keep an eye open for a few days. The symptoms sound like—But never mind. I'll let you know."

We were compelled to be satisfied with this, but for several days we lingered in anxiety. During that painful interval nothing occurred to enlighten us, except one conversation with Tish.

We had taken dinner with her, and she seemed to be all right again and more than usually active. She had given up the Bran-Nut after breaking a tooth on it, and was eating rare beef, which she had heard was digested in the spleen or some such place, thus resting the stomach for a time. She left us, however, immediately after the meal, and Hannah, her maid, tiptoed into the room.

"I'm that nervous I could scream," she said. "Do you know what she's doing now?

"No, Hannah," I said with bitter sarcasm. "Long ago I learned never to surmise what Miss Tish is doing."

"She's in the bathroom, standing on one foot and waving the other in the air. She's been doing it," Hannah said, "for weeks. First one foot, then the other. And that ain't all."

"You've been spying on Miss Tish," Aggie said. "Shame on you, Hannah!"

"I have, Miss Aggie. Spy I have and spy I will, while there's breath in my body. Twenty years have I—Do you know what she does when she come home from these sneakin' trips of hers? She sits in a hot bath until the wonder is that her blood ain't turned to water. And after that she uses liniment. Her underclothes is that stained up with it that I'm ashamed to hang 'em out."

Here Tish returned and, after a suspicious glance at Hannah, sat down. Aggie and I glanced at each other. She did not, as she had for some time past, line the chair with pillows, and there was an air about her almost of triumph.

She did not, however, volunteer any explanation. Aggie and I were driven to speculation, in which we indulged on our way home, Aggie being my guest at the time, on account of her janitor's children having measles, and Aggie never having had them, although recalling a severe rash as a child, with other measly symptoms.

"She has something in mind for next summer," said Aggie apprehensively, "and she is preparing her strength for it. Tish is forehanded if nothing else."

"Well," I remarked with some bitterness, "if we are going along it might be well to prepare us too."

"Something," Aggie continued, "that requires landing on one foot with the other in the air."

"Don't drivel," said I. "She's not likely going into the Russian ballet. She's training her muscles, that's all."

But the mystery was solved the following morning when Charlie Sands called me up.

"I've got it, beloved aunt," he said.

"Got what?" said I.

"What the old lady is up to. She's a wonder, and no mistake. Only I think it was stingy of her not to let you and Aunt Aggie in."

He asked me to get Aggie and meet him at the office as soon as possible, but he refused to explain further. And he continued to refuse until we had arrived at our destination, a large brick building in the center of the city.

"Now," he said, "take a long breath and go in. And mind—no excitement."

We went in. There was a band playing and people

circling at a mile a minute. In the center there was a cleared place, and Tish was there on ice skates. An instructor had her by the arm, and as we looked she waved him off, gave herself a shove forward with one foot, and then, with her arms waving, she made a double curve, first on one foot and then on the other.

"The outside edge, by George!" said Charlie Sands. "The old sport!"

Unluckily at that moment Tish saw us, and sat down violently on the ice. And a quite nice-looking young man fell over her and lay stunned for several seconds. We rushed round the arena, expecting to see them both carried out, but Tish was uninjured, and came skating toward us with her hands in her pockets. It was the young man who had to be assisted out.

"Well," she said, fetching up against the railing with a bang, "of course you had to come before I was ready for you! In a week I'll really be skating."

We said nothing, but looked at her, and I am afraid our glances showed disapproval, for she straightened her hat with a jerk.

"Well?" she said. "You're not tongue-tied all of a sudden, are you? Can't a woman take a little exercise without her family and friends coming snooping round and acting as if she'd broken the Ten Commandments?"

"Breaking the Ten Commandments!" I said witheringly. "Breaking a leg more likely. If you could have seen yourself, Tish Carberry, sprawled on that ice at your age, and both your arteries and your bones brittle, as the specialist told you,—and I heard him myself,—you'd take those things off your feet and go home and hide your head."

"I wish I had your breath, Lizzie," Tish said. "I'd be a submarine diver."

Saying which she skated off, and did not come near us again. A young gentleman went up to her and asked her to skate, though I doubt if she had ever seen him before. And as we left the building in disapproval they were doing fancy turns in the middle of the place, and a crowd was gathering round them.

Owing to considerable feeling being roused by the foregoing incident, we did not see much of Tish for a week. If a middle-aged woman wants to make a spectacle of herself, both Aggie and I felt that she needed to be taught a lesson. Besides, we knew Tish. With her, to conquer a thing is to lose interest.

On the anniversary of the day Aggie became engaged to Mr. Wiggins, Tish asked us both to dinner, and we buried the hatchet, or rather the skates. It was when dessert came that we realized how everything that had occurred had been preparation for the summer, and that we were not going to Asbury Park, after all.

"It's like this," said Tish. "Hannah, go out and close the door, and don't stand listening. I have figured it all out," she said, when Hannah had slammed out. "The muscles used in skating are the ones used in mountain-climbing. Besides, there may be times when a pair of skates would be handy going over the glaciers. It's not called Glacier Park for nothing, I dare say. When we went into the Maine woods we went unprepared. This time I intend to be ready for any emergency."

But we gave her little encouragement. We would go along, and told her so. But further than that I refused to prepare. I would not skate, and said so.

"Very well, Lizzie," she said. "Don't blame me if you

find yourself unable to cope with mountain hardships. I merely felt this way: if each of us could do one thing well it might be helpful. There's always snow, and if Aggie would learn to use snowshoes it might be valuable."

"Where could I practice?" Aggie demanded.

But Tish went on, ignoring Aggie's sarcastic tone. "And if you, Lizzie, would learn to throw a lasso, or lariat,—I believe both terms are correct,—it would be a great advantage, especially in case of meeting ferocious animals. The park laws will not allow us to kill them, and it would be mighty convenient, Lizzie. Not to mention that it would be an accomplishment few women possess."

I refused to make the attempt, although Tish sent for the clothesline, and with the aid of the encyclopaedia made a loop in the end of it. Finally she became interested herself, and when we left rather downhearted at ten o'clock she had caught the rocking-chair three times and broken the clock.

Aggie and I prepared with little enthusiasm, I must confess. We had as much love for the rocks and rills of our great country as Tish, but, as Aggie observed, there were rocks and rocks, and one could love them without climbing up them or falling off them.

The only comfort we had was that Charlie Sands said that we should ride ponies, and not horses. My niece's children have a pony which is very gentle and not much larger than a dog, which comes up on the porch for lumps of sugar. We were lured to a false sense of security, I must say.

As far as we could see, Tish was making few preparations for the trip. She said we could get everything we needed at the park entrance, and that the riding was merely sitting in a saddle and letting the pony do the rest. But on the 21st of June, the anniversary of the day Aggie was to have been married, we went out to decorate Mr. Wiggins's last resting-place, and coming out of the cemetery we met Tish.

She was on a horse, astride!

She was not alone. A gentleman was riding beside her, and he had her horse by a long leather strap.

She pretended not to see us, and Aggie unfortunately waved her red parasol at her. The result was most amazing. The beast she was on jerked itself free in an instant, and with the same movement, apparently, leaped the hedge beside the road. One moment there was Tish, in a derby hat and breeches, and the next moment there was only the gentleman, with his mouth open.

Aggie collapsed, moaning, in the road, and beyond the hedge we could hear the horse leaping tombstones in the cemetery.

"Oh, Tish!" Aggie wailed.

I broke my way through the hedge to find what was left of her, while the riding-master bolted for the gate. But to my intense surprise Tish was not on the ground. Then I saw her. She was still on the creature, and she was coming back along the road, with her riding-hat on the back of her head and a gleam in her eye that I knew well enough was a gleam of triumph.

She halted the thing beside me and looked down with a patronizing air.

"He's a trifle nervous this morning," she said calmly. "Hasn't been worked enough. Good horse, though,— very neat jump."

Then she rode on and out through the gates, ignoring Aggie's pitiful wail and scorning the leading-string the instructor offered.

We reached Glacier Park without difficulty, although Tish insisted on talking to the most ordinary people on the train, and once, losing her, we found her in the drawing-room learning to play bridge, although not a card-player, except for casino. Though nothing has ever been said, I believe she learned when too late that they were playing for money, as she borrowed ten dollars from me late in the afternoon and was looking rather pale.

"What do you think?" she said, while I was getting the money from the safety pocket under my skirt. "The young man who knocked me down on the ice that day is on the train. I've just exchanged a few words with him. He was not much hurt, although unconscious for a short time. His name is Bell—James C. Bell."

Soon after that Tish brought him to us, and we had a nice talk. He said he had not been badly hurt on the ice, although he got a cut on the forehead from Tish's skate, requiring two stitches.

After a time he and Aggie went out on the platform, only returning when Aggie got a cinder in her eye.

"Just think," she said as he went for water to use in my eye-cup, "he is going to meet the girl he is in love with out at the park. She has been there for four weeks. They are engaged. He is very much in love. He didn't talk of anything else."

She told him she had confided his tender secret to us, and instead of looking conscious he seemed glad to have three people instead of one to talk to about her.

"You see, it's like this," he said: "She is very good

looking, and in her town a moving-picture company has its studio. That part's all right. I suppose we have to have movies. But the fool of a director met her at a party, and said she would photograph well and ought to be with them. He offered her a salary, and it went to her head. She's young," he added, "and he said she could be as great a hit as Mary Pickford."

"How sad!" said Aggie. "But of course she refused?"

"Well, no, she liked the idea. It got me worried. Worried her people too. Her father's able to give her a good home, and I'm expecting to take that job off his hands in about a year. But girls are queer. She wanted to try it awfully."

It developed that he had gone to her folks about it, and they'd offered her a vacation with some of her school friends in Glacier Park.

"It's pretty wild out there," he went on, "and we felt that the air, and horseback riding and everything, would make her forget the movies. I hope so. She's there now. But she's had the bug pretty hard. Got so she was always posing, without knowing it."

But he was hopeful that she would be cured, and said she was to meet him at the station.

"She's an awfully nice girl, you understand," he finished. "It's only that this thing got hold of her and needed driving out."

Well, we were watching when the train drew in at Glacier Park Station, and she was there. She was a very pretty girl, and it was quite touching to see him look at her. But Aggie observed something and remarked on it.

"She's not as glad to see him as he is to see her," she said. "He was going to kiss her, and she moved back."

In the crowd we lost sight of them, but that evening, sitting in the lobby of the hotel, we saw Mr. Bell wandering round alone. He looked depressed, and Aggie beckoned to him.

"How is everything?" she asked. "Is the cure working?"

He dropped into a chair and looked straight ahead.

"Not so you could notice it!" he said bitterly. "Would you believe that there's a moving-picture outfit here, taking scenes in the park?"

"No!"

"There is. They've taken two thousand feet of her already, dressed like an Indian," he said in a tone of suppressed fury. "It makes me sick. I dare say if we tied her in a well some fool would lower a camera on a rope."

Just at that moment she sauntered past us with a reddish-haired young man. Mr. Bell ignored her, although I saw her try to catch his eye.

"That's the moving-picture man with her," he said in a low, violent tone when they had passed. "Name's Oliver." He groaned. "He's told her she ought to go in for the business. She'd be a second Mary Pickford! I'd like to kill him!" He rose savagely and left us.

We spent the night in the hotel at the park entrance, and I could not get to sleep. Tish was busy engaging a guide and going over our supplies, and at eleven o'clock Aggie came into my room and sat down on the bed.

"I can't sleep, Lizzie," she said. "That poor Mr. Bell is on my mind. Besides, did you see those ferocious Indians hanging round?"

Well, I had seen them, but said nothing.

"They would scalp one as quick as not," Aggie went

on. "And who's to know but that our guide will be in league with them? I've lost my teeth," she said with a flash of spirit, "but so far I've kept my hair, and mean to if possible. That old Indian has a scalp tied to the end of a stick. Lizzie, I'm nervous."

"If it is only hair they want, I don't mind their taking my switch," I observed, trying to be facetious, although uneasy. As to the switch, it no longer matched my hair, and I would have parted from it without a pang.

"And another thing," said Aggie: "Tish can talk about ponies until she is black in the face. The creatures are horses. I've seen them."

Well, I knew that, too, by that time. As we walked to the hotel from the train I had seen one of than carrying on. It was arching its back like a cat that's just seen a strange dog, and with every arch it swelled its stomach. At the third heave it split the strap that held the saddle on, and then it kicked up in the rear and sent saddle and rider over its head. So far as I had seen, no casualty had resulted, but it had set me thinking. Given a beast with an India-rubber spine and no sense of honor, I felt I would be helpless.

Tish came in just then and we confronted her.

"Ponies!" I said bitterly. "They are horses, if I know a horse. And, moreover, it's well enough for you, Tish Carberry, to talk about gripping a horse with your knees. I'm not built that way, and you know it. Besides, no knee grip will answer when a creature begins to act like a cat in a fit."

Aggie here had a bright idea. She said that she had seen pictures of pneumatic jackets to keep people from drowning, and that Mr. McKee, a buyer at one of the stores at home, had taken one, fully inflated, when he crossed to Paris for autumn suits.

"I would like to have one, Tish," she finished. "It would break the force of a fall anyhow, even if it did puncture."

Tish, who was still dressed, went out to the curio shop in the lobby, and returned with the sad news that there was nothing of the sort on sale.

We were late in getting started the next morning owing partly to Aggie's having put her riding-breeches on wrong, and being unable to sit down when once in the saddle. But the main reason was the guide we had engaged. Tish heard him using profane language to one of the horses and dismissed him on the spot.

The man who was providing our horses and outfit, however, understood, and in a short time returned with another man.

"I've got a good one for you now, Miss Carberry," he said. "Safe and perfectly gentle, and as mild as milk.

Only has one fault, and maybe you won't mind that. He smokes considerably."

"I don't object, as long as it's in the open air," Tish said.

So that was arranged. But I must say that the new man did not look mild. He had red hair, although a nice smile with a gold tooth, and his trousers were of white fur, which looked hot for summer.

"You are sure that you don't use strong language?" Tish asked.

"No, ma'am," he said. "I was raised strict, and very particular as to swearing. Dear, dear now, would you look at that cinch! Blow up their little tummies, they do, when they're cinched, and when they breathe it out, the saddle's as loose as the tongues of some of these here tourists."

Tish swung herself up without any trouble, but owing to a large canvas bag on the back of my saddle I was unable to get my leg across, and was compelled to have it worked over, a little at a time. At last, however, we were ready. A white pack-horse, carrying our tents and cooking-utensils, was led by Bill, which proved to be the name of our cowboy guide.

Mr. Bell came to say good-bye and to wish us luck. But he looked unhappy, and there was no sign whatever of the young lady, whose name we had learned was Helen.

"I may see you on the trail," he said sadly. "I'm about sick of this place, and I'm thinking of clearing out."

Aggie reminded him that faint heart never won fair lady, but he only shook his head.

"I'm not so sure that I want to win," he said. "Marriage is a serious business, and I don't know that

I'd care to have a wife that followed a camera like a street kid follows a brass band. It wouldn't make for a quiet home."

We left him staring wistfully into the distance.

Tish sat in her saddle and surveyed the mountain peaks that rose behind the hotel.

"Twenty centuries are looking down upon us!" she said. "The crest of our native land lies before us. We will conquer those beetling crags, or die trying. All right, Bill. Forward!"

Bill led off, followed by the pack-horse, then Tish, Aggie and myself. We kept on in this order for some time, which gave me a chance to observe Aggie carefully. I am not much of a horsewoman myself, having never been on a horse before. But my father was fond of riding, and I soon adapted myself to the horse's gait, especially when walking. On level stretches, however, where Bill spurred his horse to a trot, I was not so comfortable, and Aggie appeared to strike the saddle in a different spot every time she descended.

Once, on her turning her profile to me in a glance of despair, I was struck by the strange and collapsed appearance of her face. This was explained, however, when my horse caught up to hers on a wider stretch of road, and I saw that she had taken out her teeth and was holding them in her hand.

"Al-almost swallowed them," she gasped. "Oh, Lizzie, to think of a summer of this!"

At last we left the road and turned onto a footpath, which instantly commenced to rise. Tish called back something about the beauties of nature and riding over a carpet of flowers, but my horse was fording a small stream at the time and I was too occupied to reply. The path—or trail, which is what Bill called it—grew more steep, and I let go of the lines and held to the horn of my saddle. The horses were climbing like goats.

"Tish," Aggie called desperately, "I can't stand this. I'm going back! I'm—Lordamighty!"

Fortunately Tish did not hear this. We had suddenly emerged on the brink of a precipice. A two-foot path clung to the cliff, and along the very edge of this the horses walked, looking down in an interested manner now and then. My blood turned to water and I closed my eyes.

"Tish!" Aggie shrieked.

But the only effect of this was to start her horse into a trot. I had closed my eyes, but I opened them in time to see Aggie give a wild clutch and a low moan.

In a few moments the trail left the edge, and Aggie turned in her saddle and looked back at me.

"I lost my lower set back there," she said. "They went over the edge. I suppose they're falling yet."

"It's a good thing it wasn't the upper set," I said, to comfort her. "As far as appearance goes—"

"Appearance!" she said bitterly. "Do you suppose we'll meet anybody but desperadoes and Indians in a place like this? And not an egg with us, of course."

The eggs referred to her diet, as at different times, when having her teeth repaired, she can eat little else.

"Ham," she called back in a surly tone, "and hard tack, I suppose! I'll starve, Lizzie, that's all. If only we had brought some junket tablets!"

With the exception of this incident the morning was quiet. Tish and Bill talked prohibition, which he believed in, and the tin pans on the pack-horse clattered, and we got higher all the time, and rode through waterfalls and along the edge of death. By noon I did not much care if the horses fell over or not. The skin was off me in a number of places, and my horse did not like me, and showed it by nipping back at my leg here and there.

At eleven o'clock, riding through a valley on a trail six inches wide, Bill's horse stepped on a hornets' nest. The insects were probably dazed at first, but by the time Tish's horse arrived they were prepared, and the next thing we knew Tish's horse was flying up the mountain-side as if it had gone crazy, and Bill was shouting to us to stop.

The last we saw of Tish for some time was her horse leaping a mountain stream, and jumping like a kangaroo, and Bill was following.

"She'll be killed!" Aggie cried. "Oh, Tish, Tish!"

"Don't yell," I said. "You'll start the horses. And for Heaven's sake, Aggie," I added grimly, "remember that this is a pleasure trip."

It was a half-hour before Tish and Bill returned. Tish was a chastened woman. She said little or nothing, but borrowed some ointment from me for her face, where the branches of trees had scraped it, while Bill led the horses round the fatal spot. I recall, however, that she said she wished now that we had brought the other guide.

"Because I feel," she observed, "that a little strong language would be a relief."

We had luncheon at noon in a sylvan glade, and Aggie was pathetic. She dipped a cracker in a cup of tea, and sat off by herself under a tree. Tish, however, had recovered her spirits.

"Throw out your chests, and breathe deep of this

pure air unsullied by civilization," she cried. "Aggie, fill yourself with ozone."

"Humph!" said Aggie. "It's about all I will fill myself with."

"Think," Tish observed, "of the fools and dolts who are living under roofs, struggling, contending, plotting, while all Nature awaits them."

"With stings," Aggie said nastily, "and teeth, and horns, and claws, and every old thing! Tish, I want to go back. I'm not happy, and I don't enjoy scenery when I'm not happy. Besides, I can't eat the landscape."

As I look back, I believe it would have been better if we had returned. I think of that day, some time later, when we made the long descent from the Piegan Pass under such extraordinary circumstances, and I realize that, although worse for our bodies, which had grown strong and agile, so that I have, later on, seen Aggie mount her horse on a run, it would have been better for our nerves had we returned.

We were all perfectly stiff after luncheon, and Aggie was sulking also. Bill was compelled to lift us into our saddles, and again we started up and up. The trail was now what he called a "switchback." Halfway up Aggie refused to go farther, but on looking back decided not to return either.

"I shall not go another step," she called. "Here I am, and here I stay till I die."

"Very well," Tish said from overhead. "I suppose you don't expect us all to stay and die with you. I'll tell your niece when I see her."

Aggie thought better of it, however, and followed on, with her eyes closed and her lips moving in prayer. She happened to open them at a bad place, although safe enough, according to Bill, and nothing to what we were coming to a few days later. Opening them as she did on a ledge of rock which sloped steeply for what appeared to be several miles down on each side, she uttered a piercing shriek, followed by a sneeze. As before, her horse started to run, and Aggie is, I believe Bill said, the only person in the world who ever took that place at a canter.

We were to take things easy the first day, Bill advised. "Till you get your muscles sort of eased up, ladies," he said. "If you haven't been riding astride, a horse's back seems as wide as the roof of a church. But we'll get a rest now. The rest of the way is walking."

"I can't walk," Aggie said. "I can't get my knees together."

"Sorry, ma'am," said Bill. "We're going down now, and the animals has to be led. That's one of the diversions of a trip like this. First you ride and than you walk. And then you ride again. This here's one of the show places, although easy of access from the entrance. Be a good place for a holdup, I've always said."

"A holdup?" Tish asked. Her enthusiasm seemed to have flagged somewhat, but at this she brightened up.

"Yes'm. You see, we're near the Canadian border, and it would be easy for a gang to slip over and back again. Don't know why we've never had one. Yellowstone can boast of a number."

I observed tartly that I considered it nothing to boast of, but Bill did not agree with me.

"It doesn't hurt a neighborhood none," he observed. "Adds romance, as you might say."

He went on and, happening to slide on a piece of shale at that moment, I sat down unexpectedly and the horse put its foot on me.

I felt embittered and helpless, but the others kept on.

"Very well," I said, "go on. Don't mind me. If this creature wants to sit in my lap, well and good. I expect it's tired."

But as they went on callously, I was obliged to shove the creature off and to hobble on. Bill was still babbling about holdups, and Aggie was saying that he was sunstruck, but of course it did not matter.

We made very slow progress, owing to taking frequent rests, and late in the afternoon we were overtaken by Mr. Bell, on foot and carrying a pack. He would have passed on without stopping, but Aggie hailed him.

"Not going to hike, are you?" she said pleasantly. Aggie is fond of picking up the vernacular of a region.

"No," he said in a surly tone quite unlike his former urbane manner, "I'm merely taking this pack out for a walk."

But he stopped and mopped his face.

"To tell you the truth, ladies," he said, "I'm working off a little steam, that's all. I was afraid, if I stayed round the hotel, I'd do something I'd be sorry for. There are times when I am not a fit companion for any one, and this is one of them."

We invited him to join us, but he refused.

"No, I'm better alone," he said. "When things get too strong for me on the trail I can sling things about. I've been throwing boulders down the mountain every now and then. I'd just as soon they hit somebody as not. Also," he added, "I'm safer away from any red-headed men."

We saw him glance at Bill, and understood. Mr.

Oliver was red-headed.

"Love's an awful thing," said Bill as the young man went on, kicking stones out of his way. "I'm glad I ain't got it."

Tish turned and eyed him. "True love is a very beautiful thing," she rebuked him. "Although a single woman myself, I believe in it. 'Come live with me and be my love,'" she quoted, sitting down to shake a stone out of her riding-boot.

Bill looked startled. "I might say," he said hastily, "that I may have misled you, ladies. I'm married."

"You said you had never been in love," Tish said sharply.

"Well, not to say real love," he replied. "She was the cook of an outfit I was with and it just came about natural. She was going to leave, which meant that I'd have to do the cooking, which I ain't much at, especially pastry. So I married her."

Tish gave him a scornful glance but said nothing and we went on.

We camped late that afternoon beside Two Medicine Lake, and while Bill put up the tents the three of us sat on a log and soaked our aching feet in the water which was melted glacier, and naturally cold.

What was our surprise, on turning somewhat, to see the angry lover fishing on a point near by. While we stared he pulled out a large trout, and stalked away without a glance in our direction. As Tish, with her usual forethought, had brought a trout rod, she hastily procured it, but without result.

"Of course," Aggie said, "no fish! I could eat a piece of broiled fish. I dare say I shall be skin and bone at the end of this trip—and not much skin."

Bill had set up the sleeping-tent and built a fire, and it looked cozy and comfortable. But Tish had the young man on her mind, and after supper she put on a skirt which she had brought along and went to see him.

"I'd take him some supper, Bill," she said, "but you are correct: you are no cook."

She disappeared among the bushes, only to return in a short time, jerking off her skirt as she came.

"He says all he wants is to be let alone," she said briefly. "I must say I'm disappointed in him. He was very agreeable before."

I pass without comment over the night. Bill had put up the tent over the root of a large tree, and we disposed ourselves about it as well as we could. In the course of the night one of the horses broke loose and put its head inside the tent. Owing to Aggie's thinking it was a bear, Tish shot at it, fortunately missing it.

But the frightened animal ran away, and Bill was until noon the next day finding it. We cooked our own breakfast, and Tish made some gems, having brought the pan along. But the morning dragged, although the scenery was lovely.

At twelve Bill brought the horse back and came over to us.

"If you don't mind my saying it, Miss Carberry," he observed, "you're a bit too ready with that gun. First thing you know you'll put a hole through me, and then where will you be?"

"I've got along without men most of my life," Tish said sharply. "I reckon we'd manage."

"Well," he said, "there's another angle to it. Where would I be?"

"That's between you and your Creator," Tish retorted.

We went on again that afternoon, and climbed another precipice. We saw no human being except a mountain goat, although Bill claimed to have seen a bear. Tish was quite calm at all times, and had got so that she could look down into eternity without a shudder. But Aggie and I were still nervous, and at the steepest places we got off and walked.

The unfortunate part was that the exercise and the mountain air made Aggie hungry, and there was little that she could eat.

"If any one had told me a month ago," she said, mopping her forehead, "that I would be scaling the peaks of my country on crackers and tea, I wouldn't have believed it. I'm done out, Lizzie. I can't climb another inch."

Bill was ahead with the pack horse, and Tish, overhearing her, called back some advice.

"Take your horse's tail and let him pull you up, Aggie," she said. "I've read it somewhere."

Aggie, although frequently complaining, always does as Tish suggests. So she took the horse's tail, when a totally unexpected thing happened. Docile as the creature generally was, it objected at once, and kicked out with both rear feet. In a moment, it seemed to me, Aggie was gone, and her horse was moving on alone.

"Aggie!" I called in a panic.

Tish stopped, and we both looked about. Then we saw her, lying on a ledge about ten feet below the trail. She was flat on her back, and her riding-hat was gone. But she was uninjured, although shaken, for as we looked she sat up, and an agonized expression came over her face.

"Aggie!" I cried. "Is anything broken?"

"Damnation!" said Aggie in an awful voice. "The upper set is gone!"

I have set down exactly what Aggie said. I admit that the provocation was great. But Tish was not one to make allowances, and she turned and went on, leaving us alone. She is not without feeling, however, for from the top of the pass she sent Bill down with a rope, and we dragged poor Aggie to the trail again. Her nerves were shaken and she was repentant also, for when she found that her hat was gone she said nothing, although her eyes took on a hunted look.

At the top of the pass Tish was sitting on a stone. She had taken her mending-box from the saddle, where she always kept it handy, and was drawing up a hole in her stocking. I observed to her pleasantly that it was a sign of scandal to mend clothing while still on, but she ignored me, although, as I reflected bitterly, I had not been kicked over the cliff.

It was a subdued and speechless Aggie who followed us that afternoon along the trail. As her hat was gone, I took the spare dish towel and made a turban for her, with an end hanging down to protect the back of her neck. But she expressed little gratitude, beyond observing that as she was going over the edge piecemeal, she'd better have done it all at once and be through with it.

The afternoon wore away slowly. It seemed a long time until we reached our camping-place, partly because, although a small eater ordinarily, the air and exercise had made me feel famished. But the disagreement between Tish and Aggie, owing to the latter's unfortunate exclamation while kicked over the cliff, made the time seem longer. There was not the usual exchange of pleasant nothings between us.

But by six o'clock Tish was more amiable, having seen bear scratches on trees near the camp, and anticipating the sight of a bear. She mixed up a small cup cake while Bill was putting up our tent, and then, taking her rod, proceeded to fish, while Aggie and I searched for grasshoppers. These were few, owing to the altitude, but we caught four, which we imprisoned in a match-box.

With them Tish caught four trout and, broiling them nicely, she offered one to poor Aggie. It was a peace offering, and taken as such, so that we were soon on our former agreeable footing, and all forgotten.

The next day it rained, and we were obliged to sit in the tent. Bill sat with us, and talked mainly of desperadoes.

"As I observed before," he said, "there hasn't been any tourist holdup yet. But it's bound to come. Take the Yellowstone, now,—one holdup a year's the average, and it's full of soldiers at that."

"It's a wonder people keep on going," I observed moving out of a puddle.

"Oh, I don't know," he said. "In one way it's good business. I take it this way: When folks come West they want the West they've read about. What do they care for irrigation and apple orchards? What they like is danger and a little gunplay, the sort of thing they see in these here moving pictures."

"I'm sure I don't," Aggie remarked. It was growing dusk, and she peered out into the forest round us. "There is something crackling out there now," she said.

"Only a bear, likely," Bill assured her. "We have a sight

of bears here. No, ma'am, they want danger. And every holdup's an advertisement. You see, the Government can't advertise these here parks; not the way it should, anyhow. But a holdup's news, so the papers print it, and it sets people to thinking about the park. Maybe they never thought of the place and are arranging to go elsewhere. Then along comes a gang and raises h—, raises trouble, and the park's in every one's mouth, so to speak. We'd get considerable business if there was one this summer."

At that moment the crackling outside increased, and a shadowy form emerged from the bushes. Even Bill stood up, and Aggie screamed.

It was, however, only poor Mr. Bell.

"Mind if I borrow some matches?" he said gruffly.

"We can't lend matches," Tish replied. "At least, I don't see the use of sending them back after they've been lighted. We can give you some."

"My mistake," he said.

That was all he said, except the word "Thanks" when I reached him a box.

"He's a surly creature," Tish observed as he crackled through the brush again. "More than likely that girl's better off without him."

"He looks rather downhearted," Aggie remarked. "Much that we think is temper is due to unhappiness."

"Much of your charitable view is due to a good dinner too," Tish said. "Here we are, in the center of the wilderness, with great peaks on every hand, and we meet a fellow creature who speaks nine words, and begrudges those. If he's as stingy with money as with language she's hard a narrow escape."

"He's had kind of a raw deal," Bill put in. "The girl was stuck on him all right, until this moving-picture chap came along. He offered to take some pictures with her in them, and it was all off. They're making up a play now, and she's to be in it."

"What sort of a play?" Tish demanded.

"Sorry not to oblige," Bill replied. "Can't say the nature of it."

But all of us felt that Bill knew and would not say.

Tish, to whom a mystery is a personal affront, determined to find out for herself; and when later in the evening we saw the light of Bell's camp-fire, it was Tish herself who suggested that we go over and visit with him.

"We can converse about various things," she said, "and take his mind from his troubles. But it would be better not to mention affairs of the heart. He's probably sensitive."

So we left Bill to look after things, and went to call on Mr. Bell. It was farther to his camp than it had appeared, and Tish unfortunately ran into a tree and bruised her nose badly. When it had stopped bleeding, however, we went on, and at last arrived.

He was sitting on a log by the fire, smoking a pipe and looking very sad. Behind him was a bit of a tent not much larger than an umbrella.

Aggie touched my arm. "My heart aches for him," she said. "There is despair in his very eyes."

I do not believe that at first he was very glad to see us, but he softened somewhat when Tish held out the cake she had brought.

"That's very nice of you," he said, rising. "I'm afraid I can't ask you to sit down. The ground's wet and there is only this log."

"I've sat on logs before," Tish replied. "We thought we'd call, seeing we are neighbors. As the first comers it was our place to call first, of course."

"I see," he said, and poked up the fire with a piece of stick.

"We felt that you might be lonely," said Aggie.

"I came here to be lonely," he replied gloomily. "I want to be lonely."

Tish, however, was determined to be cheerful, and asked him, as a safe subject, how he felt about the war.

"War?" he said. "That's so, there is a war. To tell the truth, I had forgotten about it. I've been thinking of other things."

We saw that it was going to be difficult to cheer him. Tish tried the weather, which brought us nowhere, as he merely grunted. But Aggie broached the subject of desperadoes, and he roused somewhat.

"There are plenty of shady characters in the park," he said shortly. "Wolves in sheep's clothing, that's what they are."

"Bill, our guide, says there may be a holdup at any time."

"Sure there is," he said calmly. "There's one going to be pulled off in the next day or two."

We sat petrified, and Aggie's eyes were starting out of her head.

"All the trimmings," he went on, staring at the fire. "Innocent and unsuspecting tourists, lunch, laughter, boiled coffee, and cold ham. Ambush. The whole business—followed by highwaymen in flannel shirts and revolvers. Dead tourist or two, desperate resistance—everything."

Aggie rose, pale as an aspen. "You—you are joking!" she cried.

"Do I look like it?" he demanded fiercely. "I tell you there is going to be the whole thing. At the end the lovely girl will escape on horseback and ride madly for aid. She will meet the sheriff and a posse, who are out for a picnic or some such damfool nonsense, and—"

"Young man," Tish said coldly, "if you know all this, why are you sitting here and not alarming the authorities?"

"Pooh!" he said disagreeably. "It's a put-up scheme, to advertise the park. Yellowstone's got ahead of them this year, and has had its excitement, with all the papers ringing with it. That was a gag, too, probably."

"Do you mean—"

"I mean considerable," he said. "That red-headed movie idiot will be on a rise, taking the tourists as they ride through. Of course he doesn't expect the holdup—not in the papers anyhow. He happens to have the camera trained on the party, and gets it all. Result—a whacking good picture, revolvers firing blank cartridges, everything which people will crowd to see. Oh, it's good business all right. I don't mind admitting that."

Tish's face expressed the greatest rage. She rose, drawing herself to her full height.

"And the tourists?" she demanded. "They lend themselves to this imposition? To this infamy? To this turpitude?"

"Certainly not. They think it's the real thing. The whole business hangs on that. And as the sheriff, or whoever it is in the fool plot, captures the bandits, the party gets its money back, and has material for conversation for the next twenty years."

"To think," said Tish, "of our great National Government lending itself to such a scheme!"

"Wrong," said the young man. "It's a combination of Western railroads and a movie concern acting together."

"I trust," Tish observed, setting her lips firmly, "that the tourists will protest."

"The more noise, the better." The young man, though not more cheerful as to appearance, was certainly more talkative. "Trust a clergyman for yelling when his pocket's picked."

With one voice the three of us exclaimed: "Mr. Ostermaier!"

He was not sure of the name, but "Helen" had pointed the clergyman out to him, and it was Mr. Ostermaier without a doubt.

We talked it over with Bill when we got back, and he was not as surprised as we'd expected.

"Knew they were cooking up something. They've got some Indians in it too. Saw them rehearsing old Thunder Mountain the other day in nothing but a breech-clout."

Tish reproved him for a lack of delicacy of speech, and shortly afterward we went to bed. Owing to the root under the tent, and puddles here and there, we could not go to sleep for a time, and we discussed the "nefarious deed," as Tish aptly termed it, that was about to take place.

"Although," Tish observed, "Mr. Ostermaier has been receiving for so many years that it might be a good thing, for his soul's sake, to have him give up something, even if to bandits." I dozed off after a time, but awakened to find Tish sitting up, wide awake.

"I've been thinking that thing over, Lizzie," she said in a low tone. "I believe it's our duty to interfere."

"Of course," I replied sarcastically; "and be shown all over the country in the movies making fools of ourselves."

"Did you notice that that young man said they would be firing blank cartridges?"

Well, even a blank cartridge can be a dangerous thing. Then and there I reminded her of my niece's boy, who was struck on the Fourth of July by a wad from one, and had to be watched for lockjaw for several weeks.

It was at that moment that we heard Bill, who had no tent, by choice, and lay under a tree, give a loud whoop, followed by what was unmistakably an oath.

"Bear!" he yelled. "Watch out, he's headed for the tent! It's a grizzly."

Tish felt round wildly for her revolver, but it was gone! And the bear was close by. We could hear it snuffing about, and to add to the confusion Aggie wakened and commenced to sneeze with terror.

"Bill!" Tish called. "I've lost my revolver!"

"I took it, Miss Carberry. But I've been lying in a puddle, and it won't go off."

All hope seemed gone. The frail walls of our tent were no protection whatever, and as we all knew, even a tree was no refuge from a bear, which, as we had seen in the Zoological Garden at home, can climb like a cat, only swifter. Besides, none of us could climb a tree.

It was at that moment that Tish had one of those inspirations that make her so dependable in emergencies. Feeling round in the tent for a possible weapon, she touched a large ham, from which we had broiled a few slices at supper. In her shadowy form there was both purpose and high courage. With a single sweeping gesture she flung the ham at the bear so accurately that we heard the thud with which it struck.

"What the hell are you doing?" Bill called from a safe distance. Even then we realized that his restraint of speech was a pose, pure and simple. "If you make him angry he'll tear up the whole place."

But Tish did not deign to answer. The rain had ceased, and suddenly the moon came out and illuminated the whole scene. We saw the bear sniffing at the ham, which lay on the ground. Then he picked it up in his jaws and stood looking about.

Tish said later that the moment his teeth were buried in the ham she felt safe. I can still see the majestic movement with which she walked out of the tent and waved her arms.

"Now, scat with you!" she said firmly. "Scat!"

He "scatted." Snarling through his nose, for fear of dropping the ham, he turned and fled up the mountainside. In the open space Tish stood the conqueror. She yawned and glanced about.

"Going to be a nice night, after all," she said. "Now, Bill, bring me that revolver, and if I catch you meddling with it again I'll put that pair of fur rugs you are so proud of in the fire."

Bill, who was ignorant of the ham, emerged sheepishly into the open. "Where the—where the dickens did you hit him, Miss Tish?" he asked.

"In the stomach," Tish replied tartly, and taking her revolver went back to the tent.

All the next day Tish was quiet. She rode ahead,

hardly noticing the scenery, with her head dropped on her chest. At luncheon she took a sardine sandwich and withdrew to a tree, underneath which she sat, a lonely and brooding figure.

When luncheon was over and Aggie and I were washing the dishes and hanging out the dish towels to dry on a bush, Tish approached Bill, who was pouring water on the fire to extinguish it.

"Bill," she stated, "you came to us under false pretenses. You swear, for one thing."

"Only under excitement, Miss Tish," he said. "And as far as that goes, Miss Aggie herself said—"

"Also," Tish went on hastily, "you said you could cook. You cannot cook."

"Now, look here, Miss Tish," he said in a pleading tone, "I can cook. I didn't claim to know the whole cookbook. I can make coffee and fry bacon. How'd I know you ladies wanted pastry? As for them canned salmon croquettes with white sauce, I reckon to make them with a little showing, and—"

"Also," said Tish, cutting in sternly, "you took away my revolver, and left us helpless last night, and in peril of wild beasts."

"Tourists ain't allowed to carry guns."

He attempted to look injured, but Tish ignored him.

"Therefore," she said, "if I am not to send you back—which I have been considering all day, as I've put up a tent myself before this, and you are only an extra mouth to feed, which, as we are one ham short, is inconvenient—you will have to justify my keeping you."

"If you will just show me once about them gems,

Miss Tish—" he began.

But Tish cut him off. "No," she said firmly, "you are too casual about cooking. And you are no dish-washer. Setting a plate in a river and letting the current wash it may satisfy cow-punchers. It doesn't go with me. The point is this: You know all about the holdup that is going to take place. Don't lie. I know you know. Now, you take us there and tell us all you know about it."

He scratched his head reflectively. "I'll tell you," he said. "I'm a slow thinker. Give me about twenty minutes on it, will you? It's a sort of secret, and there's different ways of looking at it."

Tish took out her watch. "Twenty minutes," she said. "Start thinking now."

He wandered off and rolled a cigarette. Later on, as I have said, he showed Tish how to do it—not, of course, that she meant to smoke, but Tish is fond of learning how to do things. She got so she could roll them with one hand, and she does it now in the winter evenings, instead of rolling paper spills as formerly. When Charlie Sands comes, she always has a supply ready for him, although occasionally somewhat dry from waiting for a few weeks.

At the end of twenty minutes Tish snapped her watch shut.

"Time!" she called, and Bill came back.

"Well, I'll do it," he said. "I don't know as they'll put you in the picture, but I'll see what I can do."

"Picture nothing!" Tish snapped. "You take us there and hide us. That's the point. There must be caves round to put us in, although I don't insist on a cave. They're damp usually."

Well, he looked puzzled, but he agreed. I caught

Aggie's eye, and we exchanged glances. There was trouble coming, and we knew it. Our long experience with Tish had taught us not to ask questions. "Ours but to do and die," as Aggie later said. But I confess to a feeling of uneasiness during the remainder of that day.

We changed our course that afternoon, turning off at Saint Mary's and spending the night near the Swiss Chalet at Going-to-the-Sun. Aggie and I pleaded to spend the night in the chalet, but Tish was adamant.

"When I am out camping, I camp," she said. "I can have a bed at home, but I cannot sleep under the stars, on a bed of pine needles, and be lured to rest by the murmur of a mountain stream."

Well, we gave it up and went with her. I must say that the trip had improved us already. Except when terrified or kicked by a horse, Aggie was not sneezing at all, and I could now climb into the saddle unassisted. My waistbands were much looser, too, and during a short rest that afternoon I put a dart in my riding-breeches, during the absence of Bill after the pack-horse, which had strayed.

It was on that occasion that Tish told us as much of her plan as she thought it wise for us to know.

"The holdup," she explained, "is to be the day after to-morrow on the Piegan Pass. Bill says there is a level spot at the top with rocks all about. That is the spot. The Ostermaiers and their party leave the automobiles at Many Glaciers and take horses to the pass. It will be worth coming clear to Montana to see Mrs. Ostermaier on a horse."

"I still don't see," Aggie observed in a quavering voice, "what we have to do with it."

"Naturally not," said Tish. "You'll know as soon as is good for you."

"I don't believe it will ever be good for me," said poor Aggie. "It isn't good for anybody to be near a holdup. And I don't want to be in a moving picture with no teeth. I'm not a vain woman," she said, "but I draw the line at that."

But Tish ignored her. "The only trouble," she said, "is having one revolver. If we each had one—Lizzie, did you bring any ink?"

Well, I had, and said so, but that I needed it for postcards when we struck a settlement.

Tish waved my objection aside. "I guess it can be managed," she observed. "Bill has a knife. Yes, I think it can be done."

She and Bill engaged in an earnest conference that afternoon. At first Bill objected. I could see him shaking his head. Then Tish gave him something which Aggie said was money. I do not know. She had been short of cash on the train, but she may have had more in her trunk. Then I saw Bill start to laugh. He laughed until he had to lean against a tree, although Tish was quite stern and serious.

We reached Piegan Pass about three that afternoon, and having inspected it and the Garden Wall, which is a mile or two high at that point, we returned to a "bench" where there were some trees, and dismounted.

Here, to our surprise, we found Mr. Bell again. As Tish remarked, he was better at walking than at talking. He looked surprised at seeing us, and was much more agreeable than before.

"I'm afraid I was pretty surly the other night," he said. "The truth is, I was so blooming unhappy that I didn't give a damn for anything."

But when he saw that Bill was preparing to take the pack off the horse he looked startled.

"I say," he said, "you don't mean to camp here, do you?"

"Such is my intention," Tish observed grimly.

"But look here. Just beyond, at the pass, is where the holdup is to take place to-morrow."

"So I believe," said Tish. "What has that to do with us? What are you going to do?"

"Oh, I'm going to hang round."

"Well, we intend to hang round also."

He stood by and watched our preparations for camp. Tish chose a small grove for the tent, and then left us, clambering up the mountain-side. She finally disappeared. Aggie mixed some muffins for tea, and we invited the young man to join us. But he was looking downhearted again and refused.

However, when she took them out of the portable oven, nicely browned, and lifting the tops of each one dropped in a teaspoonful of grape jelly, he changed his mind.

"I'll stay, if you don't mind," he said. "Maybe some decent food will make me see things clearer."

When Tish descended at six o'clock, she looked depressed. "There is no cave," she said, "although I have gone where a mountain goat would get dizzy. But I have found a good place to hide the horses, where we can get them quickly when we need them."

Aggie was scooping the inside out of her muffin, being unable to eat the crust, but she went quite pale.

"Tish," she said, "you have some desperate plan in view, and I am not equal to it. I am worn with travel and soft food, and am not as young as I once was."

"Desperate nothing!" said Tish, pouring condensed milk into her tea. "I am going to teach a lot of idiots a lesson, that's all. There should be one spot in America free from the advertising man and his schemes, and this is going to be it. Commercialism," she went on, growing oratorical, "does not belong here among these mighty mountains. Once let it start, and these towering cliffs will be defaced with toothpowder and intoxicating-liquor signs."

The young man knew the plans for the holdup even letter than Bill. He was able to show us the exact spot which had been selected, and to tell us the hour at which the Ostermaier party was to cross the pass.

"They'll lunch on the pass," he said, "and, of course, they suspect nothing. The young lady of whom I spoke to you will be one of their party. She, however, knows what is coming, and is, indeed, a party to it. The holdup will take place during luncheon."

Here his voice broke, and he ate an entire muffin before he went on: "The holdup will take place on the pass, the bandits having been hidden on this 'bench' right here. Then the outlaws, having robbed the tourists, will steal the young lady and escape down the trail on the other side. The guide, who is in the plot, will ride ahead in this direction and raise the alarm. You understand," he added, "that as it's a put-up job, the tourists will get all their stuff back. I don't know how that's to be arranged."

"But the girl?" Tish asked.

"She's to make her escape later," Mr. Bell said grimly, "and will be photographed galloping down the trail, by another idiot with a camera, who, of course, just happens to be on the spot. She'll do it too," he added with a pathetic note of pride in his voice. "She's got nerve enough for anything."

He drew a long breath, and Aggie poured him a third cup of tea.

"I dare say this will finish everything," he said dejectedly. "I can't offer her any excitement like this. We live in a quiet suburb, where nobody ever fires a revolver except on the Fourth of July."

"What she needs," Tish said, bending forward, "is a lesson, Mr. Bell—something to make her hate the very thought of a moving picture and shudder at the sound of a shot."

"Exactly," said Mr. Bell. "I've thought of that. Something to make her gun-shy and camera-shy. It's curious about her. In some ways she's a timid girl. She's afraid of thunder, for one thing."

Tish bent forward. "Do you know," she said, "the greatest weapon in the world?"

"Weapon? Well, I don't know. These new German guns—"

"The greatest weapon in the world," Tish explained, "is ridicule. Man is helpless against it. To be absurd is to be lost. When the bandits take the money, where do they go?"

"Down the other side from the pass. A photographer will photograph them there, making their escape with the loot."

"And the young lady?"

"I've told you that," he said bitterly. "She is to be captured by the attacking party."

"They will all be armed?"

"Sure, with blanks. The Indians have guns and

arrows, but the arrows have rubber tips."

Tish rose majestically. "Mr. Bell," she said, "you may sleep to-night the sleep of peace. When I undertake a thing, I carry it through. My friends will agree with me. I never fail, when my heart is set on it. By the day after to-morrow the young lady in the case will hate the sight of a camera."

Although not disclosing her plan, she invited the young man to join us. But his face fell and he shook his head.

Tish said that she did not expect to need him, but that, if the time came, she would blow three times on a police whistle, which she had, with her usual foresight, brought along. He agreed to that, although looking rather surprised, and we parted from him.

"I would advise," Tish said as he moved away, "that you conceal yourself in the valley below the pass on the other side."

He agreed to this, and we separated for the night. But long after Aggie and I had composed ourselves to rest Tish sat on a stone by the camp-fire and rolled cigarettes.

At last she came into the tent and wakened us by prodding us with her foot.

"Get all the sleep you can," she said. "We'll leave here at dawn to-morrow, and there'll be little rest for any of us to-morrow night."

At daylight next morning she roused us. She was dressed, except that she wore her combing-jacket, and her hair was loose round her face.

"Aggie, you make an omelet in a hurry, and, Lizzie, you will have to get the horses."

"I'll do nothing of the sort," I said, sitting up on the

ground. "We've got a man here for that. Besides, I have to set the table."

"Very well," Tish replied, "we can stay here, I dare say. Bill's busy at something I've set him to doing."

"Whose fault is it," I demanded, "that we are here in 'Greenland's Icy Mountains'? Not mine. Id never heard of the dratted place. And those horses are five miles away by now, most likely."

"Go and get a cup of tea. You'll have a little sense then," said Tish, not unkindly. "And as for what Bill's doing, he's making revolvers. Where's your writing ink?"

I had none! I realized it that moment. I had got it out at the first camp to record in my diary the place, weather, temperature, and my own pulse rate, which I had been advised to watch, on account of the effect of altitude on the heart, and had left the bottle sitting on a stone.

When I confessed this to Tish, she was unjustly angry and a trifle bitter.

"It's what I deserve, most likely, for bringing along two incompetents," was her brief remark. "Without ink we are weaponless."

But she is a creature of resource, and a moment later she emerged from the tent and called to Bill in a cheerful tone.

"No ink, Bill," she said, "but we've got blackberry cordial, and by mixing it with a little soot we may be able to manage."

Aggie demurred loudly, as there are occasions when only a mouthful of the cordial enables her to keep doing. But Tish was firm. When I went to the fire, I found Bill busily carving wooden revolvers, copying

Tish's, which lay before him. He had them done well enough, and could have gone for the horses as easy as not, but he insisted on trimming them up. Mine, which I still have, has a buffalo head carved on the handle, and Aggie's has a wreath of leaves running round the barrel.

In spite of Aggie's wails Tish poured a large part of the blackberry cordial into a biscuit pan, and put in a chip of wood.

"It makes it red," she said doubtfully. "I never saw a red revolver, Bill."

"Seems like an awful waste," Bill said. But having now completed the wreath he placed all three weapons—he had made one for himself—in the pan. The last thing I saw, as I started for the horses, was the three of them standing about, looking down, and Aggie's face was full of misery.

I was gone for a half-hour. The horses had not wandered far, and having mounted mine, although without a saddle, I copied as well as I could the whoop Bill used to drive them in, and rounded them up. When I returned, driving them before me, the pack was ready, and on Tish's face was a look of intense satisfaction. I soon perceived the reason.

Lying on a stone by the fire were three of the shiniest black revolvers any one could want. I eyed Tish and she explained.

"Stove polish," she said. "Like a fool I'd forgot it. Gives a true metallic luster, as it says on the box."

Tish is very particular about a stove, and even on our camping-trips we keep the portable stove shining and clean.

"Does it come off?"

"Well, more or less," she admitted. "We can keep the box out and renew when necessary. It is a great comfort," she added, "to feel that we are all armed. We shall need weapons."

"In an emergency," I observed rather tartly, "I hope you will not depend on us too much. While I don't know what you intend to do, if it is anything desperate, just remember that the only way Aggie or I can do any damage with these things is to thrust them down somebody's throat and strangle him to death."

She ignored my remark, however, and soon we were on our horses and moving along the trail toward the pass.

II

It will be unnecessary to remind those familiar with Glacier Park of the trail which hugs the mountain above timber-line, and extends toward the pass for a mile or so, in a long semicircle which curves inward.

At the end it turns to the right and mounts to an acre or so of level ground, with snow and rocks but no vegetation. This is the Piegan Pass. Behind it is the Garden Wall, that stupendous mass of granite rising to incredible heights. On the other side the trail drops abruptly, by means of stepladders which I have explained.

Tish now told us of her plan.

"The unfortunate part is," she said, "that the Ostermaiers will not see us. I tried to arrange it so they could, but it was impossible. We must content ourselves with the knowledge of a good deed done."

Her plan, in brief, was this: The sham attacking party was to turn and ride away down the far side of the pass, up which the Ostermaiers had come. They were, according to the young man, to take the girl with them, with the idea of holding her for ransom. She was to escape, however, while they were lunching in some secluded fastness, and, riding back to the pass, was to meet there a rescue party, which the Ostermaiers were to meet on the way down to Gunsight Chalet.

Tish's idea was this: We would ride up while they were lunching, pretend to think them real bandits, paying no attention to them if they fired at us, as we knew they had only blank cartridges, and, having taken them prisoners, make them walk in ignominy to the nearest camp, some miles farther.

"Then," said Tish, "either they will confess the ruse, and the country will ring with laughter, or they will have to submit to arrest and much unpleasantness. It will be a severe lesson."

We reached the pass safely, and on the way down the other side we passed Mr. Oliver, the moving-picture man, with his outfit on a horse. He touched his hat politely and moved out on a ledge to let us by.

"Mind if I take you as you go down the mountain?" he called. "It's a bully place for a picture." He stared at Aggie, who was muffled in a cape and had the dish towel round her head. "I'd particularly like to get your Arab," he said. "The Far East and the Far West, you know."

Aggie gave him a furious glance. "Arab nothing!" she snapped. "If you can't tell a Christian lady from a heathen, on account of her having lost her hat, then you belong in the dirty work you're doing."

"Aggie, be quiet!" Tish said in an awful voice.

But wrath had made Aggie reckless. "'dirty work' was

what I said," she repeated, staring at the young man.

"I beg your pardon. I'm sure I—"

"Don't think," Aggie went on, to Tish's fury, "that we don't know a few things. We do."

"I see," he said slowly. "All right. Although I'd like to know—"

"Good-morning," said Aggie, and kicked her horse to go on.

I shall never forget Tish's face. Round the next bend she got off her horse and confronted Aggie.

"The older I get, Aggie Pilkington," she said, "the more I realize that to take you anywhere means ruin. We are done now. All our labor is for nothing. There will be no holdup, no nothing. They are scared off."

But Aggie was still angry. "Just let some one take you for a lousy Bedouin, Tish," she said, "and see what you would do. I'm not sorry anyhow. I never did like the idea."

But Tish dislikes relinquishing an idea, once it has taken hold. And, although she did not speak to Aggie again for the next hour, she went ahead with her preparations.

"There's still a chance, Lizzie," she said. "It's not likely they'll give up easy, on account of hiring the Indians and everything."

About a mile and a half down the trail, she picked out a place to hide. This time there was a cave. We cleared our saddles for action, as Tish proposed to let them escape past us with the girl, and then to follow them rapidly, stealing upon them if possible while they were at luncheon, and covering them with the one real revolver and the three wooden ones.

The only thing that bothered us was Bill's attitude. He kept laughing to himself and muttering, and when he was storing things in the cave, Tish took me aside.

"I don't like his attitude, Lizzie," she said. "He's likely to giggle or do something silly, just at the crucial moment. I cannot understand why he thinks it is funny, but he does. We'd be much better without him."

"You'd better talk to him, Tish," I said. "You can't get rid of him now."

But to tell Tish she cannot do a thing is to determine her to do it.

It was still early, only half-past eight, when she came to me with an eager face.

"I've got it, Lizzie," she said. "I'll send off Mona Lisa, and he will have to search for her. The only thing is, she won't move unless she's driven. If we could only find a hornet's nest again, we could manage. It may be cruel, but I understand that a hornet's sting is not as painful to a horse as to a human being."

Mona Lisa, I must explain, was the pack-horse. Tish had changed her name from Jane to Mona Lisa because in the mornings she was constantly missing, and having to be looked for.

Tish disappeared for a time, and we settled down to our long wait. Bill put another coat of stove polish on the weapons, and broke now and then into silent laughter. On my giving him a haughty glance, however, he became sober and rubbed with redoubled vigor.

In a half-hour, however, I saw Tish beckoning to me from a distance, and I went to her. I soon saw that she was holding her handkerchief to one cheek, but when I mentioned the fact she ignored me.

"I have found a nest, Lizzie," she cried. "Slip over and unfasten Mona Lisa. She's not near the other horses, which is fortunate."

I then perceived that Tish's yellow slicker was behind her on the ground and tied into a bundle, from which emerged a dull roaring. I was wondering how Tish expected to open it, when she settled the question by asking me to cut a piece from the mosquito netting which we put in the doorway of the tent at night, and to bring her riding-gloves.

Aggie was darning a hole in the tablecloth when I went back and Bill was still engaged with the weapons. Having taken what she required to Tish, under pretense of giving Mona Lisa a lump of sugar, I untied her. What followed was exactly as Tish had planned. Mona Lisa, not realizing her freedom, stood still while Tish untied the slicker and freed its furious inmates. She then dropped the whole thing under the unfortunate animal, and retreated, not too rapidly, for fear of drawing Bill's attention. For possibly sixty seconds nothing happened, except that Mona Lisa raised her head and appeared to listen. Then, with a loud scream, she threw up her head and bolted. By the time Bill had put down the stove brush she was out of sight among the trees, but we could hear her leaping and scrambling through the wood.

"Jumping cats!" said Bill, and ran for his horse. "Acts as though she'd started for the Coast!" he yelled to me, and flung after her.

When he had disappeared, Tish came out of the woods, and, getting a kettle of boiling water, poured it over the nest. In spite of the netting, however, she was stung again, on the back of the neck, and spent the rest of the morning holding wet mud to the affected parts.

Her brain, however, was as active as ever, and by half-past eleven, mounting a boulder, she announced that she could see the Ostermaier party far down the trail, and that in an hour they would probably be at the top. She had her field-glasses, and she said that Mrs. Ostermaier was pointing up to the pass and shaking her head, and that the others were arguing with her.

"It would be just like the woman," Tish said bitterly, "to refuse to come any farther and spoil everything."

But a little later she announced that the guide was leading Mrs. Ostermaier's horse and that they were coming on.

We immediately retreated to the cave and waited, it being Tish's intention to allow them to reach the pass without suspecting our presence, and only to cut off the pseudo-bandits in their retreat, as I have explained.

It was well that we had concealed the horses also, for the party stopped near the cave, and Mrs. Ostermaier was weeping. "Not a step farther!" she said. "I have a family to consider, and Mr. Ostermaier is a man of wide usefulness and cannot be spared."

We did not dare to look out, but we heard the young lady speaking, and as Aggie remarked later, no one would have thought, from the sweetness of her voice, that she was a creature of duplicity.

"But it is perfectly safe, dear Mrs. Ostermaier," she said "And think, when you go home, of being able to say that you have climbed a mountain pass."

"Pass!" sniffed Mrs. Ostermaier. "Pass nothing! I don't call a wall a mile high a pass."

"Think," said the girl, "of being able to crow over those three old women who are always boasting of the things they do. Probably you are right, and they never do them at all, but you—there's a moving-picture man waiting, remember, and you can show the picture before the Dorcas Society. No one can ever doubt that you have done a courageous thing. You'll have the proof."

"George," said Mrs. Ostermaier in a small voice, "if anything happens, I have told you how I want my things divided."

"Little devil!" whispered Aggie, referring to the girl. "If that young man knows when he is well off, he'll let her go."

But beyond rebuking her for the epithet, Tish made no comment, and the party moved on. We lost them for a time among the trees, but when they moved out above timber-line we were able to watch them, and we saw that Mrs. Ostermaier got off her horse, about halfway up, and climbed slowly on foot. Tish, who had the glasses, said that she looked purple and angry, and that she distinctly saw the guide give her something to drink out of a bottle. It might, however, have been vichy or some similar innocent beverage, and I believe in giving her the benefit of the doubt.

When at last they vanished over the edge of the pass, we led out our horses and prepared for what was to come. Bill had not returned, and, indeed, we did not see him until the evening of the second day after that, when, worn but triumphant, we emerged from the trail at the Many Glaciers Hotel. That, however, comes later in this narrative.

With everything prepared, Tish judged it best to have luncheon. I made a few mayonnaise-and-lettuce sandwiches, beating the mayonnaise in the cool recesses of the cave, and we drank some iced tea, to which Aggie had thoughtfully added sliced lemon and a quantity of ginger ale. Feeling much refreshed, we grasped our weapons and waited.

At half-past twelve we heard a loud shriek on the pass, far overhead, followed almost immediately by a fusillade of shots. Then a silence, followed by more shots. Then a solitary horseman rode over the edge of the pass and, spurring his horse, rode recklessly down the precipitous trail. Aggie exclaimed that it was Mr. Ostermaier, basely deserting his wife in her apparent hour of need. But Tish, who had the glasses, reported finally that it was the moving-picture man.

We were greatly surprised, as it had not occurred to us that this would be a part of the program.

As he descended, Tish announced that there must be another photographer on top, as he was "registering" signs of terror—a moving-picture expression which she had acquired from Charlie Sands—and looking back frequently over his shoulder.

We waited until he reached timber-line, and then withdrew to a group of trees. It was not our intention to allow him to see us and spoil everything. But when he came near, through the woods, and his horse continued at unabated speed, Tish decided that the animal, frightened by the shots, was running away.

She therefore placed herself across the trail to check its headlong speed, but the animal merely rushed round her. Mr. Oliver yelled something at us, which we were, however, unable to hear, and kept madly on.

Almost immediately four men, firing back over their shoulders, rode into sight at the pass and came swiftly down toward us.

"Where's the girl?" Tish cried with her glasses to her eyes. "The idiots have got excited and have forgotten to steal her."

That was plainly what had happened, but she was determined to be stolen anyhow, for the next moment she rode into view, furiously following the bandits.

"She's kept her head anyhow," Tish observed with satisfaction. "Trust a lot of men to go crazy and do the wrong thing. But they'll have to change the story and make her follow them."

At timber-line the men seemed to realize that she was behind them, and they turned and looked up. They seemed to be at a loss to know what to do, in view of the picture. But they were quick thinkers, too, we decided. Right then and there they took her prisoner, surrounding her.

She made a desperate resistance, even crying out, as we could plainly see. But Tish was irritated. She said she could not see how the story would hold now. Either the girl should have captured them, they being out of ammunition, or the whole thing should have been done again, according to the original plan. However, as she said, it was not our affair. Our business was to teach them a lesson not to impose on unsuspecting tourists, for although not fond of Mrs. Ostermaier, we had been members of Mr. Ostermaier's church, and liked him, although his sermons were shorter than Tish entirely approved of.

We withdrew again to seclusion until they had passed, and Tish gave them ten minutes to get well ahead. Then we rode out.

Tish's face was stern as she led off. The shriek of Mrs. Ostermaier was still, as she said in a low tone, ringing in her ears. But before we had gone very far, Tish stopped and got off her horse. "We've got to pad the horses' feet," she said. "How can we creep up on them when on every stony place we sound like an artillery engagement?"

Here was a difficulty we had not anticipated. But Tish overcame it with her customary resource, by taking the blanket from under her saddle and cutting it into pieces with her scissors, which always accompany her. We then cut the leather straps from our saddles at her direction, and each of us went to work. Aggie, however, protested.

"I never expected," she said querulously, "to be sitting on the Rocky Mountains under a horse, tying a piece of bed quilt on his feet. I wouldn't mind," she added, "if the creature liked me. But the way he feels toward me he's likely to haul off and murder me at any moment."

However, it was done at last, and it made a great change. We moved along silently, and all went well except that, having neglected to draw the cinch tight, and the horse's back being slippery without the padding, my saddle turned unexpectedly, throwing me off into the trail. I bruised my arm badly, but Tish only gave me a glance of scorn and went on.

Being above carelessness herself, she very justly resents it in others.

We had expected, with reason, that the so-called highwaymen, having retreated to a certain distance, would there pause and very possibly lunch before returning. It was, therefore, a matter of surprise to find that they had kept on.

Moreover, they seemed to have advanced rapidly, and Tish, who had read a book on signs of the trail, examined the hoofprints of their horses in a soft place beside a stream, and reported that they had been going at a lope.

"Now, remember," she said as she prepared to mount again, "to all intents and purposes these are real bandits and to be treated accordingly. Our motto is 'No quarter.' I shall be harsh, and I expect no protest from either of you. They deserve everything they get."

But when, after another mile or two, we came to a side trail, leading, by Tish's map, not to Many Glaciers, but up a ravine to another pass, and Tish saw that they had taken that direction, we were puzzled.

But not for long.

"I understand now," she said. "It is all clear. The photographer was riding ahead to get them up this valley somewhere. They've probably got a rendezvous all ready, with another camera in place. I must say," she observed, "that they are doing it thoroughly."

We rode for two hours, and no sign of them. The stove polish had come off the handles of our revolvers by that time, and Aggie, having rubbed her face ever and anon to remove perspiration, presented under her turban a villainous and ferocious expression quite at variance with her customary mildness.

I urged her to stop and wash, but Tish, after a glance, said to keep on.

"Your looking like that's a distinct advantage, Aggie," she said. "Like as not they'll throw up their hands the minute they see you. I know I should. You'd better ride first when we get near."

"Like as not they'll put a hole in me," Aggie objected. "And as to riding first, I will not. This is your doing, Tish Carberry, and as for their having blank cartridges—how do we know someone hasn't made a mistake and got a real one?"

Tish reflected on that. "It's a possibility," she agreed. "If we find that they're going to spend the night out, it might be better to wait until they've taken off all the hardware they're hung with."

But we did not come up with them. We kept on finding traces of the party in marshy spots, and once

Tish hopped off her horse and picked up a small handkerchief with a colored border and held it up to us.

"It's hers," she said. "Anybody would know she is the sort to use colored borders. They're ahead somewhere."

But it seemed strange that they would go so far, and I said so.

"We're far enough off the main trail, Tish," I said. "And it's getting wilder every minute. There's nothing I can see to prevent a mountain lion dropping on us most any time."

"Not if it gets a good look at Aggie!" was Tish's grim response.

It began to grow dark in the valley, and things seemed to move on either side of the trail. Aggie called out once that we had just passed a grizzly bear, but Tish never faltered. The region grew more and more wild. The trail was broken with mudholes and crossed by fallen logs. With a superb disdain Tish rode across all obstacles, not even glancing at them. But Aggie and I got off at the worst places and led our horses. At one mudhole I was unfortunate enough to stumble. A horse with a particle of affection for a woman who had ridden it and cared for it for several days would have paused.

Not so my animal. With a heartlessness at which I still shudder the creature used me as a bridge, and stepped across, dryfoot, on my back. Owing to his padded feet and to the depth of the mud—some eight feet, I believe—I was uninjured. But it required ten minutes of hard labor on the part of both Tish and Aggie to release me from the mud, from which I was finally raised with a low, hissing sound.

"Park!" said Aggie as she scraped my obliterated features with a small branch. "Park, indeed! It's a howling wilderness. I'm fond of my native land," she went on, digging out my nostrils, so I could breathe, "but I don't calculate to eat it. As for that unfeeling beast of yours, Lizzie, I've never known a horse to show such selfishness. Never."

Well, we went on at last, but I was not so enthusiastic about teaching people lessons as I had been. It seemed to me that we might have kept on along the trail and had a mighty good time, getting more and more nimble and stopping now and then to bake a pie and have a decent meal, and putting up our hair in crimps at night, without worrying about other folks' affairs.

Late in the afternoon of that day, when so far as I could see Tish was lost, and not even her gathering a bunch of wild flowers while the horses rested could fool me, I voiced my complaint.

"Let me look at the map, Tish," I suggested. "I'm pretty good at maps. You know how I am at charades and acrostics. At the church supper—"

"Nonsense, Lizzie," she returned. "You couldn't make head or tail of this map. It's my belief that the man who made it had never been here. Either that or there has been an earthquake since. But," she went on, more cheerfully, "if we are lost, so are the others."

"If we even had Bill along!"

"Bill!" Tish said scornfully. "It's my belief Bill is in the whole business, and that if we hadn't got rid of him we'd have been the next advertising dodge. As far as that goes," she said thoughtfully, "it wouldn't surprise me a particle to find that we've been taken, without our knowing it, most any time. Your horse just now, walking across that bridge of size, for one thing."

Tish seldom makes a pun, which she herself has said is the lowest form of humor. The dig at my figure was unkind, also, and unworthy of her. I turned and left her.

At last, well on in the evening, I saw Tish draw up her horse and point ahead.

"The miscreants!" she said.

True enough, up a narrow side canon we could see a camp-fire. It was a small one, and only noticeable from one point. But Tish's keen eye had seen it. She sat on her horse and gazed toward it.

"What a shameful thing it is," she said, "to prostitute the beauties of this magnificent region to such a purpose. To make of these beetling crags a joke! To invade these vast gorges with the spirit of commercialism and to bring a pack of movie actors to desecrate the virgin silence with ribald jests and laughter! Lizzie, I wish you wouldn't wheeze!"

"You would wheeze, too, Tish Carberry," I retorted, justly indignant, "if a horse had just pressed your spinal column into your breast bone. Goodness knows," I said, "where my lungs are. I've missed them ever since my fall."

However, she was engrossed with larger matters, and ignored my petulance. She is a large-natured woman and above pettiness.

We made our way slowly up the canon. The movie outfit was securely camped under an overhanging rock, as we could now see. At one point their position commanded the trail, which was hardly more than a track through the wilderness, and before we reached this point we dismounted and Tish surveyed the camp through her glasses.

"We'd better wait until dark," Tish said. "Owing to the padding they have not heard us, but it looks to me as if one of them is on a rock, watching."

It seemed rather strange to me that they were keeping a lookout, but Tish only shrugged her shoulders.

"If I know anything of that red-headed Oliver man," she said, "he hates to let a camera rest. Like as not he's got it set up among the trees somewhere, taking flashlights of wild animals. It's rather a pity," she said, turning and surveying Aggie and myself, "that he cannot get you two. If you happen to see anything edible lying on the ground, you'd better not pick it up. It's probably attached to the string that sets off the flash."

We led our horses into the woods, which were very thick at that point, and tied them. My beast, however, lay down and rolled, saddle and all, thus breaking my mirror—a most unlucky omen—and the bottle of olive oil which we had brought along for mayonnaise dressing. Tish is fond of mayonnaise, and, besides, considers olive oil most strengthening. However, it was gone, and although Aggie comforted me by suggesting that her boiled salad dressing is quite tasty, I was disconsolate.

It was by that time seven o'clock and almost dark. We held a conference. Tish was of the opinion that we should first lead off their horses, if possible.

"I intend," she said severely, "to make escape impossible. If they fire, when taken by surprise, remember that they have only blank cartridges. I must say," she added with a confession of unusual weakness, "that I am glad the Indians escaped the other way.

I would hardly know what to do with Indians, even quite tame ones. While I know a few letters of the deaf-and-dumb language, which I believe all tribes use in common, I fear that in a moment of excitement I would forget what I know."

The next step, she asserted, was to secure their weapons.

"After all," she said, "the darkness is in our favor. I intend to fire once, to show them that we are armed and dangerous. And if you two will point the guns Bill made, they cannot possibly tell that they are not real."

"But we will know it," Aggie quavered. Now that the quarry was in sight she was more and more nervous, sneezing at short intervals in spite of her menthol inhaler. "I am sorry, Tish, but I cannot feel the same about that wooden revolver as I would about a real one. And even when I try to forget that it is only wood the carving reminds me."

But Tish silenced her with a glance. She had strangely altered in the last few minutes. All traces of fatigue had gone, and when she struck a match and consulted her watch I saw in her face that high resolve, that stern and matchless courage, which I so often have tried to emulate and failed.

"Seven o'clock," she announced. "We will dine first. There is nothing like food to restore failing spirits."

But we had nothing except our sandwiches, and Tish suggested snaring some of the stupid squirrels with which the region abounded.

"Aggie needs broth," she said decidedly. "We have sandwiches, but Aggie is frail and must be looked to."

Aggie was pathetically grateful, although sorry for the squirrels, which were pretty and quite tame. But

Tish was firm in her kindly intent, and proceeded at once to set a rabbit snare, a trick she had learned in the Maine woods. Having done this, and built a small fire, well hidden, we sat down to wait.

In a short time we heard terrible human cries proceeding from the snare, and, hurrying thither, found in it a young mountain lion. It looked dangerous, and was biting in every direction. I admit that I was prepared to leave in haste, but not so Tish. She fetched her umbrella, without which she never travels, and while the animal set its jaws in it—a painful necessity, as it was her best umbrella—Tish hit it on the head—not the umbrella, but the lion—with a large stone.

Tish's satisfaction was unbounded. She stated that the flesh of the mountain lion was much like veal, and so indeed it proved. We made a nourishing soup of it, with potatoes and a can of macedoine vegetables, and within an hour and a half we had dined luxuriously, adding to our repast what remained of the sandwiches, and a tinned plum pudding of English make, very nutritious and delicious.

For twenty minutes after the meal we all stood. Tish insists on this, as aiding digestion. Then we prepared for the night's work.

I believe that our conduct requires no defense. But it may be well again to explain our position. These people, whose camp-fire glowed so brazenly against the opposite cliff, had for purely mercenary motives committed a cruel hoax. They had posed as bandits, and as bandits they deserved to be treated. They had held up our own clergyman, of a nervous temperament, on a mountain pass, and had taken from him a part of his stipend. It was heartless. It was barbarous. It was cruel.

My own courage came back with the hot food, which I followed by a charcoal tablet. And the difference in Aggie was marked. Possibly some of the courage of the mountain lion, that bravest of wild creatures, had communicated itself to her through the homely medicine of digestion.

"I can hardly wait to get after them," she said.

However, it was still too early for them to have settled for the night. We sat down, having extinguished our fire, and I was just dozing off when Tish remembered the young man who was to have listened for the police whistle.

"I absolutely forgot him," she said regretfully. "I suppose he is hanging round the foot of Piegan's Pass yet. I'm sorry to have him miss this. I shall tell him, when I see him, that no girl worth having would be sitting over there at supper with four moving-picture actors without a chaperon. The whole proceeding is scandalous. I have noticed," she added, "that it is the girls from quiet suburban towns who are really most prone to defy the conventions when the chance comes."

We dozed for a short time.

Then Tish sat up suddenly. "What's that?" she said.

We listened and distinctly heard the tramp of horses' feet. We started up, but Tish was quite calm.

"They've turned their horses out," she said. "Fortune is with us. They are coming this way."

But at first it did not seem so fortunate, for we heard one of the men following them, stumbling along, and, I regret to say, using profane language. They came directly toward us, and Aggie beside me trembled. But Tish was equal to the emergency.

She drew us behind a large rock, where, spreading out a raincoat to protect us from the dampness, we sat down and waited.

When one of the animals loomed up close to the rock Aggie gave a low cry, but Tish covered her mouth fiercely with an ungentle hand.

"Be still!" she hissed.

It was now perfectly dark, and the man with the horses was not far off. We could not see him, but at last he came near enough so that we could see the flare of a match when he lighted a cigarette. I put my hand on Aggie, and she was shaking with nervousness.

"I am sure I am going to sneeze, Lizzie," she gasped.

And sneeze she did. She muffled it considerably, however, and we were not discovered. But, Tish, I knew, was silently raging.

The horses came nearer.

One of them, indeed, came quite close, and took a nip at the toe of my riding-boot. I kicked at it sharply, however, and it moved away.

The man had gone on. We watched the light of his cigarette, and thus, as he now and then turned his head, knew where he was. It was now that I felt, rather than heard, that Tish was crawling out from the shelter of the rock. At the same time we heard, by the crunching of branches, that the man had sat down near at hand.

Tish's progress was slow but sure. For a half-hour we sat there. Then she returned, still crawling, and on putting out my hand I discovered that she had secured the lasso from her saddle and had brought it back. How true had been her instinct when she practiced its use! How my own words, that it was all foolishness, came back and whispered lessons of humility in my ear!

At this moment a deep, resonant sound came from the tree where the movie actor sat. At the same moment a small creature dropped into my lap from somewhere above, and ran up my sleeve. I made frantic although necessarily silent efforts to dislodge it, and it bit me severely.

The necessity for silence taxed all my strength, but managing finally to secure it by the tail, I forcibly withdrew it and flung it away. Unluckily it struck Aggie in the left eye and inflicted a painful bruise.

Tish had risen to her feet and was standing, a silent and menacing figure, while this event transpired. The movements of the horses as they grazed, the soft breeze blowing through the pines, were the only sounds. Now she took a step forward.

"He's asleep!" she whispered. "Aggie, sit still and watch the horses. Lizzie, come with me."

As I advanced to her she thrust her revolver into my hand.

"When I give the word," she said in a whisper, "hold it against his neck. But keep your finger off the trigger. It's loaded."

We advanced slowly, halting now and then to listen. Although brush crackled under our feet, the grazing horses were making a similar disturbance, and the man slept on. Soon we could see him clearly, sitting back against a tree, his head dropped forward on his breast. Tish surveyed the scene with her keen and appraising eye, and raised the lasso.

The first result was not good. The loaded end struck a branch, and, being deflected, the thing wrapped itself perhaps a dozen times round my neck. Tish, being unconscious of what had happened, drew it up with a jerk, and I stood helpless and slowly strangling. At last, however, she realized the difficulty and released me. I was unable to breathe comfortably for some time, and my tongue felt swollen for several hours.

Through all of this the movie actor had slept soundly. At the second effort Tish succeeded in lassoing him without difficulty. We had feared a loud outcry before we could get to him, but owing to Tish's swiftness in tightening the rope he was able to make, at first, only a low, gurgling sound. I had advanced to him, and was under the impression that I was holding the revolver to his neck. On discovering, however, that I was pressing it to the trunk of the tree, to which he was now secured by the lariat, I corrected the error and held it against his ear.

He was now wide awake and struggling violently. Then, I regret to say, he broke out into such language as I have never heard before. At Tish's request I suppress his oaths, and substitute for them harmless expressions in common use.

"Good gracious!" he said. "What in the world are you doing anyhow? Jimminy crickets, take that thing away from my neck! Great Scott and land alive, I haven't done anything! My word, that gun will go off if you aren't careful!"

I am aware that much of the strength of what he said is lost in this free translation. But it is impossible to repeat his real language.

"Don't move," Tish said, "and don't call out. A sound, and a bullet goes crashing through your brain."

"A woman!" he said in most unflattering amazement. "Great Jehoshaphat, a woman!"

This again is only a translation of what he said.

"Exactly," Tish observed calmly. She had cut the end off the lasso with her scissors, and was now tying his feet together with it. "My friend, we know the whole story, and I am ashamed, ashamed," she said oratorically, "of your sex! To frighten a harmless and well-meaning preacher and his wife for the purpose of publicity is not a joke. Such hoaxes are criminal. If you must have publicity, why not seek it in some other way?"

"Crazy!" he groaned to himself. "In the hands of lunatics! Oh, my goodness!" Again these were not exactly his words.

Having bound him tightly, hand and foot, and taken a revolver from his pocket, Tish straightened herself.

"Now we'll gag him, Lizzie," she said. "We have other things to do to-night than to stand here and converse." Then she turned to the man and told him a deliberate lie. I am sorry to record this. But a tendency to avoid the straight and narrow issues of truth when facing a crisis is one of Tish's weaknesses, the only flaw in an otherwise strong and perfect character.

"We are going to leave you here," she said. "But one of our number, fully armed, will be near by. A sound from you, or any endeavor to call for succor, will end sadly for you. A word to the wise. Now, Lizzie, take that bandanna off his neck and tie it over his mouth."

Tish stood, looking down at him, and her very silhouette was scornful.

"Think, my friend," she said, "of the ignominy of your position! Is any moving picture worth it? Is the pleasure of seeing yourself on the screen any reward for such a shameful position as yours now is? No. A thousand times no."

He made a choking sound in his throat and writhed helplessly. And so we left him, a hopeless and miserable figure, to ponder on his sins.

"That's one," said Tish briskly. "There are only three left. Come, Aggie," she said cheerfully—"to work! We have made a good beginning."

It is with modesty that I approach that night's events, remembering always that Tish's was the brain which conceived and carried out the affair. We were but her loyal and eager assistants. It is for this reason that I thought, and still think, that the money should have been divided so as to give Tish the lion's share. But she, dear, magnanimous soul, refused even to hear of such a course, and insisted that we share it equally.

Of that, however, more anon.

We next proceeded to capture their horses and to tie them up. We regretted the necessity for this, since the unfortunate animals had traveled far and were doubtless hungry. It went to my heart to drag them from their fragrant pasture and to tie them to trees. But, as Tish said, "Necessity knows no law," not even kindness. So we tied them up. Not, however, until we had moved them far from the trail.

Tish stopped then, and stared across the canon to the enemy's camp-fire.

"No quarter, remember," she said. "And bring your weapons."

We grasped our wooden revolvers and, with Tish leading, started for the camp. Unluckily there was a stream between us, and it was necessary to ford it. It shows Tish's true generalship that, instead of removing her shoes and stockings, as Aggie and I were about to do, she suggested getting our horses and riding across.

This we did, and alighted on the other side dryshod.

It was, on consulting my watch, nine o'clock and very dark. A few drops of rain began to fall also, and the distant camp-fire was burning low. Tish gave us each a little blackberry cordial, for fear of dampness, and took some herself. The mild glow which followed was very comforting.

It was Tish, naturally, who went forward to reconnoiter. She returned in an hour, to report that the three men were lying round the fire, two asleep and one leaning on his elbow with a revolver handy. She did not see Mr. Oliver, and it was possible that it was he we had tied to the tree. The girl, she said, was sitting on a log, with her chin propped in her hands.

"She looked rather low-spirited," Tish said. "I expect she liked the first young man better than she thought she did. I intend to give her a piece of my mind as soon as I get a chance. This playing hot and cold isn't maidenly, to say the least."

We now moved slowly forward, after tying our horses. Toward the last, following Tish's example, we went on our hands and knees, and I was thankful then for no skirts. It is wonderful the freedom a man has. I was never one to approve of Doctor Mary Walker, but I'm not so sure she isn't a wise woman and the rest of us fools. I haven't put on a skirt braid since that time without begrudging it.

Well, as I have stated, we advanced, and at last we were in full sight of the camp. I must say I'd have thought they'd have a tent. We expected something better, I suppose, because of the articles in the papers about movie people having their own limousines, and all that. But there they were, open to the wrath of the heavens, and deserving it, if I do say so.

The girl was still sitting, as Tish had described her. Only now she was crying. My heart was downright sore for her. It is no comfort, having made a wrong choice, to know that it is one's own fault.

Having now reached the zone of firelight Tish gave the signal, and we rose and pointed our revolvers at them. Then Tish stepped forward and said:—

"Hands up!"

I shall never forget the expression on the man's face.

He shouted something, but he threw up his hands also, with his eyes popping out of his head. The others scrambled to their feet, but he warned them.

"Careful, boys!" he yelled. "They're got the drop on us."

Just then his eyes fell on Aggie, and he screeched:—

"Two women and a Turk, by ——." The blank is mine.

"Lizzie," said Tish sternly, as all of them, including the girl, held their hands up, "just give me your weapon and go over them."

"Go over them?" I said, not understanding.

"Search them," said Tish. "Take everything out of their pockets. And don't move," she ordered them sternly. "One motion, and I fire. Go on, Lizzie."

Now I have never searched a man's pockets, and the idea was repugnant to me. I am a woman of delicate instincts. But Tish's face was stern. I did as commanded, therefore, the total result being:—

Four revolvers.

Two large knives.

One small knife.
One bunch of keys.
One plug of chewing-tobacco.
Four cartridge belts.
Two old pipes.

Mr. Ostermaier's cigar-case, which I recognized at once, being the one we had presented to him.

Mrs. Ostermaier's wedding-ring and gold bracelet, which her sister gave her on her last birthday.

A diamond solitaire, unknown, as Mrs. Ostermaier never owned one, preferring instead earrings as more showy.

And a considerable sum of money, which I kept but did not count.

There were other small articles, of no value.

"Is that all the loot you secured during the infamous scene on Piegan Pass?" Tish demanded, "You need not hide anything from us. We know the facts, and the whole story will soon be public."

"That's all, lady," whined one of the men. "Except a few boxes of lunch, and that's gone. Lady, lemme take my hands down. I've got a stiff shoulder, and I—"

"Keep them up," Tish snapped. "Aggie, see that they keep them up."

Until that time we had been too occupied to observe the girl, who merely stood and watched in a disdainful sort of way. But now Tish turned and eyed her sternly.

"Search her, Lizzie," she commanded.

"Search me!" the girl exclaimed indignantly. "Certainly not!"

"Lizzie," said Tish in her sternest manner, "go over that girl. Look in her riding-boots. I haven't come across Mrs. Ostermaier's earrings yet."

At that the girl changed color and backed off.

"It's an outrage," she said. "Surely I have suffered enough."

"Not as much," Tish observed, "as you are going to suffer. Go over her, Lizzie."

While I searched her, Tish was lecturing her.

"You come from a good home, I understand," she said, "and you ought to know better. Not content with breaking an honest heart, you join a moving-picture outfit and frighten a prominent divine—for Mr. Ostermaier is well known—into what may be an illness. You cannot deny," she accused her, "that it was you who coaxed them to the pass. At least you needn't. We heard you."

"How was I to know—" the girl began sullenly.

But at that moment I found Mrs. Ostermaier' chamois bag thrust into her riding-boot, and she suddenly went pale.

Tish held it up before her accusingly. "I dare say you will not deny this," she exclaimed, and took Mrs. Ostermaier's earrings out of it.

The men muttered, but Aggie was equal to the occasion. "Silence!" she said, and pointed the revolver at each in turn.

The girl started to speak. Then she shrugged her shoulders. "I could explain," she said, "but I won't. If you think I stole those hideous earrings you're welcome to."

"Of course not," said Tish sarcastically. "No doubt she gave them to you—although I never knew her to give anything away before."

The girl stood still, thinking. Suddenly she said "There's another one, you know. Another man."

"We have him. He will give no further trouble," Tish observed grimly. "I think we have you all, except your Mr. Oliver."

"He is not my Mr. Oliver," said the girl. "I never want to see him again. I—I hate him."

"You haven't got much mind or you couldn't change it so quickly."

She looked sulky again, and said she'd thank us for the ring, which was hers and she could prove it.

But Tish sternly refused. "It's my private opinion," she observed, "that it is Mrs. Ostermaier's, and she has not worn it openly because of the congregation talking quite considerably about her earrings, and not caring for jewelry on the minister's wife. That's what I think."

Shortly after that we heard a horse loping along the road. It came nearer, and then left the trail and came toward the fire. Tish picked up one of the extra revolvers and pointed it. It was Mr. Oliver!

"Throw up your hands!" Tish called. And he did it. He turned a sort of blue color, too, when he saw us, and all the men with their hands up. But he looked relieved when he saw the girl.

"Thank Heaven!" he said. "The way I've been riding this country—"

"You rode hard enough away from the pass," she replied coldly.

We took a revolver away from him and lined him up with the others. All the time he was paying little attention to us and none at all to the other men. But he was pleading with the girl.

"Honestly," he said, "I thought I could do better for everybody by doing what I did. How did I know," he pleaded, "that you were going to do such a crazy thing as this?"

But she only stared at him as if she hated the very ground he stood on.

"It's a pity," Tish observed, "that you haven't got your camera along. This would make a very nice picture. But I dare say you could hardly turn the crank with your hands in the air."

We searched him carefully, but he had only a gold watch and some money. On the chance, however, that the watch was Mr. Ostermaier's, although unlikely, we took it.

I must say he was very disagreeable, referring to us as highwaymen and using uncomplimentary language. But, as Tish observed, we might as well be thorough while we were about it.

For the nonce we had forgotten the other man. But now I noticed that the pseudo-bandits wore a watchful and not unhopeful air. And suddenly one of them whistled—a thin, shrill note that had, as Tish later remarked, great penetrative power without being noisy.

"That's enough of that," she said. "Aggie, take another of these guns and point them both at these gentlemen. If they whistle again, shoot. As to the other man, he will not reply, nor will he come to your assistance. He is gagged and tied, and into the bargain may become at any time the victim of wild beasts."

The moment she had said it, Tish realized that it was but too true, and she grew thoughtful. Aggie, too, was far from comfortable. She said later that she was uncertain what to do. Tish had said to fire if they whistled again. The question in her mind was, had it been said purely for effect or did Tish mean it? After all, the men were not real bandits, she reflected, although guilty of theft, even if only for advertising purposes. She was greatly disturbed, and as agitation always causes a return of her hay fever, she began to sneeze violently.

Until then the men had been quiet, if furious. But now they fell into abject terror, imploring Tish, whom they easily recognized as the leader, to take the revolvers from her.

But Tish only said: "No fatalities, Aggie, please. Point at an arm or a leg until the spasm subsides."

Her tone was quite gentle.

Heretofore this has been a plain narrative, dull, I fear, in many places. But I come now to a not unexciting incident—which for a time placed Tish and myself in an unpleasant position.

I refer to the escape of the man we had tied.

We held a brief discussion as to what to do with our prisoners until morning, a discussion which Tish solved with her usual celerity by cutting from the saddles which lay round the fire a number of those leather thongs with which such saddles are adorned and which are used in case of necessity to strap various articles to the aforesaid saddles.

With these thongs we tied them, not uncomfortably, but firmly, their hands behind them and their feet fastened together. Then, as the night grew cold, Tish suggested that we shove them near the fire, which we did.

The young lady, however, offered a more difficult problem. We compromised by giving her her freedom, but arranging for one of our number to keep her covered with a revolver.

"You needn't be so thoughtful," she said angrily, and

with a total lack of appreciation of Tish's considerate attitude. "I'd rather be tied, especially if the Moslem with the hay fever is going to hold the gun."

It was at that moment that we heard a whistle from across the stream, and each of the prostrate men raised his head eagerly. Before Tish could interfere one of them had whistled three times sharply, probably a danger signal.

Without a word Tish turned and ran toward the stream, calling to me to follow her.

"Tish!" I heard Aggie's agonized tone. "Lizzie! Come back. Don't leave me here alone. I—"

Here she evidently clutched the revolver involuntarily, for there was a sharp report, and a bullet struck a tree near us.

Tish paused and turned. "Point that thing up into the air, Aggie," she called back. "And stay there. I hold you responsible."

I heard Aggie give a low moan, but she said nothing, and we kept on.

The moon had now come up, flooding the valley with silver radiance. We found our horses at once, and Tish leaped into the saddle. Being heavier and also out of breath from having stumbled over a log, I was somewhat slower.

Tish was therefore in advance of me when we started, and it was she who caught sight of him first.

"He's got a horse, Lizzie," she called back to me. "We can get him, I think. Remember, he is unarmed."

Fortunately he had made for the trail, which was here wider than ordinary and gleamed white in the moonlight. We had, however, lost some time in fording the stream, and we had but the one glimpse of him as the trail curved.

Tish lashed her horse to a lope, and mine followed without urging. I had, unfortunately, lost a stirrup early in the chase, and was compelled, being unable to recover it, to drop the lines and clutch the saddle.

Twice Tish fired into the air. She explained afterward that she did this for the moral effect on the fugitive, but as each time it caused my horse to jump and almost unseat me, at last I begged her to desist.

We struck at last into a straight piece of trail, ending in a wall of granite, and up this the trail climbed in a switchback. Tish turned to me.

"We have him now," she said. "When he starts up there he is as much gone as a fly on the wall. As a matter of fact," she said as calmly as though we had been taking an afternoon stroll, "his taking this trail shows that he is a novice and no real highwayman. Otherwise he would have turned off into the woods."

At that moment the fugitive's horse emerged into the moonlight and Tish smiled grimly.

"I see why now," she exclaimed. "The idiot has happened on Mona Lisa, who must have returned and followed us. And no pack-horse can be made to leave the trail unless by means of a hornet. Look, he's trying to pull her off and she won't go."

It was true, as we now perceived. He saw his danger, but too late. Mona Lisa, probably still disagreeable after her experience with the hornets, held straight for the cliff.

The moon shone full on it, and when he was only thirty feet up its face Tish fired again, and the fugitive stopped.

"Come down," said Tish quietly.

He said a great many things which, like his earlier language, I do not care to repeat. But after a second shot he began to descend slowly.

Tish, however, approached him warily, having given her revolver to me.

"He might try to get it from me, Lizzie," she observed. "Keep it pointed in our direction, but not at us. I'm going to tie him again."

This she proceeded to do, tying his hands behind him and fastening his belt also to the horn of the saddle, but leaving his feet free. All this was done to the accompaniment of bitter vituperation. She pretended to ignore this, but it made an impression evidently, for at last she replied.

"You have no one to blame but yourself," she said. "You deserve your present humiliating position, and you know it. I've made up my mind to take you all in and expose your cruel scheme, and I intend to do it. I'm nothing if I am not thorough," she finished.

He made no reply to this, and, in fact, he made only one speech on the way back, and that, I am happy to say, was without profanity.

"It isn't being taken in that I mind so much," he said pathetically. "It's all in the game, and I can stand up as well under trouble as any one. It's being led in by a crowd of women that makes it painful."

I have neglected to say that Tish was leading Mona Lisa, while I followed with the revolver.

It was not far from dawn when we reached the camp again. Aggie was as we had left her, but in the light of the dying fire she looked older and much worn. As a matter of fact, it was some weeks before she looked like her old self.

The girl was sitting where we had left her, and sulkier than ever. She had turned her back to Mr. Oliver, and Aggie said afterward that the way they had quarreled had been something terrible.

Aggie said she had tried to make conversation with the girl, and had, indeed, told her of Mr. Wiggins and her own blasted life. But she had remained singularly unresponsive.

The return of our new prisoner was greeted by the other men with brutal rage, except Mr. Oliver, who merely glanced at him and then went back to his staring at the fire. It appeared that they had been counting on him to get assistance, and his capture destroyed their last hope. Indeed, their language grew so unpleasant that at last Tish hammered sharply on a rock with the handle of her revolver.

"Please remember," she said, "that you are in the presence of ladies!"

They jeered at her, but she handled the situation with her usual generalship.

"Lizzie," she said calmly, "get the tin basin that is hanging to my saddle, and fill it with the water from that snowbank. On the occasion of any more unseemly language, pour it over the offender without mercy."

It became necessary to do it, I regret to state. They had not yet learned that Tish always carries out her threats. It was the one who we felt was the leader who offended, and I did as I had been requested to. But Aggie, ever tender-hearted, feared that it would give the man a severe cold, and got Tish's permission to pour a little blackberry cordial down his throat.

Far from this kindness having a salubrious effect, it had the contrary. They all fell to bad language again, and, realizing that they wished the cordial, and our supply being limited, we were compelled to abandon the treatment.

It had been an uncomfortable night, and I confess to a feeling of relief when "the rift of dawn" broke the early skies.

We were, Tish calculated, some forty miles from breakfast, and Aggie's diet for some days had been light at the best, even the mountain-lion broth having been more stimulating than staying. We therefore investigated the camp, and found behind a large stone some flour, baking-powder, and bacon. With this equipment and a frying-pan or two we were able to make some very fair pancakes—or flapjacks, as they are called in the West.

Tish civilly invited the girl to eat with us, but she refused curtly, although, on turning once, I saw her eyeing us with famished eyes. I think, however, that on seeing us going about the homely task of getting breakfast, she realized that we were not the desperate creatures she had fancied during the night, but three gentlewomen on a holiday—simple tourists, indeed.

"I wish," she said at last almost wistfully—"I wish that I could understand it all. I seem to be all mixed up. You don't suppose I want to be here, do you?"

But Tish was not in a mood to make concessions. "As for what you want," she said, "how are we to know that? You are here, aren't you?—here as a result of your own cold-heartedness. Had you remained true to the very estimable young man you jilted you would not now be in this position."

"Of course he would talk about it!" said the girl darkly.

"I am convinced," Tish went on, dexterously turning a pancake by a swift movement of the pan, "that sensational movies are responsible for much that is wrong with the country to-day. They set false standards. Perfectly pure-minded people see them and are filled with thoughts of crime."

Although she had ignored him steadily, the girl turned now to Mr. Oliver.

"They don't believe anything I tell them. Why don't you explain?" she demanded.

"Explain!" he said in a furious voice. "Explain to three lunatics? What's the use?"

"You got me into this, you know."

"I did! I like that! What in the name of Heaven induced you to ride off the way you did?"

Tish paused, with the frying-pan in the air. "Silence!" she commanded. "You are both only reaping what you have sowed. As far as quarreling goes, you can keep that until you are married, if you intend to be. I don't know but I'd advise it. It's a pity to spoil two houses."

But the girl said that she wouldn't marry him if he was the last man on earth, and he fell back to sulking again.

As Aggie observed later, he acted as if he had never cared for her, while Mr. Bell, on the contrary, could not help his face changing when he so much as mentioned her name.

We made some tea and ate a hearty breakfast, while the men watched us. And as we ate, Tish held the moving-picture business up to contumely and scorn.

"Lady," said one of the prostrate men, "aren't you going to give us anything to eat?"

"People," Tish said, ignoring him, "who would

ordinarily cringe at the sight of a wounded beetle sit through bloody murders and go home with the obsession of crime."

"I hope you won't take it amiss," said the man again, "if I say that, seeing it's our flour and bacon, you either ought to feed us or take it away and eat it where we can't see you."

"I take it," said Tish to the girl, pouring in more batter, "that you yourself would never have thought of highway robbery had you not been led to it by an overstimulated imagination."

"I wish," said the girl rudely, "that you wouldn't talk so much. I've got a headache."

When we had finished Tish indicated the frying-pan and the batter. "Perhaps," she said, "you would like to bake some cakes for these friends of yours. We have a long trip ahead of us."

But the girl replied heartlessly that she hoped they would starve to death, ignoring their pitiful glances. In the end it was our own tender-hearted Aggie who baked pancakes for them and, loosening their hands while I stood guard, saw that they had not only food but the gentle refreshment of fresh tea. Tish it was, however, who, not to be outdone in magnanimity, permitted them to go, one by one, to the stream to wash. Escape, without horses or weapons, was impossible, and they realized it.

By nine o'clock we were ready to return. And here a difficulty presented itself. There were six prisoners and only three of us. The men, fed now, were looking less subdued, although they pretended to obey Tish's commands with alacrity.

Aggie overheard a scrap of conversation, too, which

seemed to indicate that they had not given up hope. Had Tish not set her heart on leading them into the great hotel at Many Glaciers, and there exposing them to the taunts of angry tourists, it would have been simpler for one of us to ride for assistance, leaving the others there.

In this emergency Tish, putting her hand into her pocket for her scissors to trim a hangnail, happened to come across the policeman's whistle.

"My gracious!" she said. "I forgot my promise to that young man!"

She immediately put it to her lips and blew three shrill blasts. To our surprise they were answered by a halloo, and a moment later the young gentleman himself appeared on the trail. He was no longer afoot, but was mounted on a pinto pony, which we knew at once for Bill's.

He sat on his horse, staring as if he could not believe his eyes. Then he made his way across the stream toward us.

"Good Heavens!" he said. "What in the name of—" Here his eyes fell on the girl, and he stiffened.

"Jim!" cried the girl, and looked at him with what Aggie afterward characterized as a most touching expression.

But he ignored her. "Looks as though you folks have been pretty busy," he observed, glancing at our scowling captives. "I'm a trifle surprised. You don't mind my being rather breathless, do you?"

"My only regret," Tish said loftily, "is that we have not secured the Indians. They too should be taught a lesson. I am sure that the red man is noble until led away by civilized people who might know better."

It was at this point that Mr. Bell's eyes fell on Mr. Oliver, who with his hands tied behind him was crouching over the fire.

"Well!" he said. "So you're here too! But of course you would be." This he said bitterly.

"For the love of Heaven, Bell," Mr. Oliver said, "tell those mad women that I'm not a bandit."

"We know that already," Tish observed.

"And untie my hands. My shoulders are about broken."

But Mr. Bell only looked at him coldly. "I can't interfere with these ladies," he said. "They're friends of mine. If they think you are better tied, it's their business. They did it."

"At least," Mr. Oliver said savagely, "you can tell them who I am, can't you?"

"As to that," Mr. Bell returned, "I can only tell them what you say you are. You must remember that I know nothing about you. Helen knows much more than I do."

"Jim," cried the girl, "surely you are going to tell these women that we are not highway robbers. Tell them the truth. Tell them I am not a highway robber. Tell them that these men are not my accomplices, that I never saw them before."

"You must remember," he replied in an icy tone, "that I no longer know your friends. It is some days since you and I parted company. And you must admit that one of them is a friend of yours—as well as I can judge, a very close friend."

She was almost in tears, but she persisted. "At least," she said, "you can tell them that I did not rob that woman on the pass. They are going to lead us in to

Many Glaciers, and—Jim, you won't let them, will you? I'll die of shame."

But he was totally unmoved. As Aggie said afterward, no one would have thought that, but a day or two before, he had been heartbroken because she was in love with someone else.

"As to that," he said, "it is questionable, according to Mrs. Ostermaier, that nothing was taken from you, and that as soon as the attack was over you basely deserted her and followed the bandits. A full description of you, which I was able to correct in one or two trifling details, is now in the hands of the park police."

She stared at him with fury in her eyes. "I hope you will never speak to me again," she cried.

"You said that the last time I saw you, Helen. If you will think, you will remember that you addressed me first just now."

She stamped her foot.

"Of course," he said politely, "you can see my position. You maintain and possibly believe that these—er—acquaintances of yours"—he indicated the men—"are not members of the moving-picture outfit. Also that your being with them is of an accidental nature. But, on the other hand—"

She put her fingers in her ears and turned her back on him.

"On the other hand," he went on calmly, "I have the word of these three respectable ladies that they are the outfit, or part of it, that they have just concluded a cruel hoax on unsuspecting tourists, and that they justly deserve to be led in as captives and exposed to the full ignominy of their position."

Here she faced him again, and this time she was

quite pale. "Ask those—those women where they found my engagement ring," she said. "One of those wretches took it from me. That ought to be proof enough that they are not from the moving-picture outfit."

Tish at once produced the ring and held it out to him. But he merely glanced at it and shook his head.

"All engagement rings look alike," he observed. "I cannot possibly say, Helen, but I think it is unlikely that it is the one I gave you, as you told me, you may recall, that you had thrown it into a crack in a glacier. It may, of course, be one you have recently acquired."

He glanced at Mr. Oliver, but the latter only shrugged his shoulders.

Well, she shed a few tears, but he was adamant, and helped us saddle the horses, ignoring her utterly. It was our opinion that he no longer cared for her, and that, having lost him, she now regretted it. I know that she watched him steadily when he was not looking her way. But he went round quite happily, whistling a bit of tune, and not at all like the surly individual we had at first thought him.

The ride back was without much incident. Our prisoners rode with their hands tied behind them, except the young lady.

"We might as well leave her unfastened," the young man said casually. "While I dare say she would make her escape if possible, and particularly if there was any chance of getting filmed while doing it, I will make myself personally responsible."

As a matter of fact she was exceedingly rude to all of us, and during our stop for luncheon, which was again bacon and pancakes, she made a dash for her horse. The young man saw her, however, in time, and brought her back. From that time on she was more civil, but I saw her looking at him now and then, and her eyes were positively terrified.

It was Aggie, at last, who put in a plea for her with him, drawing him aside to do so. "I am sure," she said, "that she is really a nice girl, and has merely been led astray by the search for adventure. Naturally my friends, especially Miss Tish, have small sympathy with such a state of mind. But you are younger—and remember, you loved her once."

"Loved her once!" he replied. "Dear lady, I'm so crazy about her at this minute that I can hardly hold myself in."

"You are not acting much like it."

"The fact is," he replied, "I'm afraid to let myself go. And if she's learned a lesson, I have too. I've been her doormat long enough. I tried it and it didn't work. She's caring more for me now, at this minute, than she has in eleven months. She needs a strong hand, and, by George! I've got it—two of them, in fact."

We reached Many Glaciers late that afternoon, and Tish rode right up to the hotel. Our arrival created the most intense excitement, and Tish, although pleased, was rather surprised. It was not, however, until a large man elbowed his way through the crowd and took possession of the prisoners that we understood.

"I'll take them now," he said. "Well, George, how are you?"

This was to the leader, who merely muttered in reply.

"I'd like to leave them here for a short time," Tish stated. "They should be taught a severe lesson and nothing stings like ridicule. After that you can turn them free, but I think they ought to be discharged."

"Turn them free!" he said in a tone of amazement. "Discharged! My dear madam, they will get fifteen years' hard labor, I hope. And that's too good for them."

Then suddenly the crowd began to cheer. It was some time before Tish realized that they were cheering us. And even then, I shall have to confess, we did not understand until the young man explained to me.

"You see," he said, "I didn't like to say anything sooner, for fear of making you nervous. You'd done it all so well that I wanted you to finish it. You're been in the right church all along, but the wrong pew. Those fellows aren't movie actors, except Oliver, who will be freed now, and come after me with a gun, as like as not! They're real dyed-in-the-wool desperadoes and there's a reward of five thousand dollars for capturing them."

Tish went rather white, but said nothing. Aggie, however, went into a paroxysm of sneezing, and did not revive until given aromatic ammonia to inhale.

"I was fooled at first too," the young man said. "We'd been expecting a holdup and when it came we thought it was the faked one. But the person"—he paused and looked round—"the person who had the real jolt was Helen. She followed them, since they didn't take her for ransom, as had been agreed in the plot.

"Then, when she found her mistake, they took her along, for fear she'd ride off and raise the alarm. All in all," he said reflectively, "it has been worth about a million dollars to me."

We went into the hotel, with the crowd following us, and the first thing we saw was Mrs. Ostermaier, sitting dejectedly by the fire. When she saw us, she sprang to her feet and came to meet us.

"Oh, Miss Tish, Miss Tish!" she said. "What I have been through! Attacked on a lonely mountain-top and robbed of everything. My reason is almost gone. And my earrings, my beautiful earrings!"

Tish said nothing, but, reaching into her reticule, which she had taken from the horn of her saddle, she drew out a number of things.

"Here," she said. "Are your earrings. Here also is Mr. Ostermaier's cigar-case, but empty. Here is some money too. I'll keep that, however, until I know how much you lost."

"Tish!" screeched Mrs. Ostermaier. "You found them!"

"Yes," Tish said somewhat wearily, "we found them. We found a number of things, Mrs. Ostermaier,—four bandits, and two lovers, or rather three, but so no longer, and your things, and a reward of five thousand dollars, and an engagement ring. I think," she said, "that I'd like a hot bath and something to eat."

Mrs. Ostermaier was gloating over her earrings, but she looked up at Tish's tired and grimy face, at the mud encrusted on me from my accident the day before, at Aggie in her turban.

"Go and wash, all of you," she said kindly, "and I'll order some hot tea."

But Tish shook her head. "Tea nothing!" she said firmly. "I want a broiled sirloin steak and potatoes. And"—she looked Mrs. Ostermaier full in the eye—"I am going to have a cocktail. I need it."

Late that evening Aggie came to Tish's room, where I was sitting with her. Tish was feeling entirely well, and more talkative than I can remember her in years.

But the cocktail, which she felt, she said, in no other way, had gone to her legs.

"It is not," she observed, "that I cannot walk. I can, perfectly well. But I am obliged to keep my eyes on my feet, and it might be noticed."

"I just came in," Aggie said, "to say that Helen and her lover have made it up. They are down by the lake now, and if you will look out you can see them."

I gave Tish an arm to the window, and the three of us stood and looked out. The moon was rising over the snow-capped peaks across the lake, and against its silver pathway the young people stood outlined. As we looked he stooped and kissed her. But it was a brief caress, as if he had just remembered the strong hand and being a doormat long enough.

Tish drew a long breath.

"What," she said, "is more beautiful than young love? It will be a comfort to remember that we brought them together. Let go of me now, Lizzie. If I keep my eye on the bedpost I think I can get back."

We hope that you have enjoyed reading this book from The Large Print Book Company.

If you are interested in other titles we publish, please get in touch with us and we will be happy to send you our latest catalogue.

You can write to us at P.O. Box 970, Sanbornville, NH 03872-0970.

Or you can visit our website at www.largeprintbookco.com.

Our website contains a copy of our latest catalogue.

THE LARGE PRINT BOOK COMPANY